Paris

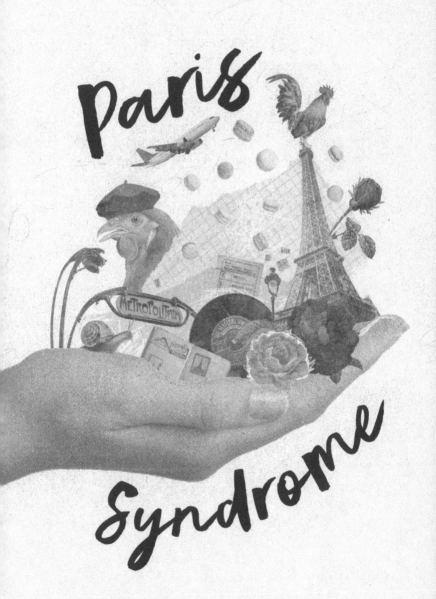

Syndrome

LISA WALKER

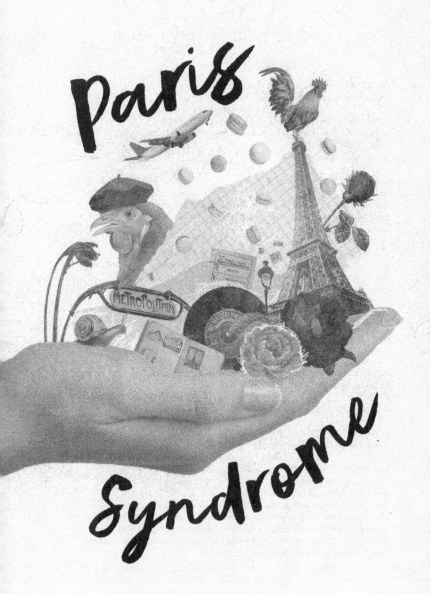

Paris
Syndrome

Angus&Robertson
An imprint of HarperCollins*Publishers*

Angus&Robertson

An imprint of HarperCollins *Publishers*, Australia

First published in Australia in 2018
by HarperCollins *Publishers* Australia Pty Limited
ABN 36 009 913 517
harpercollins.com.au

HarperCollins *Publishers*
Level 13, 201 Elizabeth Street, Sydney NSW 2000, Australia
Unit D1, 63 Apollo Drive, Rosedale, Auckland 0632, New Zealand
A 53, Sector 57, Noida, UP, India
1 London Bridge Street, London SE1 9GF, United Kingdom
2 Bloor Street East, 20th floor, Toronto, Ontario M4W 1A8, Canada
195 Broadway, New York NY 10007, USA

A catalogue record for this book is available from the National Library of Australia

ISBN 978 1 4607 5524 2 (paperback)
ISBN 978 1 4607 0956 6 (ebook)

Cover design by Steph Spartels, Studio Spartels
Cover images by Adobe Stock
Typeset in Sabon LT Std by Kirby Jones
Printed and bound in Australia by McPherson's Printing Group
The papers used by HarperCollins in the manufacture of this book are a natural,
recyclable product made from wood grown in sustainable plantation forests.
The fibre source and manufacturing processes meet recognised international
environmental standards, and carry certification.

For Judy and Eric who first took me to Paris

Chapter One

Today is a portentous and long-awaited day. I, Veronica Happiness Glass, am about to get my first tattoo.

When I discussed tattoos with Rosie, she said two pm was a good time for tattoo parlours. 'Most of the school kids don't get there until about three-thirty, so they're not expecting you. And they're tired after the morning. Act cool and you'll be fine.' As it is now the first week of the absurdly long summer holidays it is possible different rules apply, but I'm not willing to risk waiting.

Rosie had a line from *The Great Gatsby* – *You can't repeat the past? Why, of course you can* – inscribed on her inner forearm as a seventeenth birthday present from her boyfriend. They both wish they'd been born into the Jazz Age so this quote has special resonance. I did tell Rosie she wouldn't have got a tattoo if she'd been a flapper, but she said that wouldn't matter if she could have danced in one of those slinky dresses and worn a headband like Daisy in *The Great Gatsby*. Rosie would have made a good flapper.

She posted a picture of her tattoo on Facebook and it looked very elegant. Rosie is the main thing I miss about Sydney. I've been the Lone Ranger since Mum and I moved to Brisbane four months ago. The girls in my new class at school are all a year younger than me. They need less schooling in Queensland than we do south of the border. They are also strangely obsessed by reality TV shows like *Glamour in the Wild*. I tried to engage with them on this topic – I'm quite interested in desert-island survival – but it came out sounding cynical and now they think I am a 'hater'. Which I suppose I am. I haven't found one person yet who I can talk to about *Amélie* – a subject that never ran dry between Rosie and me.

Rosie also posted a picture on Facebook of her second tattoo, obtained three months after the first. This one was on her foot and said *Je suis une Parisienne*. It looked even more elegant than *The Great Gatsby* quote. This tattoo was a contract of intent. 'You need to get one too, Happy,' she said. 'Seeing as we're plasma sisters.'

Rosie and I have a pact that requires us to include an unusual word choice in every conversation. It's a hangover from our Year Nine English essay-writing class. 'Be creative in your word choices, girls,' our teacher Mrs Jenkins used to say. After a year of using *amiable* instead of *friendly*, *tedious* instead of *boring* and *malevolent* instead of *dangerous*, the habit stuck. Why say *blood*, when you can say *plasma*? It's so much more offbeat and interesting, or should I say beguiling?

It is time to get ready. I dress for the occasion in my Number Two Amélie outfit – a dark blue polka-dotted op shop dress with a scoop neck and low waist, but instead of my usual boots, I add a pair of high heels borrowed from Mum's wardrobe. Her bathroom cabinet also supplies fire-engine red lipstick and mascara to tart up my usually naked face. I'm sure I look eighteen. Even older maybe. I know most seventeen-year-olds wouldn't have to raid their mother's supplies for high heels and make-up, but I've never been much into that stuff. I pin The Gatsbys' badge to my chest before I leave. The Gatsbys are Rosie's band and I am obliged to promote them. Every bit of stealth marketing helps.

On the train into town, excitement pulsates in my chest. I can't wait to post a picture of my new tatt on Facebook. That will get Rosie's attention. Getting out at Roma Street, I head straight for the tattoo parlour.

As I stride past a shop window, I catch a glimpse of myself. I look streetwise and sophisticated like the Veronica I am about to become. Except for my hair. It is so unfair that I have ended up with this ridiculous mop – Mum and Dad both have sleek, straight hair.

'If I didn't know better, I'd think your mother had taken up with one of the cast of *Hair*,' my father used to tease. *Hair* is an old musical he likes that was notable for the follicular volume of its cast. This is tres ironic, considering. My father, who is a human rights lawyer, left Mum last year to take up with a refugee advocate called Hannah. Hannah, like me, has hair that in its natural state would be a perfect fit for *Hair*. She is also an incredible person who is fearless in defence of the rights of all refugees.

This is a total bummer as it makes it hard to complain about her in a way that doesn't come across as politically incorrect. Hannah and her refugees clearly need Dad more than Mum and I do. Hannah has offered to give me hair grooming tips – and her hair looks fantastic – but I would feel disloyal to Mum if I took her up on it.

'Be proud,' Mum says when I despair of my rampant locks. 'You're the spitting image of my great-grandmother.'

A photograph of my great-great-grandmother Billy hangs on my bedroom wall. Billy wasn't her real name, but it is the only one I know. The picture was taken in 1915, during the Great War, to send to Billy's brother, who was fighting in France. It shows a teenage Billy and her six sisters outside their old Queenslander house. They have formed a V shape, like a flock of flying geese, with Billy, who stands half a head higher than the others, at the apex. All the other sisters have their hair neatly coiffed but Billy's poodle-like mane is not the slightest bit tamed by the white ribbon that hangs over her temple in a big floppy bow.

Family lore has it that Billy disappeared in Paris while on a secret mission in World War II. So it is not just the hair and the height I have inherited. I too have ambitions to make my mark in the international arena. Specifically, I have set my sights on becoming the Australian Ambassador to France.

Due to my physical resemblance and the fact she disappeared in Paris, I feel a psychic bond with Billy. Whenever I am unsure of what course to take in life, I ask myself, *What would Billy do?* While I never knew Billy, I know she was an adventurer who wasn't afraid to take hold of life and make something of it. That is the kind of person I aspire to be.

Billy agrees with me that my new tattoo will be a positive step towards becoming the ambassador to France. An unconventional step, true, but one that will demonstrate and cement my commitment to the cause. If tattoos had been de rigueur in Billy's day, she would have got one too. In fact, it is entirely possible that Billy's flowing white dress conceals her own tattoo.

The hundred dollars I won in the essay competition is burning a hole in my pocket. I hope it is enough to get *Je suis une Parisienne* tattooed on my foot like Rosie. As I am facing the prospect of a long, boring summer in Brisbane followed by a long, boring year of school, I will need the tattoo to give me strength. I owe it to myself. One last year of school, then I am Paris bound.

Rosie and I have spent a lot of time making plans for Paris. We aim to work as au pairs, or if that fails, do fruit picking outside Paris or teach English. The main thing is to get to Paris. The rest will follow. I have been saving my pocket money and birthday money for years. It goes straight into the special Paris account that I can only access after completing Year Twelve. The tattoo money is a windfall and the usual saving rules do not apply. 'Happy is a very determined young lady,' said my last school report. I'm used to people saying that, but it still surprises me that they think it worthy of note. If you don't have goals and work towards them, how do you ever get anywhere?

Chapter Two

I pause outside the tattoo parlour. Its name, Trev's Tatts, is probably an ironic nod to the tattoo industry's seedy past. In fact, Trev's Tatts is uber hip and staffed by a master tattooist all the way from Sydney – so it says on the door. As if we Brisbanites should be honoured. Truth be told, I suppose I am mildly honoured. It is rumoured (on the Trev's Tatts Facebook page and Twitter feed) that when Angelina Jolie comes to Australia she jets straight to Brisbane for some new tatts. I find that hard to believe, but I guess it's possible.

I go past this shop every day on my way to and from school and always stop to admire the window display, which they update regularly. Today it has an occult theme – a crow's skull, a few black feathers and a silver goblet, artfully arrayed on a black cloth. A shiver of anticipation runs down my spine as I push open the door – the door to a new me.

The shop counter is empty so I hover, trying to maintain the aura of a cool, calm eighteen-year-old, rather than an illegal seventeen-year-old. It's ridiculous that I shouldn't be able to get a tattoo if I want one. What is this, North Korea?

A boy in a black T-shirt pushes open the door and comes in. He has olive skin, a small goatee beard and dazzlingly white teeth that are displayed to outstanding effect when he smiles. 'Well, 'ello,' he says, in a friendly way. He gives the impression we have met before.

I have no idea who he is, which is a crying shame, or as Rosie would have me say, a snivelling humiliation. I would certainly remember if we'd met before.

'You 'ave no idea who I am, do you?' He is still smiling.

Ooh la la – is that a French accent? I ponder further. This boy, I decide, is memorable, ipso facto I have not met him or I would remember. Unless … 'Were you at the French Tourism Board last night?'

'Well done.' His smile broadens. 'I'm Alex.'

I smile back, pleased to have solved the riddle. Alex must have been one of the stick figures in the audience when I read my essay. The fact I didn't notice him, when he's so noticeable, goes to show the astonishing power of my tunnel vision. 'I'm Happy.'

'I know.'

'Why were you at the presentation for the essay competition? Are you an essay groupie?'

He laughs. 'No. I am doing an internship at the Tourism Board.'

'That explains the accent.' I blush, as if I've said something unseemly. His accent kills me. My legs are doing that stupid Jane Austenish weak-kneed thing. I believe I may swoon in a moment. 'It was a fantastic evening,' I gush.

He gives me a dubious look. Perhaps he is having trouble putting 'essay presentation' and 'fantastic evening' together in his mind.

Oh no, I have inadvertently betrayed the tragedy of my sad social life. 'As far as essay presentations go,' I add. Though in fact it had been the highlight of my year.

Chapter Three

The essay competition had come out of the blue in the middle of last term. It was open to any school student in Brisbane and seemed purpose-made for me. 'Why I Love Paris' – I mean, come on – I challenge anyone in Brisbane to love Paris more than me. So, two weeks ago, when I found out I had won, I wasn't all that surprised.

The letter made the awards ceremony sound exciting. I envisaged an undiscovered mini-Paris, right here in Brisbane, that I could enter through a secret portal. By the time the evening came around I was at a fever pitch of anticipation.

The essay presentation was to be held at six-thirty pm in the French Tourism Board's office in the Brisbane CBD. Clutching my invitation, I climbed the stairs to a grey, high-rise in the middle of town at the fashionably late hour of six-thirty-one. I inspected the sign next to the lift and pressed the 'down' button for the basement. My pulse raced and I slipped into a fantasy as the doors opened …

Looking each way, I dart inside and pick up the receiver.

'Bonjour,' says a sultry male voice on the end of the line.

'Je suis 'Appy Glass. I am 'ere for the essay presentation.'

'Ah, Mademoiselle Glass, we 'ave been expecting you.'

The doors closed and the lift juddered into action. I inspected myself in the mirror as I descended and patted at my head. If I wasn't above such things, my hair could be a real downer. I had, however, accustomed myself to it. It was only on a bad day, after one too many people had stepped aside to make way for my hair as I passed, or murmured something uncalled for about Guy Sebastian, that I pondered the injustice of my lot. 'First World problem,' Rosie always said, and she was right of course.

I was wearing my Number One Amélie outfit – a sleeveless red high-necked dress with a blue ribbon for a belt and black boots. If I crossed my eyes so my reflection blurred I looked almost like her from the neck down. I had, of course, pinned a badge to my chest advertising The Gatsbys.

Mum was working late again so I had to rock up to the prize presentation on my own. Not that I minded, because she was way too thrilled about it all and would have totally brought down my cool factor. Ha. That was a joke. If me and cool ever appeared in a sentence together, the world would shake on its axis.

Dad had even rung to give me some gratuitous advice. 'Picture the audience naked,' he'd said. 'It's what I always do when I have a presentation.' I reminded myself not to go along to any of Dad's presentations.

As the lift dropped, I slipped my hand inside my bag and touched the printed pages of my essay. My heart gave a panicky leap at the thought of reading it out loud.

The telephone booth drops like an elevator and the doors open. I find myself on a narrow cobbled street, lined with high terraced houses and charming shopfronts. Hordes of sharply dressed Parisians jostle beneath colourful awnings. Not one of them looks anything less than fabulous. Rosie is there too in a gorgeous twenties-style flapper dress. Everyone raises their glasses and cheers as I step out of the telephone booth.
'The winner. 'Ooray!'

The doors opened and I stepped out into an empty grey-carpeted corridor. In the distance I spied a lone sandwich board with *Why I Love Paris Essay Award* written on it in red, white and blue chalk. A murmur of conversation drifted towards me.

Next to the sandwich board an open door led into a crowded and fairly boring meeting room. In place of coloured awnings and cobblestone streets they had a French flag on the wall and a table of petits fours and cheeses. This made it tres thrilling in my book.

I scuttled into a corner near the food table, picked up a petit four and waited for the formalities. The closer my reading loomed, the more my stomach rebelled. I downed several petits fours then turned to the cheese and biscuits in an effort to placate it.

''Ello.'

I dragged my attention from the cheese plate to a sleek, blonde woman in a dark blue suit next to me.

'I am Marie, the 'ead of the Tourism Board.' She put out her hand.

Marie appeared to have burst from the cobbled street of my imagination. A chunky necklace dangled around her neck and her hair was pulled back in a stylish chignon. The French always had sleek hair, I'd noticed. I chewed, swallowed and thrust out my hand. 'I am Happy, that is Veronica, Glass.'

'Ah, our winner.' She gave me a ravishing smile. Seriously. Ravishing. It was something to do with her red lipstick and white teeth.

After I had filled her in on where I went to school and why I entered the competition, an awkward silence fell. *Oh no.* I chewed my lip for a second, trying to resist. I knew I shouldn't … But what else were we going to talk about?

'I have face blindness,' I blurted, then immediately wished I hadn't. *Damn.* It's this weird urge that overcomes me when I run out of small talk, particularly when I'm nervous. Confessing to an obscure ailment is not a conversational ploy I would recommend. It does stimulate conversation but can have unforeseen repercussions. When I was ten, I had to spend a whole summer camp indoors after telling the trainee teacher on the bus I had Polymorphous Light Eruption. I was only trying to make her comfortable – she looked a little shy. I won't be making that mistake again.

On this occasion though, Marie was politely interested and our chat about face blindness filled in the time nicely. This positive reinforcement made me more likely to reoffend in the future.

'Ah, time for the prize-giving ceremony,' she said eventually.

A buzzing sensation filled my ears. The other thing that happens when I'm nervous is I get tunnel vision. If someone was to be murdered later that night – which I hoped wouldn't happen – there would be no point in getting me in to look at a line-up. When Marie called me to the front to read my essay the sea of faces in the room may as well have been stick figures. There was no need to picture them naked; to me they were wallpaper.

I coughed, turned bright red, then spoke into the microphone. 'I'd like to dedicate this essay to my friend Rosie who first inspired my love of Paris.'

Chapter Four

'I am a Parisian' by Veronica Happiness Glass
[Winning Entry in the 'Why I love Paris' Essay Competition]

Ever since I was ten, I have dreamed of The City of Light, the most
romantic city in the world. Has any other city inspired authors,
filmmakers, artists and lovers as much as Paris? Paris is a city built on
stories.

My Parisian passion started with Madeline *and* The Aristocats.
In Paris, even schoolgirls and cats lead elegant lives in chic apartments.
While others yearned for hidden doors to Narnia or to cast spells with
Harry Potter, I wished only to stroll along the Champs-Élysées and the
Boulevard Saint-Michel.

When I was fourteen I watched Midnight in Paris. *How I longed*
to be Owen Wilson as he mingled with Hemingway, Picasso and those
wild and crazy Fitzgeralds in the Paris nightclubs. When I was fifteen
I watched Before Sunset. *The next day I woke up and cried because I*

wasn't *Julie Delpy living in a little walk-up apartment off a cobbled courtyard in the Marais.*

But these movies were just the warm-up. At sixteen, I found Amélie. *My life has never been the same since. I instantly went out and asked a hairdresser to cut my hair exactly like hers. She laughed, but I insisted. My hair could never be gorgeously elfin like Amélie's, but for a year I tried.*

I dream constantly of walking the streets of Montmartre. Of skipping stones in St Martin's Canal. Of popping into a photo booth in the Metro and of flirting with an eccentric Frenchman at the Sacre-Coeur Cathedral. Whenever I think of Amélie, a warm feeling spreads through me and I know my life won't be complete until I have sipped café au lait in Café des 2 Moulins where she waitressed.

I acknowledge all is not champagne and roses in the City of Light. I have cried over The Elegance of the Hedgehog *and* The Hunchback of Notre Dame. *I have read about beggars in* Down and Out in Paris and London *and* A Tale of Two Cities.

But still — to walk along the Seine with a freshly baked baguette under my arm singing 'Alouette' is my mission in life. As soon as I finish school I plan to live in Paris.

I believe when I am in Paris I will become my true self. My hair will morph into an elfin bob as I ride on the back of a scooter past the Arc de Triomphe. I will acquire a sense of style and spend my day in fierce discussions about existentialism with earnest and handsome young men. I might smoke the odd Gauloise, though of course I will never inhale.

When I live in Paris, accordion players will pop out from quaint little wooden-shuttered shops to serenade me as I pass. I will buy flowers at a street stall and sip espresso at a café while watching elegant women

walk their poodles. I will climb the Eiffel Tower at sunset — no lift for
me — and look out on the City of Light at night. I will shop for cheese and
croissants at a little market off the Rue de Passy. I will bask in the sun by
the Seine with a glass of Chablis in my hand.

No other city in the world stirs me so. My passion for Paree is a
burning ember that will never be extinguished. At heart, je suis une
Parisienne.

A round of applause greeted me as I finished. I was shocked to
find myself still in a grey-carpeted meeting room in Brisbane and
not a dusty bookshop in Paris. Reading my essay was an out of
body experience. I was panting like a marathon runner and my
cheeks were burning. On consideration, it was lucky I wasn't in a
bookshop in Paris. Hopefully I would have more savoir-faire by
the time that came around.

Bizarrely, a tiny, elderly Japanese woman in a kimono stepped
forward to present my prize. This multi-cultural juxtaposition
confused me and her connection to the French Tourism Board
was never explained. Or perhaps it was and I missed it, which
was entirely possible. I did catch her name, however: Professor
Tanaka.

When she handed me the envelope with my prize money in it,
she bowed, then smiled and squeezed my hand, which was nice of
her. 'Make sure you spend it wisely, Veronica.' She pronounced the
'l' of *wisely* in that adorable Japanese way. *Wisry.*

'I certainly will.' I remembered to bow back, which was pretty
awesome as I had come prepared for cheek-kissing. I already knew
what I was going to do with this windfall.

Chapter Five

'Great essay, by the way,' says Alex.

I drag my focus back to the tattoo shop and the boy in front of me. He is so good looking. And French! I can't believe I didn't notice him last night. I must have been like a deer in the headlights. I control an urge to tell him I have Alien Hand Syndrome – what a great excuse that would be for fondling his goatee beard. 'It was nothing,' I murmur.

'I love that movie *Before Sunset* too.'

I open and close my mouth. If this were a movie, the camera would zoom in on my goldfish-like face. 'Really?'

'Mm-hm. Did you like that bookshop where they meet, Shakespeare and Company? When I'm in Paris I go there all the time.'

'Me too.' I flush. 'I mean, I'm going to go there all the time. Next year, when I go to Paris.' I swallow. 'With my friend Rosie.'

'You're going to Paris next year?'

I nod. 'As soon as I finish school.'

'Maybe I'll see you there.'

'Maybe.' I try to sound casual, as if meeting good-looking boys in Parisian bookshops is part of my daily routine. Oh my, how life is looking up. 'When do you go back to Paris?'

'When university starts again, in January.'

I smile at him like Julie Delpy the first time she met Ethan Hawke in *Before Sunrise*. I can already sense what is going to happen ...

Alex and I roam the streets of Brisbane all night long. It is clear we have a deeply deep relationship that only comes along once in a lifetime. We talk about the meaning of life and fall irreversibly in love before the sun rises. Tragically, we then fail to exchange phone numbers and have to wait nine years before meeting again by chance in a Parisian bookshop ...

I stop my fantasy right there. 'What are you doing here?' I gesture at the shop.

'The usual, getting a tattoo. 'Ow about you?'

'Same.'

'What sort of–?'

Alex stops abruptly as a rake-thin man with the dark tan of a sun worshipper brushes through the curtain at the back of the counter. He surveys us both. 'Here for a tattoo?'

We both nod.

'Got proof of age?' he asks me.

A deep heat descends all the way from my forehead to my toes. I shake my head.

He flicks his head towards the street.

'Sorry, 'Appy,' whispers Alex as I turn to scuttle out.

As I get to the entrance one of my high heels snags in the thick doormat. Alex and Trev the tattooist watch as I struggle without success to free it. Eventually I take off my shoe, wrench it free and stumble out the door half-shod. My cool factor melts behind me like a blob of ice cream in the sun.

On the train back home I message Rosie to tell her about my thrilling encounter (leaving out the blobby ending) but she doesn't reply. She and Luke must be out on the town. I fiddle with the badge on my dress and try not to let this get me down. Moping isn't going to get me anywhere.

My mind returns to the way Alex said my name. 'Appy. Once I am in Paris that's what everyone will call me. 'Appy. The prospect is electrifying.

I suppose I should talk about my name, because it's confusing, right? My parents had been trying for a child for a long time before I arrived. As a result, when I finally did, Mum was so overjoyed she decided to call me Happiness. My mum reads a lot of period novels featuring heroines with names like Faith, Chastity and Patience, so I am well aware things could have been much worse.

My father persuaded her to make Happiness my middle name, which was a good move, but since neither of them has ever called me anything except Happy, it's more or less a moot point. Veronica is my formal name – used only by doctors, banks and the Department of Education.

Having a name like Happy does impact on one's life in ways my parents didn't think through properly. It makes it hard to express emotions other than good cheer without someone making

19

a crack like, 'Happy's not happy' or bursting into 'If you're Happy and you know it clap your hands'. The additional opportunities offered by my surname Glass, when combined with half-full or half-empty, are hardly worth expanding upon.

It would be easy enough to drop the Happiness from my name and become Veronica, but that would be strange, like changing my identity. Still, I'm keeping the possibility of a name change in reserve and if I ever have a child, I plan to call them Jane or John. Simplicity is underrated.

I get off the train at Toowong and tramp up the street to our new apartment. It's nice, I suppose. It has a giant fig tree out the front with vines hanging all the way to the ground and a small swimming pool out the back, shared by all the units. It isn't home though. Home is the old house in Glebe with Rosie just around the corner. Someone else is there now.

By the time I reach the door, sweat is dribbling down my back. Brisbane summer sucks – there isn't even a beach so you can cool off. I don't count that fake beach on the river at South Bank. It might have a lifeguard tower but there's no salt and no waves.

Mum is still at work of course, so I let myself in. She has bought in as a partner in a medical practice – her excuse for our move to Brisbane – and is required to work relentlessly. I would never be a doctor.

If I sound like I think Mum has other reasons for wanting to move to Brisbane, that's because I do. I'm sure she could have bought into a practice in Sydney instead of being a fill-in at the local medical centre. But Dad is in Sydney and, after everything she's been through, a fresh start is needed.

At least it's cool inside. I gulp down a glass of cold water but it doesn't improve my mood. I am exceedingly disgruntled by my treatment at the tattoo parlour. I bet that wouldn't have happened in Sydney. This town is so boring. I am undeterred, however. I decide to make a list of tattoo parlours in Brisbane. There has to be one that won't ask for proof of age.

I am in my bedroom Googling Brisbane tattoo parlours when there is a knock on the door. I get sluggishly to my feet. This had better be important; I'm busy here.

Stomping to the front door, I open it to reveal a girl wearing blue denim overalls and a white singlet. She is about my age and her short black hair has a vivid blue streak dyed into the front. I find this intriguing and wonder if I should dye part of my hair a different colour.

The girl gives a small smile. Her teeth are very straight. She coughs and says, 'Hi,' in a friendly way, as if she knows me.

This is the second time today this has happened to me. I have no idea who she is. Based on the straightness of her teeth, and despite the denim overalls and the blue streak, I decide she is a Mormon or a Scientologist. 'Sorry, we're all Buddhists in this house.' I point at the little Buddha on our porch and start to shut the door.

She puts her foot out to stop the door closing.

I can't believe she did that. I glare at her and she removes her foot.

I recommence door closing.

'Wait,' she says. 'Do I look like a Mormon? I've got something for you. You don't remember me, do you?'

I inspect her through the narrow gap in the door. I have no recollection of ever seeing her before in my life. Can face blindness strike out of the blue like this, just because you *said* you had it? I make a mental note to Google it.

'Professor Tanaka asked me to give you this.' She thrusts an envelope into my hand.

Aha, this girl is another of the stick figures from last night. I hope I'm not going to be ambushed by any more people who expect me to know them. There were a lot of people there, but apart from Professor Tanaka, Marie, and now sexy Alex the Frenchman, I have no memory of any of them.

'Thanks.' I take the envelope and start to close the door again. It's probably a certificate to say I won the competition. Why didn't she just stick it in the mail?

The girl frowns, as if our interaction isn't going as expected.

I waver. At this stage I have a range of options. I can say, 'Can I help you?' But I've done this in the past and it upsets people, I'm not sure why. I can keep shutting the door and accept she may be offended. Or I can chat for a while and hope things become clearer. It's like a choose-your-own-adventure – I choose option three. I open the door again. 'Hot day, isn't it?' Weather is a safer bet for small talk than unusual ailments.

The girl smiles again in a slightly ironic way, as if there's more to this interaction than I can possibly imagine. I think she might be a little shy. Shyness is not a personality trait I would normally associate with blue hair but you should never stereotype. That would be like saying that redheads have hot tempers and look at Ros– Well in Rosie's case, the stereotype has some truth.

The blue-haired girl looks very fit – as if she does physical things for a living. Perhaps this is a clue. I follow this line of thought but it doesn't get me anywhere.

Having exhausted the weather I am tempted to tell her I have face blindness to kick things along but I decide to keep that in reserve in case the situation deteriorates. 'How do you know Professor Tanaka?'

'I work for her. She's, um, expecting a reply.'

Why didn't she say so in the first place? 'Oh, right.' I open the envelope. 'I'm Happy, by the way.'

'I know. I'm Alex.'

I look at her sharply. It's a little coincidental that I suddenly have two Alexes in my life. But the other Alex had a French accent, a goatee and no blue streak. He was also a boy. 'Have you shaved lately?'

'No.' She puts her hand to her chin. 'Should I?'

'No, no, you're fine. Just double-checking.' Okay, good, I haven't got face blindness. This morning I had no Alexes in my life and now I have two. Get over it and move on. I slide the paper out of the envelope. The letter from Professor Tanaka is written in a precise and beautiful hand.

Dear Veronica,

Would you like to join me for morning tea tomorrow? I have some information I believe will be of interest to you.

If this suits you, please come to my house at eleven am. The address is below.

Yours sincerely,

Prof Michiko Tanaka

How enigmatic. I read the letter again. I feel like Harry Potter being summoned to Hogwarts. But on the other hand, she could be a crazy woman who lures people to her home for some nefarious purpose.

I look at Alex, who from now on to save confusion shall be known as Alex Two. 'Do you know what this is about?'

'Yes.' Annoyingly, she fails to elaborate.

'And?'

'It's better if you let Professor Tanaka explain.'

'She's not a nutcase, is she?'

'No. Of course not.' She sounds a tad snippy.

'In that case, tell her yes.'

'Okay then.' She still looks like she is expecting something more but all I have left to offer is unusual syndromes and I'm reluctant to go there right now.

'Well, I'd better …' I gesture inside in a way that implies I have urgent things to do. Which obviously I do.

Alex Two raises her hand. 'Maybe I'll see you round.'

'Yes, absolutely.' I wave and shut the door.

I put the letter on the kitchen bench and read it again while I make myself a baguette with Camembert cheese. How eccentric of Professor Tanaka to send me a letter via personal messenger, rather than email. So I now have a mysterious assignation with a Japanese woman and have met two Alexes. Both of these Alexes, I take a large bite of my baguette, have made an impression on me. In the case of Alex Two, this impression is mixed – the foot in the door and the snippy tone – but she is intriguing.

'This summer is looking up,' I say to Billy's photo when I go back to my bedroom. She looks pleased to hear it. I have been rather hermit-like of late. Given a choice between reality TV recaps and solitude, I choose solitude every time.

The bang of the front door announces Mum's return and I thrust the letter into my bedside drawer. She is intensely interested in my affairs and more than a mite protective. I don't want her ringing Professor Tanaka to interrogate her. A girl has to have some secrets.

Chapter Six

On Wednesday morning I stroll to the Toowong ferry terminal, catch the ferry up-river to St Lucia and follow Google Maps towards Professor Tanaka's door. I am cautiously excited. Maybe she was so impressed by my essay that she wants to offer me a job blogging about Paris. I'd be good at that. Or maybe even send me over to Paris on a secret mission. Rosie could come too. My mind wanders as I stroll along the footpath …

> *Rosie and I wrap our chic black raincoats around our waists, straighten our sunglasses, look each way and dart across the Champs-Élysées.*
>
> *In a café on the other side sits a young man with dark floppy hair and a goatee beard. A red rose in his buttonhole identifies him as our contact.*
>
> *We sit down and murmur the password — Camembert — and he slides an envelope across the table …*

I arrive at my destination. Professor Tanaka's house is in a quiet street near the river and close to the university. Rose bushes in various states of bloom line her paved footpath. I sniff, inhaling waves of luscious scent, before stepping up to knock on the door.

There is a long silence, then a shuffling noise and the door creaks open.

Professor Tanaka looks even tinier and older today, but she is stylishly dressed in a silky blue shirt. Her face lights up when she sees me. 'Ah, Veronica.'

I decide not to correct her. Perhaps this will be the start of the new me.

'Come in, come in.' She shuts the door behind me and shuffles down the narrow hallway.

I follow, a little nervous. I Googled her of course, so I know she is a professor of psychology. Perhaps she wants to interrogate me about the underlying Freudian themes in my essay? I should have prepared some notes. My musings stop as we enter the lounge room. 'Holy Dooley.'

Professor Tanaka's lounge room is a shrine to Paris. Photographs cover the walls – the Eiffel Tower, the Arc de Triomphe, the Champs-Élysées, the Louvre, the Seine. There is also that famous image, *The Kiss*, of two lovers in Paris, and a print of a colourful mass of water lilies. My eyes scan her bookcase. It is crammed with books about France, many written in French. I spy a copy of *The Great Gatsby* there too. It appears to be the odd one out, although of course F Scott Fitzgerald did have a Parisian connection. A vinyl record, of all things, plays Edith Piaf singing 'La Vie en rose'. My French teacher used to play it in class so I recognise it immediately.

I circle slowly. 'This is awesome. When were you last in Paris?'

Professor Tanaka looks out the window. 'A long, long time ago.' Her voice is soft. 'And I can never go back.'

'Why not?' My spine tingles. Has she been banned? Perhaps she is more dangerous than she looks.

Professor Tanaka gestures to an armchair. 'Why don't you sit down, Veronica, and I will explain.'

I am a little wary, but I am much bigger and stronger than her so I plonk myself down in a worn leather armchair.

Professor Tanaka takes a seat opposite me. She nods her head to the music and smiles vaguely at me, but doesn't talk.

The atmosphere is kind of weird. I wish I hadn't come. Everywhere I look I see more French memorabilia. Even the curtains have little Eiffel Towers on them. No one loves France more than me but still, this is a little over the top. I am reminded of Miss Havisham from *Great Expectations*, preserved in her wedding dress for years and years. I shuffle my feet and try to find an excuse to leave.

As the song finishes Professor Tanaka picks up a silver pot. 'Coffee?'

I shake my head and speak in a rush due to nervousness. 'No, thank you. I never drink coffee. My mother says that girls my age shouldn't have too much caffeine, which is dumb but doctors are like that. I'm not that fussed about it anyway.'

Professor Tanaka's eyelids flutter. 'Croissant?' She lifts a cloth from a tray on the table to reveal a pile of golden croissants. 'I get them from the French pâtisserie down the road.'

I can never say no to a croissant. I pick one up and the Miss Havisham aura recedes as I smell its freshness. There's no rotting wedding feast here.

'Jam?' She holds out a glass dish.

The glistening red condiment looks too good to refuse, so I spoon some onto my plate.

Once we are both settled with our plates on our knees, Professor Tanaka clears her throat. 'Have you ever heard of Paris Syndrome, Veronica?'

'No.' My scalp tingles. How did she know that syndromes are my favourite things? 'Is that like Stockholm Syndrome? I've always thought that if I were kidnapped I would probably end up in love with my captors. Although it would be preferable if they got Lima Syndrome and fell in love with me, wouldn't it?' I stop talking because I run out of breath. When I glance at my plate, I am surprised to see I have eaten a whole croissant already.

Professor Tanaka blinks. 'These are both psychological syndromes associated with a particular city, but Paris Syndrome is different. It is an affliction which particularly, although not uniquely, strikes Japanese visitors to Paris.' She pauses to sip her coffee.

It's always nice to learn about a new syndrome. Someone is now singing 'Non, Je Ne Regrette Rien'. It's not Edith Piaf anymore, but it sounds familiar, like a movie soundtrack I can't quite identify. Was the record changed? I didn't notice. A breeze blows the curtains and as I listen to the music I imagine I'm in Paris. A wheelbarrow rumbles on the pathway outside as if a farmer is wheeling a load of cheeses to the Paris morning market.

'Ah, my gardener has arrived.' Professor Tanaka fixes her dark eyes on me. 'Paris Syndrome is a debilitating psychological condition characterised by agitation, hysteria, paranoia and in extreme cases, suicidal behaviour.'

'Goodness.' It seems I have been summoned here to make small talk about obscure ailments. Maybe Marie from the Tourism Board tipped Professor Tanaka off that this is one of my main interests. Perhaps I should tell her I have Fainting Goat Disease. I haven't used that one before.

'It is hypothesised that the syndrome is suffered by Japanese visitors who have an idealised vision of Paris.' The professor gestures at her walls and smiles in a knowing way. 'Young women are particularly susceptible.'

'Mainly Japanese women?'

'That is true. These young women arrive in Paris with their heads full of designer clothes and waiters playing accordions. Perhaps they have watched too many French movies, read too many French books ...'

My gaze trails towards the bookcase.

'They are expecting to be charmed, romanced, to fall in love with the city. They have carried this image in their heads since childhood. In Paris, they think, they will be their true selves.' Professor Tanaka looks at me in a pointed way.

I take another croissant. She clearly needs to get this syndrome out of her system.

'But when they get to Paris, it is not as they thought. Perhaps the taxi driver or the waiter is rude. They do not speak French and they feel isolated. In shops, they are treated like second-class citizens. The food doesn't agree with them. The streets are dirtier than they expected and the women not as well dressed. There are no poodles, only mangy mongrels that snap at them, and the baker gives them the burnt baguette from the bottom of his pile.'

Professor Tanaka pauses to draw breath. 'And the Seine is brown and muddy and the weather is drizzly and cold and the flowers in the flower shops are wilted and the–'

A quick knock on the door interrupts her. She looks up. 'Ah, Alex.'

Alex Two, the blue-haired girl from yesterday, not my French heartthrob Alex One, is at the door, a bunch of roses in her hands. She is wearing a white singlet, blue work shorts and socks – her shoes must have been left at the door. 'Hi,' she says to me. Her manner is a little distant.

'You met Alex yesterday, of course,' says Professor Tanaka.

'Yes.' I wonder if I was inadvertently rude to Alex Two. That would explain her distant manner.

Professor Tanaka gestures at the table. 'You can put them there, dear. Alex is my gardener,' she adds.

Alex arranges the flowers in a vase on the table and departs.

'So,' Professor Tanaka continues. 'You can see how Paris Syndrome works. There is a disconnection between expectation and reality, leading to shock and mental breakdown.'

'What happens to the people who get it?' I picture a troop of dejected Japanese zombies shuffling along the Champs-Élysées.

'It manifests in different ways. In some cases people lock themselves in their room and refuse to come out. One young man started carjacking, which was completely out of character. Some become delirious. Perhaps I should tell you about my own case ...'

I stop mid-chew, my mouth full of pastry.

The professor nods, takes another sip of coffee and dabs at her lips before continuing.

'I was twenty-five years old when I first arrived in Paris.' Her voice takes on a dreamy tone. 'It was 1967. Like you, I had longed to go there for years. I had been studying so hard, working on my PhD. Finally, I decided it was time to follow my dream. I didn't think of it as a holiday, more as a pilgrimage, an opportunity for transformation. I had lined up some post-doctoral work with a professor at the Sorbonne.' A faraway look comes over her.

'There was a poster in the Tokyo subway I went past every day. It showed a girl in a red dress standing beside the Eiffel Tower. *Find Yourself in Paris*, it said. She looked so happy, that girl. So free and full of promise. Paris was a symbol of everything I longed to be – free, individual, non-conformist. Japan was so rigid: it was important to follow the rules, be part of the team.

'I was so excited, getting on the plane, arriving at Orly airport. Even the name, Orly, sent shivers up my spine. It was a fantasy come to life. But the train ride into the city wasn't what I expected. It was crowded and the people seemed irritable. The woman who sold me my ticket scowled at me. I told myself I wasn't in the real Paris yet.' The professor sighs. 'Well, you can probably guess the rest. So much had been building to that moment.'

'How long were you in Paris?'

Professor Tanaka puts down her coffee cup. 'I prefer not to think of that time. It was devastating to me. When it didn't work out, I felt so alienated, such a failure. As if I didn't fit in anywhere.

'I was ... medically repatriated. They sent me to a hospital in Tokyo and I got better slowly once I was there. But returning home did not resolve my sense of alienation. I felt like I could not live in Japan anymore, but I knew I could not live in Paris. So that is why I came to Australia. Here, where it is not Paris, and not Japan, I feel more like myself. But not quite. My real self is still in Paris.'

'Wow. But there must be a cure?'

Professor Tanaka shakes her head. 'I long to visit Paris one more time. But I can't. I am too sensitive.'

I finish my second croissant, which is as light and buttery as the first. It may be time to introduce her to a syndrome of my own. She is a prime candidate for Alice in Wonderland Syndrome, I've been dying to try that one out.

'Have another,' says Professor Tanaka.

'Thank you.' I take a third croissant and spread butter and jam on it, while I ponder how to segue into Alice in Wonderland Syndrome. The syndrome is named after that scene where Alice eats a mushroom that makes her grow larger. Sufferers see objects as either smaller or larger than they are. 'I myself–' I interrupt myself by taking a large bite of my croissant.

'I like to see a girl with a good appetite.' Professor Tanaka nods with approval. 'So many, pick, pick, pick. So, I suppose you are wondering why I'm telling you all this?'

I nod, as my mouth is too full for an intelligent response. Seems like there's only room for one syndrome in this conversation anyway.

'I don't want to see anyone else suffer the way I did, Veronica. It is too awful, having your illusions crushed. I thought there must be a way to find people who are susceptible and temper their sensitivity before they reach Paris, or to warn them off. There must be a way to predict who will get Paris Syndrome, but it is complicated, there are so many variables. And what is the main risk factor? I do not know. Is it an interest in French history or French architecture, or is it more to do with relating to French philosophers or artists? Is someone who wears French fashion more at risk than someone who watches French movies …?' Professor Tanaka trails off at last.

I lean forward on my seat. My mouth is empty and I am ready to share. 'Fascinating. I myself have–'

Professor Tanaka smiles and claps her hands. 'I knew you would leap ahead of me. I could tell from your essay what a smart girl you are.'

I give her an *aw shucks* look. 'Would you like to hear abou–?'

'Some of the other essays were very good, but only yours showed the true hallmarks of someone at extreme risk of Paris Syndrome.'

I am mid-bite again and swallow the rest of my croissant with difficulty. 'Pardon?'

'Yes, yes.' Professor Tanaka chuckles. 'No one else came close.' She takes a piece of paper with writing highlighted in red and blue from the table behind her. It is my essay. 'Look.' She unpins a sheet of paper from the back and hands it to me. 'Here is my scoring.'

I run my eyes down the paper.

Veronica Happiness Glass
Books: 6
Roads: 3
Movies: 3
Song: 1
Historical figures: 3

Aesthetics: 5
Food: 4
Intellectualism: 1
Art: 1
Architecture: 1
Miscellaneous: 1
Delusional statements: 8
Total: 37

Professor Tanaka smiles at me. 'Your essay was exceptional. The next closest score was fifteen.'

I look from my essay to the score sheet and back again. 'What was miscellaneous?'

'The Gauloise.'

'And the delusional statements?'

'Highlighted in red.'

Is she implying my essay was exceptional only for its delusions? I scan the essay with a mounting sense of indignation, noting the following red-highlighted phrases.

I woke up and cried because I wasn't Julie Delpy living in a little walk-up apartment off a cobbled courtyard

How I longed to be Owen Wilson as he mingled with Hemingway, Picasso and those wild and crazy Fitzgeralds in the Paris nightclubs.

My hair could never be gorgeously elfin like Amélie's, but for a year I tried.

I believe when I am in Paris I will become my true self.

I stop reading at that point. It's embarrassing.

Professor Tanaka frowns. 'Sorry, I added up wrong.'

'Oh.' What a relief. 'That's what I thou–'

'The elfin bob is different from the sense of style and the accordion players, flowers, espresso and poodles are different delusions.' She reaches out with her pen and changes the eight to a twelve. 'Forty-one in total. Extraordinary. Veronica, I'm afraid I have some bad news for you.' She fixes me with her kindly brown eyes.

I wipe the croissant crumbs from my face. I feel like I'm at the doctor.

'In your current state, it would not be safe for you to travel to Paris.'

Chapter Seven

Professor Tanaka's words linger in the room. She places my essay back on the side table and steeples her fingers, gazing at me sympathetically, as a doctor would at a patient with a terminal diagnosis.

I stare back at her, chewing the inside of my lip. The three croissants sit heavily in my stomach. I have Paris Syndrome and it's not safe for me to travel to Paris? But the prospect of Paris with Rosie is the only thing that will keep me going through Year Twelve. It's the only thing I want in life.

I put my crumb-strewn plate on the table with a bang and fold my arms. This is ridiculous. Just because she can't handle Paris doesn't mean I won't be able to. Professor Tanaka can take her croissants and her Edith Piaf and her Paris Syndrome and … I am too polite to follow that line of thought.

Professor Tanaka puts her hand on my arm. 'Veronica, you are too sensitive. Paris would break you. This is why I run the essay competition.'

I pull my arm away. 'What? So you can crush people's dreams, the way yours were crushed?'

Professor Tanaka closes her eyes for a moment then opens them again. 'I am trying to help you.' She leans forward to stack the plates. 'Maybe we should leave our conversation there for today. I am a little tired.'

I stand. 'Well. Thanks for the prize. And the croissants.'

She stands too, the plates in her hands. 'You are welcome, Veronica. Please let yourself out.'

I sniff. I am still in a snit. Flouncing through the front door, I close it behind me with a bang. Paris Syndrome – what rubbish. And my essay was delusional? Sexy Alex the Frenchman didn't think so, did he? Professor Tanaka clearly doesn't understand the romantic Gallic temperament as I do.

'Hi, Happy.' Out in the garden, Alex Two is standing near a rose bed with a hose in her hand.

'Hi.' I walk towards the gate. I'm not in the mood for conversation.

'Do you want to talk about it?'

I pause with my hand on the garden gate, then swing around. 'Have you read my essay?'

'Yes. I mean I was at the prize ceremony. I heard you read it out.'

'So what do you think?'

She waters the roses for a few moments. 'It was passionate.'

'She said I was delusional.'

Her mouth twitches.

'Do you think I'm delusional?'

She shakes her head but it doesn't look like she means it.

I take a step towards her. 'Do you?'

She laughs. 'Yes, okay, maybe a bit.'

I put my hands on my hips. A takedown retort eludes me.

'Thanks for that.' I roll my eyes, swing on my heel and stomp towards the gate again.

'Are you going to the ferry?' she calls from behind me.

'Yeah.'

'Well, so am I.'

Despite my head start, we arrive at the gate at the same time. 'After you,' I say.

'No, after you.'

I step ahead.

So Alex Two and I walk down to the ferry terminal, not exactly together, but in the same vicinity. Considering our minor altercation, it's a little awkward, but short of deliberately taking a longer route, it's hard to know what else to do. When we get there, I sit down on one end of a seat and she sits at the other.

I hum 'Alouette' and she gazes out at the river, pretending to ignore me.

'If you're delusional, maybe I'm delusional too,' she says eventually. 'I'm pretty into Paris myself. I'd like to go there one day.'

I swing around and look at her. 'Of course you're into Paris. Who isn't into Paris? Paris Syndrome.' I snort. 'That's the stupidest thing I've ever heard. She said herself it's mainly Japanese women who get it.'

'It does seem to have affected her badly though.' Alex blinks and I notice her eyes are the same shade of blue as her hair. 'She doesn't like to talk about it.'

I laugh. 'Yeah, that's what she said. Then she went on to talk about it for, like, half an hour. So she's told you about how she went totally nutso in Paris, huh?'

'Very sensitively put.' Her face is impassive and it's hard to know what she's thinking.

'Not my strong point, sorry. Is she okay now do you think?'

Alex Two half-shrugs. 'She's still kind of nutso I guess. You saw her lounge room.'

I meet her eyes. I'm not sure what to say. Does she mean really nutso, or just slightly?

'It's okay. She's not certifiable or anything. Just highly strung. A bit obsessive.' She gives me a small smile. 'But who isn't, right?'

'True.' I grimace. 'Do you think I'll ever make a diplomat?'

She looks amused. 'You seem like the kind of person who does what she sets out to do.'

'Yes. I do. That's why I'm so dirty on this Paris Syndrome thing. It's stupid. As if something like that would stop me going to Paris. I'm going next year, when I finish school.' I hesitate. 'With my friend. With Rosie.'

Alex glances at me then looks out at the water. 'Not everything works out the way you think it's going to.'

I frown. 'It does if you put your mind to it.'

'I don't know. Sometimes shit happens.'

I snort. 'I hate that defeatist sort of attitude.'

She snorts too.

'Excuse me? Are you snorting at me?'

'Maybe.' Her voice is deadpan, but her mouth curls.

We sit there in silence for a while, looking out at the muddy water. The ferry turns up and disgorges a few passengers. Alex and I get on and sit out the front.

'Hey, this is like *Before Sunset*,' I say as the ferry leaves the wharf. 'You know how they take that boat ride through Paris?'

Alex looks at me out of the corner of her eye. 'I haven't seen it.'

'Why not?'

She smiles and shrugs. 'Don't sound so horrified. It's just one of those things. Maybe I should.'

'Not maybe. You totally should. I mean it's not on a par with *Amélie* of course but it's still awesome.'

'I haven't seen *Amélie* either.'

'What? You're into Paris and you haven't seen *Amélie*? That's bizarre. I'm lost for words.'

Alex tucks her blue fringe behind one ear. 'You make it sound like I've admitted to having a creepy fetish.'

'It's worse than that. Way worse. You have a huge, gaping hole in your life that can only be filled by watching *Amélie*.'

Alex leans back on her seat. She looks unconvinced. 'So what's it about?'

I take a deep breath. 'It's about this girl who does anonymous good deeds for everyone around her. It's funny and romantic and it makes you feel good. And it's set in Paris. You need to see it as soon as possible.'

'Okay, I'll schedule it in.'

'Just do it.'

'You'd make a good personal trainer.'

'Yeah, I would. Motivation is my middle name. So, this Paris Syndrome thing. You're not taking it lying down, are you?'

Alex frowns. 'How do you mean?'

'You're going to go to Paris one day, right? Or have you just gone, *Oh well, guess I'm never going to drive through Paris with the wind in my hair? It's too dangerous, I might get Paris Syndrome.*'

She readjusts a stray lock of hair, then for some reason she chuckles.

I glare at her. 'I'm serious.'

Her chuckle turns into a guffaw.

Nothing I've said merits a chuckle, let alone a guffaw. 'What's with the guffawing?'

'You.' She guffaws some more. She's got a weird snorty nose thing going on. It's pretty amusing.

I imitate her, snorting and swaying forward. 'This is you.'

She snorts even more explosively.

Her laugh is so peculiar it's contagious and my imitation turns into the real thing even though I have no idea what's funny. A snorty explosion erupts from my mouth. Heads turn, but there's nothing I can do. 'Stop it. My stomach ...'

Our laughter subsides into giggles. I breathe deeply until I recover. 'What was that all about?'

Alex shakes her head. 'You're a hard case, Happy. What do you do when you wake up in the morning? Memorise another song about Paris, so you can be ready to misquote it at the right moment?'

'Is that what we were laughing at? Yes. I do know a few songs about Paris as it happens.'

'Paris, wind, car ... Marianne Faithfull, right?'

'Yep. *Ballad of Lucy Jordan*. How tragic, to realise at the age of thirty-seven you're never going to ride through Paris in a sports car.'

'First World problem.'

I look at her. 'My friend Rosie always says that. But anyway, that's not going to happen to me.'

Alex smiles. 'No, you definitely strike me as a Paris sports car kind of girl.'

I meet her eyes, but look away before the giggles start again. 'Still, back before you started with the guffawing, I was serious. You don't give up your dreams like that.' I snap my fingers. 'Aren't they worth fighting for?'

'Yes, but ... Sometimes life doesn't run to plan. Look at Professor Tanaka. Seems like Paris broke her.'

A gust of wind blows my hair all over the place and I wrestle it down. 'Damn you, poodle hair.'

Alex watches with amusement, her own hair rising politely in the breeze like a silky blue horse mane.

I hold my hair bunched in my fist. 'So, what are you doing now? Gardening for Professor Tanaka? You planning to do that for the rest of your life?'

'Give me a break, I've just finished school. I'm enrolled at uni for the new year. It doesn't start until March though.' The ferry slows down as West End wharf approaches.

'Cool. So, what are you studying?'

'Psychology.' Alex picks up her bag.

'That's interesting. Psychology. Is that because of your, um, background?'

43

'Working as a gardener for someone who went nutso in Paris you mean?'

'Sorry.'

'That's okay. I like your blunt style, but you may need to adapt it if you want to be a diplomat. Maybe it is. Well, this is my stop.' Alex stands. 'Bye then.' The wind blows her fringe across her eyes but she doesn't try to restrain it.

'Bye.'

'It was nice guffawing with you.' Alex shoulders her backpack and walks across the gangplank to shore.

I lift my hand to wave, but she doesn't look back. Meh – she needn't think I care.

Chapter eight

'What are you going to do with yourself all summer?' asks Mum at dinner that night. 'School holidays in Queensland are so long. I can't believe it's nearly eight weeks until you go back.'

I shrug and attempt to look excited about the meal on my plate, which is allegedly spaghetti carbonara. To be frank, Mum has many talents but cooking is not one of them. Back in Sydney, Dad was in charge of kitchen affairs. Mum and I share the burden now and I try to encourage her as much as possible as I don't want to damage her confidence. 'This is yum.' I load my fork with a greyish-looking mixture.

Mum smiles. 'I got the recipe from an old magazine we had in the surgery. Cooking's not that hard, is it? Your father always used to make such a fuss about it.'

'I know.' I chew with necessary enthusiasm. 'I like what you've done with the spaghetti.' I struggle to find something else to say about the meal. 'Cool haircut.' Mum is looking sharp these days. If the divorce has dented her self-esteem she tries not to let it show.

She has taken up Zumba and developed muscles I've never seen before and is taking extra care with her appearance. I hope that doesn't mean there's a man on the scene. None of my business of course, but still.

Mum touches her spiky red-tipped hair. 'Do you like it?'

'Yeah. You look super-hot. No one would ever imagine you have a seventeen-year-old daughter.'

She smiles. 'Almost eighteen.'

'I wish. Then I could get a tattoo.'

Mum squawks. She does. Like a chicken.

'What? There's no way you're getting a tattoo, Happy.'

'Soon as I'm eighteen. Sooner maybe.'

'I forbid it.'

I laugh. 'You and whose army? What are you going to do, confine me to my room? Cut me out of your will?'

Mum sighs and takes a sip of wine. 'Well, I hope you come to your senses before you ruin your beautiful body by putting ink all over it. The only thing that would upset me more is if you took up smoking.'

Mum feels very strongly about smoking. I suppose most doctors do, but she has taken it to a whole new level. My grandfather died of lung cancer and this is why she is a little scary on the topic. I have known her to deliver a twenty-minute lecture to random strangers who are unlucky enough to be smoking when she passes by.

'Happy?'

'What?'

Mum has an expectant look. 'You never answered my question. What are you going to do with yourself this summer?'

I ponder. I'd like to run into sexy Alex One again. Alex Two was kind of fun too. I remember her snorty laugh. 'I've got a few ideas. I've got some reading to do for Year Twelve too.' Things are going to have to get awfully dull around here before that rises to the top of my 'to do' list though.

'You could get a job.'

'Mm. Maybe.'

'Don't you have some friends you can hang out with?'

'My friends are in Sydney, Mum.'

Her shoulders droop. 'I know you and Rosie were so close ...' Her voice peters out.

Were. I stare at her.

She takes another sip of wine and runs her hand through her hair. Rosie's name hangs in the room. 'It's going to take a while to make new connections,' she murmurs.

I swallow the lump of spaghetti that has lodged in my throat and change the topic. 'Do you think I'm delusional?'

Mum's forkful of food freezes halfway to her mouth. 'Why do you ask? In what way?'

'Um, I don't know.' I poke at my food. 'Like, wanting to be the Australian Ambassador to France.'

Mum looks relieved. 'Happy, you know I've always told you: you can be whatever you want to be. Anything the human mind can perceive and believe it can achieve.'

'Well, if I am delusional, it is clearly your fault.'

After dinner I do the dishes. It's funny at home now there's just me and Mum. The dynamic's changed. We watch each other's backs. And it doesn't matter what a fabulous person Hannah is, I still think Dad's a frigging idiot for leaving Mum.

Back in my room, I Google Paris Syndrome. I want to check Professor Tanaka hasn't cooked it up for obscure reasons of her own, but Google confirms it is indeed a syndrome afflicting visitors to Paris. The Japanese Embassy has apparently set up a twenty-four-hour hotline for sufferers to call. I imagine a flood of distressed Japanese tourists ricocheting from encounters with rude waiters to the hotline. How bizarre.

While I am there on the syndrome site, I tool around looking for some new material. Luckily for me, there is no shortage of syndromes. Today I learn about Jerusalem Syndrome, a religious mania vexing visitors to the holy city. Scrolling down I find Florence Syndrome, an intense reaction to an excess of beautiful art. *No, no, not one more Da Vinci. I can't take it!*

It seems to me this city syndrome thing is way under-diagnosed. What about Brisbane Syndrome – where people believe they are living in the world's most liveable city? Or Sydney Syndrome – where people think they'll fall off the edge of the world if they venture north of Newcastle or south of Wollongong? This is the sort of thing I might enjoy discussing with Alex Two if I ever run into her again.

I return to my list of tattoo parlours from yesterday. I will not let Mum or Professor Tanaka deflect me from my mission of getting *Je suis une Parisienne* tattooed on my foot. I print out a list of twenty tattoo parlours. I'm sure one of them will take my money. It's not for nothing I have earned my reputation as A Very Determined Young Lady.

Before bed, I message Rosie: *Do you think I'm delusional?*

Yes, but all the preeminent people are. Look at Gatsby.

Gatsby is not a good advertisement for the delusional. I don't want to end up deceased in a swimming pool, mourned by no one.

Gatsby was a dreamer. He held onto his bright star. It wasn't his fault those around him couldn't see the beauty of his vision.

True. Je ne regrette rien, baby.

That's my girl xxx

I lie in bed staring at the ceiling. Sometimes it's like things are just the way they used to be between Rosie and me. How they were before she started hanging out with that uni crowd and drinking and taking drugs. We still have a special connection. One more year and we'll be plasma sisters again in Paris.

Rosie and I met at dance class in Year Five. She was new to the school. I noticed her hair first – that tumble of red right down her back. She beamed at me as we did our routine. Such a cheeky grin. It said, *Stick with me and we'll have a blast.*

She rocketed into my life, taking me with her on a burning trail of excitement. She was fickle sometimes, but that was the price I paid for the thrill of being swept up in her orbit.

As I roll over in bed I see her well-thumbed copy of *The Great Gatsby* on my bookshelf. Poor Gatsby. He loved Daisy so much and she deserved his love so little. Perhaps it's better to be a realist than a dreamer.

But it is Gatsby who we remember, isn't it? Because he never stopped believing.

Chapter Nine

My pillow is wet when I wake. This confuses me until I remember my dream.

> *I am chasing Rosie down a laneway in Paris. She keeps looking back and laughing. 'Come on, Happy, you're so slow.'*
>
> *I'm running as fast as I can, trying to keep her in sight. But when I turn the corner she is gone. I call her name, but she doesn't reply.*
>
> *I spin in a circle, looking for her, but see only closed doors. She has gone.*

I turn my pillow over to the dry side and lie there for a while. When I dream about Rosie I have trouble getting out of bed. I finally emerge at the crack of ten am.

Over breakfast I inspect my list of tattoo parlours and circle three that are accessible by public transport. One of the tattoo parlours, fortuitously, is not far from the French Tourism Board where Alex One works. I underline it. I will try this one first.

I suppose this brings me to the regrettable topic of me and boys. Regrettable, because I've not had a lot of success in that department. Boys always seem scared of me, like they suspect I'll mate with them and then eat them alive. They're pretty feeble, most of them. Anyone who thinks females are the weaker sex has been moving in different circles from me.

I didn't help matters when I was younger by challenging any boy who showed interest to beat me in an arm wrestle followed by a simple maths quiz. I was trying to sort out the sheep from the goats but ended up with neither.

I should have been born as a warrior queen, like Cleopatra or Boadicea. Then men would have fought to win my hand and I would have chosen only the bravest and most brilliant. But that doesn't work in my world. Even when I relaxed the requirement for arm wrestling and maths skills, boys still didn't beat a path to my door.

Perhaps it's my hair, or maybe my height – I'm taller than a lot of boys I meet. I try not to get hung up about it. Plenty of important women in history were chaste – Joan of Arc, Queen Elizabeth I, the Bronte sisters, Jane Austen and of course the Virgin Mary. Not to mention nuns and vestal virgins. Being a virgin is a sensible lifestyle choice in many situations.

However, considering the average age for French girls to have their first sexual experience is sixteen, and also considering that at heart *Je suis une Parisienne*, it's time I got started. A sophisticated Parisienne should have a string of lovers.

Virginity is such an icky word. For me it conjures images of pale girls in white dresses playing the piano and doing needlepoint

51

while their parents try to marry them off. I decide to banish the 'v' word from my vocabulary. It's a negative value, like being untravelled or not speaking a second language. I plan to travel a lot, speak many languages and have a plethora of lovers.

Alex One would be a suitable first candidate. He is French. And everyone knows the French are fantastic lovers. Yes, Alex One would be an auspicious start to my amorous future.

Today I select my Number Three Amélie outfit – another polka-dot dress, but this one is green with a white Peter Pan collar. Rosie and I used to spend a lot of time scouring op shops in Sydney. In preparation for my visit to the tattoo parlour, I put on Mum's high-heeled shoes, do my make-up again and look in the mirror. I definitely look older than eighteen. My eyes fall on one of Mum's redundant hair clips and I decide to try something new. I gather my hair and pin it to the top of my head. The result is interesting – a puffball sprouts from my crown. With the heels and the hair I am even more imposing than usual.

As I pick up my bus pass and stride through the door, my hair brushes the top of the doorjamb.

My second tattoo parlour, located on a side street in the CBD, is more downmarket than Trev's Tatts and has no claims to celebrity clients. There are no customers inside and its run-down air suggests they need business. I figure they'll be a soft touch. I am feeling confident as I push open the door.

The tattooist, a dark-haired woman with tattoos all the way down her arms and pierced eyebrows, looks up from a paperback book as I enter. She doesn't say anything. Customer service does not appear to be a high priority for tattooists.

'I'd like to get a tattoo.'

Her eyes rest on me for a moment. 'No.' She looks back at her book, which has a female vampire on the cover.

'Why?' I cross my arms. 'You don't look like you're busy.'

She lifts her gaze. 'I am. I'm in an exciting part. How old are you, anyway?'

I can't believe what sticklers to the law these tattooists are. I snort and roll my eyes as if I can't believe she's asking.

'Seventeen?'

I don't reply.

'Thought so. You'll change your mind and hate it. You'll upset your parents. Don't even think about it.'

'So why have you got so many tattoos?'

She smiles at me – a pretty smile that makes the corners of her blue eyes crinkle. 'You want to end up working in a tattoo shop in Queen Street?'

'No, but ...'

'So get out of here and never come back.' She flicks her hand, looks down and turns the page of her book.

'What about when I'm eighteen?'

'I still won't tattoo you.' She turns the page again; she must be speed-reading.

'Why not?'

She smooths down her page and looks up again. 'You're the wrong type.'

'How do you know? You don't even know me.' She is getting me so peeved. 'Maybe I want to be a singer in a rock band. Maybe I'm trying to change my image. Have you thought of that?'

'I'm clairvoyant, right? You're going to go on to big things. You don't want a tattoo holding you back.'

'I want it on my foot. No one will see it.'

'They'll sense it.'

'Wow. I thought tattooists would be daring nonconformists, but you're almost as bad as school teachers.'

'Funny you should say that. I would have liked to have been a school teacher, but do you think I'd get a job looking like this?' She picks up her phone, holds it up and takes a photo of me, before typing rapidly with her thumbs.

'What are you doing?'

'I'm posting this to the Brisbane tattooists' Facebook group.' Her thumbs keep moving. '*Don't tattoo this girl*,' she reads. '*She's only seventeen*. There.' She looks up and winks. 'You'll thank me one day.'

'You've just ruined my life.' I stomp out, slamming the door behind me, then turn around and glare at her through the window.

She waves at me.

I stick out my tongue in reply.

Soon after, I am staked out in a café opposite the French Tourism Board with an espresso. After my exceptionally aggravating run-in with the tattooist, I'm in a defiant mood. I'm cutting loose, living life on the edge. Stuff the effects of caffeine on growing girls.

*

As I lift my little cup to my lips I pretend I'm in the Cafe de Flore, the most famous literary café in Paris, gazing out at all the passers-by on the Boulevard Saint-Germain. I put my coffee cup down after one sip. As it turns out, I still don't like espresso. I add a few teaspoons of sugar to make it drinkable. This doesn't detract too much from my rebellious statement.

I drum my fingers on the table. Boy, that tattooist was annoying. I'd have thought she'd be glad to take my money, and maybe offer me some heroin on the side. The world is so politically correct these days. I guess I'll have to make a special interstate trip to get tattooed. Maybe I'll go to Sydney ... I could visit Rosie. Either that or work on a disguise.

I sip my coffee and frown. It's still kind of disgusting, but I'll need to get used to it if I'm going to fit in in Paris.

'It's not very good, is it?' says a male voice. A male voice with a French accent.

I look up and my heart jumps sky-high. How did he sneak in here without me noticing?

"Ello 'Appy,' says Alex One.

'Ello. I could listen to him say that all day long.

'Can I sit?'

'Of course.' I act nonchalant, as if I regularly share café tables with incredibly good-looking Frenchmen.

'We meet again,' he says.

I nod, take a big gulp of my coffee and almost spit it out again. My heart gives a rapid thump, thump. I may be having an attack of Caffeine-induced Anxiety Disorder, a surprisingly common affliction affecting–

'Are you okay?'

'Yes. Why? Don't I look okay?'

His eyebrows twitch. 'You seem tense.'

'Oh.' I concentrate on being calm. An overwhelming urge to get up from the table and run away strikes me. Instead I say the first thing that comes into my head. 'What's eight minus one times zero plus two divided by two.' *Aargh.* I so wish I hadn't said that.

He smiles. 'Do you expect me to answer?'

'No. Um, the answer's nine. If you care.'

He shrugs. 'Maths is not my strong point.'

'That's okay. There's more to life than maths I guess.'

He cocks his head and looks at me. 'You are unusual.'

I want to sink under the table. *Unusual.* He means strange. At least I didn't challenge him to an arm wrestle. 'Has anyone ever told you that you look like Johnny Depp?' I say and immediately wish I hadn't. If only my brain had better control over my mouth.

'Yes, it 'appens frequently.' He looks out the window. 'It's a nice day, isn't it? I was going to get a sandwich 'ere, but it might be nice to 'ave lunch by the river.'

Lunch by the river ... I sigh. Déjeuner au bord du fleuve.

Cue: Romantic French music. Mood lighting. My hair falls in soft ringlets around my face. I am wearing a floaty summer dress. He stands and takes my hand and magically a picnic basket holding a baguette, a selection of cheeses, some figs and a bottle of wine materialises in his other hand. We float down Queen Street and shopkeepers smile and wave as

we pass. One presses a bunch of roses towards me — 'For the beautiful
mademoiselle.' We find a shady patch of grass beside the river. He feeds
me pieces of soft cheese and after we have eaten we sink into a bed of
autumn leaves and ...

He stands.

'Maybe I will see you around,' he says.

My ringlets and floaty dress self-combust and vanish in a puff of smoke. I am left with a polka-dot dress and a bunch of fuzzy hair that sticks up from my head. So much for my plans of becoming sexually active.

''Ave you eaten yet?'

'No.' Even if I'd just had a twelve-course lunch I would have said the same thing.

'Well, why don't you come?'

Cue: Romantic French music. Mood lighting ... 'Sure.' I smile in a charming French way and toss my head. My puffball bounces.

We select our lunch from the display at the front of the café, stroll down the street, cross the road and find a spot in the shade near the river. There are no smiling shopkeepers and no picnic basket. I eat my ham sandwich and he has a salad wrap. We compare our lunches and make small talk about the brownness of the river, but after we have eaten, an awkward silence falls. At this stage a French girl would no doubt introduce Jean-Paul Sartre into the conversation, but as I have never read him – a shocking omission on my part – that would be challenging. I expect everyone in Paris converses about *Being and Nothingness* with no trouble at all.

Alex leans on his elbow and looks at me. 'Your 'air is amazing. Why don't you take it out of that clip?'

I flush and a queasy warmth rises from my stomach. Putting my hand up, I pull out the clip and my 'air bounces everywhere.

He reaches out and touches it with his finger. 'Fantastic.'

His touch freezes me. It's like one of those dreams where you know you're awake, but you can't move. If he decided to eat me alive I couldn't lift a finger to save myself.

He glances at his watch. 'I 'ad better get back to work.' He gets to his feet.

The spell breaks. I unfreeze and scramble up too. I am disappointed in myself. I have failed to engage him in an earnest philosophical discussion, such as he is accustomed to at home. On the positive side, I still haven't challenged him to an arm wrestle.

'Want to go see a French film some time?' he asks casually.

Sacrebleu. That is the last thing I expected after my poor conversational performance. I nod, dumbly.

He pulls out his phone. 'What is your number?'

I tell him and he enters it in.

'Okay. I'll be in touch. Salut.' He smiles, raises his hand and strides off towards his office.

'Salut,' I murmur as I watch the faded denim encasing his long legs get further and further away. My brain is as addled as a sun-drunk butterfly. Je suis amoureuse. I think I am in love.

Chapter Ten

Over the next few days something strange happens – a half-wit, lovesick fool takes up residence in my head. The old Happy watches from afar, shaking her head and rolling her eyes. *He didn't even pass the maths test*, she mutters in a judgemental way. *I don't know what you see in him.*

Look at her, checking her phone again in case she has missed a message, she tut tuts. *There she is again – gazing off into the distance like a moonstruck cow. Thinking about how he touched her hair. Pathetic.*

'Shut up,' I say to the old Happy. 'You have no idea what it's like.' I'm not interested in gaining perspective.

This is torment, I message Rosie. *Why didn't anyone inform me?*

Welcome to insanity. About time. Thought you'd never get here.

Mum catches me checking my messages over dinner. She reaches over and takes hold of my phone. 'No phones at the table.'

I hold on and we have a short tussle, but eventually I give in. 'Fine. Ruin my life.'

Mum places the phone on the kitchen bench and sits again. 'Are you okay, Happy? You've been off in a dream the last few days. What's up?'

I shrug, eyeing my phone. 'Nothing.' Perhaps I can go and hang around in the café opposite his work … *No, pathetic. It will be so obvious.* But what if he never rings? What if he's lost my number? A deep sigh wells up from the depths of my body and emerges through my nose.

Mum frowns. 'The cinema down the road is looking for staff. Why don't you go and enquire? It'd give you something to do.'

I consider this for a moment but decide I am too busy thinking about Alex to take on a job. 'I don't think so. I'm too busy.'

Mum rolls her eyes but declines to comment.

On Monday, after checking my phone about ten million times, I decide to cheer myself up by walking down the road to buy some Milo. I have a sudden craving for cold milk with Milo piled on top. Since falling in love, I have been strangely hungry. Desire must burn up calories.

On the way to the corner store I pass the local cinema. I glance at it, then stop in my tracks. Above the entrance hangs a large banner showing an attractive couple kissing in front of the Eiffel Tower. *French Film Festival*, it says.

I stand there, smitten by a vision like Joan of Arc. The only difference is that I am called to work in a cinema, not to lead the French army to battle. I can't believe it – what incredible luck.

I cross the road to inspect the banner more closely. The festival starts tomorrow. Does Alex know about this? He wanted to take me to a French film and here are two weeks of them. He must know. Why hasn't he asked me? He must have lost my phone number.

I inspect the notice stuck to the window – *Staff wanted, enquire within*. If I work here, I will see him when he comes and we will be reunited like the couple in *Before Sunset*, only not after so long. It is the perfect solution.

Milo forgotten, I rush home and revamp my resume, giving pride of place to winning the French essay competition. Under *interests* I add *French films*. I also provide some helpful dot points of the skills I can bring to the position.

French speaking

Efficient ... and ... I struggle for a third one.

Personable?

I'm not sure if I am personable, but I expect I could be if I put my mind to it. I hit print and get out my Number Four Amélie outfit – a green swing skirt with a stretchy red button-up top and red ballet shoes. Picking up my resume, I race from the house. I couldn't bear it if someone beat me to the position. As I get closer to the cinema, a nervous flutter fills my stomach and the familiar tunnel vision takes hold. I have to get this job. My love life depends on it.

I straighten my shoulders and smooth my hair as I climb the stairs to the cinema. My hair is a lost cause, but one has to try to put one's best foot forward.

As it turns out, my second-best foot would have been perfectly fine. The manager, Kevin, an ageing hippy in a Hawaiian shirt with a string of beads around his neck, scarcely glances at my resume. He leans over the counter and pushes my papers back towards me. 'Can you start tomorrow? My last assistant slipped on some popcorn and broke his arm so he's out of action for the summer.'

'Absolument.' The word bursts from my mouth.

'Speak French, do you?' He smooths his floppy hair across his head, which only brings attention to a thin spot he must be trying to cover.

'Mais oui, un petit peu.' I am firing on all cylinders.

He gives me a long look. 'Well, don't do it here.'

I am chastened and instantly downcast. I've blown it already. 'Pardo– I mean sorry. I won't do it again.' But despite my inappropriate French, I am hired. On my way to the door I pass a box full of rolled-up posters next to the rubbish bin. 'Are you throwing these out?'

Kevin glances over from the counter. 'Yeah. It's all old stuff I found out the back. Left by the previous owner.'

'Can I have a look through?'

He waves his hand dismissively and pulls a packet of cigarettes from his top pocket. 'I pay fortnightly.'

'Okay.'

With a cough, he goes outside for a smoke.

The first few posters are Hollywood blockbusters, but as I unroll the third, the room quiets around me. If this was a movie, the soundtrack would indicate awe and revelation. In my hands is the poster from *Amélie*.

I study it. Amélie's so-familiar face is tilted to one side and she gives me a mischievous smile. I smile back and she seems to wink –

We're going to have some fun, I imagine her saying. I carefully roll the poster back up again and tuck it under my arm.

Out on the street, Kevin draws heavily on his cigarette and coughs again. 'Which poster did you take? *Hunger Games*?'

I shake my head and unroll the poster to show him. 'I adore *Amélie*.'

'Oh yeah?' He puts out the stub of his cigarette on the wall and walks back inside without another word.

I stare after him. I don't think he's the right person to be running a French Film Festival. It's lucky for him he's got me. As I walk home I imagine the opening night …

> *A well-dressed crowd is gathered in the foyer sipping French champagne. Rosie is there; she would never miss an occasion like this. She is wearing a headband with a bright green feather on the side.*
>
> *'Here she comes.' The murmur spreads through the crowd. Everyone jostles for position.*
>
> *I am wearing a tight black dress with high heels and a black beret. My hair is miraculously straight. I emerge from a limousine and walk elegantly down the red carpet.*
>
> *I hear my name being called by the paparazzi. 'A comment please, director.'*
>
> *I smile graciously as the flashbulbs go off.*

At home I find some Blu-tack and stick up my *Amélie* poster on my bedroom wall. 'There you go, Amélie. Now you can work your magic here.' I stand back and admire the effect. My room looks much brighter with the addition of her smiling face.

I see we've got company, says Billy's photo.

'Billy, this is Amélie; Amélie, this is Billy.' I turn from one to the other. 'I'm sure we're all going to get along together fine.'

Billy is conspicuously silent.

I message Rosie to tell her about my new job and the *Amélie* poster, but she doesn't reply. This makes me feel bad and I wish I hadn't messaged her at all. If only I could see her I'm sure everything would be fine.

'Got a job at the cinema,' I mutter to Mum through a mouthful of macaroni cheese at dinner that night.

She looks delighted and tactfully refrains from probing me about my change of heart.

The phone rings as I am doing the washing up so I dry my hands on the tea towel and head out to the lounge room. There is only one person, apart from telemarketers, who calls our landline. I don't know how Dad settled on Mondays, but Mondays it is.

'That'll be your father.' Mum's voice is neutral.

Mum always calls Dad 'your father' these days, like he's no relation to her. This is understandable. Thinking about the way he dropped out of our lives gives me a funny feeling in my stomach. It's like neither of us were worth sticking around for.

But I answer the phone and tell him about my job. He sounds impressed, though I can tell he isn't. He's too tied up with Hannah and all his important human rights work to care that his daughter has a job in a cinema.

'How's your mum going?' he asks.

There it is again. She used to be Rhonda, now she's 'your mum'.

'She's going great. She's doing Zumba and she's got a new haircut and she looks fantastic.'

Dad is silent for a while. Eventually he coughs. 'Right, well, I'd better get back to it.' We say our goodbyes.

After the phone call, I lie in bed looking up at my *Amélie* poster. I don't know why I didn't get one ages ago. Looking at her makes me feel good. I take a photo and send it to Rosie but she still doesn't reply. I guess, like Dad, she has more important things on her mind.

Unlike me, Rosie has always had boyfriends, but until Luke they never got in the way. All of a sudden I had to compete for her time and attention. She said we should double date, but it didn't work out. She set me up with one of Luke's friends and all he wanted to do was get stoned and take my top off. His tongue was like a sea slug. It was horrible.

I guess I never really felt like I needed a boyfriend. I had so much fun with Rosie, I didn't feel like there was a hole in my life. I was happy to wait for the right boy to come along. And now he has. Not even Rosie has had a French boyfriend. She is going to be super-impressed.

'My life is taking a new course now I have a job at the French Film Festival,' I say to Amélie. Just the words French Film Festival make me feel very classy. They are like a magic spell. Hopefully Alex One will come by and, noticing my new French Film Festival sophistication, will fall head over heels in love with me.

'What would you do,' I ask Amélie, 'if you thought the man of your dreams might have lost your phone number?'

I would pick up his photograph album on the street where he dropped it while riding his scooter, then leave him anonymous clues that would lead him to the Sacre-Coeur Cathedral, where I would be waiting in disguise ...

In the absence of a photograph album, a scooter or a cathedral, none of Amélie's methods are pertinent at this point.

Pull yourself together, girl, I hear Billy say as I close my eyes. I'm not sure if she's talking to Amélie or to me.

Chapter Eleven

On Tuesday I am at the cinema at nine am, ready for the first screening at ten. I have gone to some trouble with my appearance.

Kevin stares at me as I come in. 'It's not fancy dress.'

This is rich as he, himself, is wearing yet another Hawaiian shirt with beads. I am only the hired help, so I don't comment on his similarity to a seedy Honolulu bartender in a Hollywood movie. Instead, I straighten my beret and glance at my blue-striped T-shirt and jaunty blue neck kerchief. 'I thought, for the festival …'

His mouth twitches. 'Well, as long as you do what you're paid for, I suppose it's okay.'

'Eh bien.'

He scowls. 'I warned you about that.'

'Pard– sorry.' He's such a stick in the mud. You'd think he'd be grateful I'm bringing a touch of class to his run-down establishment.

Kevin explains my duties to me. I am to sell tickets, ice creams and lollies and clean up in the cinema after each showing.

That is all as I expected, but not much of a challenge for someone with my indomitable qualities. I glance around the foyer. The ambience is a little disappointing. Kevin clearly has no idea about marketing. If it were up to me, I'd have decorated the cinema in red, white and blue. I'd have sliced up some baguettes, topped them with Camembert and put on Edith Piaf. Maybe I can talk to him about my ideas later. Once we've bonded.

Kevin coughs and wanders outside for a smoke. He smokes an awful lot. Mum would be horrified.

While I wait for Kevin to come back in I ferret around in the box of posters, which he has not yet thrown out. What luck – another *Amélie* poster emerges. I find some Blu-tack under the counter and fasten it to the wall behind me. It's not much, but it lifts the decor immediately.

Satisfied, I stand self-importantly behind the counter and inspect the program. The first movie today is an old one, *Three Colours: Blue*. According to the program, it is about a woman whose family has been killed in a car crash. This sounds intense and I'm not sure I want to watch it. The underlying theme, apparently, is about liberty.

The following films in the series, *Three Colours: White* and *Three Colours: Red*, which are showing later in the week, are about equality and fraternity. Those French. They're so profound. So intellectual. Who else but the French would make a series of movies about the founding values of their country?

I try to imagine an Australian version of *Three Colours* and fail. What are our founding values anyway? *Mateship, holidays and ...*

'Happy?'

I focus on the figure in front of me. It is an Alex, but not Alex One, who I crave, but Alex Two – she of the Paris Syndrome conversation. Today she is wearing cut-off denim shorts and a blue singlet that coordinates nicely with her blue hair and eyes.

'What are you doing here?' I ask.

She speaks over me at the same time, possibly asking the same question.

We smile, pause, and interrupt each other again in a jumble of words – 'working ... seeing a movie ... festival ... selling tickets ...'

My competitive streak surfaces and I raise my voice so as to get the upper hand. 'Is it safe for you to watch French movies? With your possibly latent Paris Syndrome? Aren't you worried about activating it?'

Alex shrugs. 'I'm experimenting. I'm working on something.'

'Something?'

'An idea.'

'Want to share it?'

Kevin has come back inside. He glares at me as he replaces his packet of smokes in his top pocket and I notice a line has formed behind Alex.

'Student? Nine dollars.' I hold out my hand. 'I get a break before the afternoon session. Do you want to have lunch?'

Alex adjusts her backpack and looks thoughtful. 'Okay, yes, that would be good.' She hands over her money.

I present her ticket with a flourish – 'One to *Three Colours: Blue*' – and turn to the next person in the queue. Despite Kevin's ban, I can't resist the odd s'il vous plaît and merci beaucoup when he is out of earshot. It goes down well with the audience, who are an eclectic mix of young student-looking types and retirees. I suppose that's what you get on a December weekday.

After everyone is in and I've cleaned the snack area, Kevin steps outside for yet another smoke. I open the cinema door and step quietly inside, standing still while my eyes adjust to the dark. It's hard to work out what's going on but perhaps that's because I missed the beginning, which hopefully was the car-crash scene. Luckily I've read the program so I know that Juliette Binoche is trying to free herself from attachments following the death of her family. She looks sultry and Gallic in close-up as she watches television.

On the screen in front of her, people fall from the sky. This must be symbolic of Juliette's desire to be free. I can relate to that part. The blue chandelier must also be symbolic – it keeps reappearing. Maybe the chandelier is beautiful but cold, like Juliette herself. I am proud of my film-analysis skills – I may have a future as a critic. The elderly woman recycling bottles must be significant too. My brain starts to hurt at this stage. Maybe I don't have a future as a film critic.

Over the next forty-five minutes I feel increasingly confused. A vague discomfort surfaces. Yes, the movie is stylish and sexy and seductive, but by the time Juliette tries to stop her husband's assistant from finishing his music I just want it to be over. This is disconcerting. I should love this movie. Why don't I?

I message Rosie to ask if she's ever watched *Three Colours: Blue*, but she doesn't reply again. She's going through a quiet patch. This has been happening a lot lately.

The movie closes with a beautiful scene of Juliette Binoche crying – symbolising (I think) that her heart has at last unfrozen – and by the time the lights come up I am again convinced it was a masterpiece.

'Like that stuff, do you?' asks Kevin, as I walk outside, ready to open the doors. He has styled his sandy-coloured hair with a wet comb, upgrading him to the appearance of a Honolulu cocktail maker. He reeks of cigarette smoke.

'French films? Yes. Doesn't everyone?' I have almost forgotten my existential crisis.

Kevin hitches up his shorts. 'To be honest, nah. Give me a good old Yankee blockbuster any day. But I get the French films cheap for the festival. Sponsored by the French government. And they go okay with the uni crowd and the pensioners. What do you like about them? Every time I took a look, nothing was happening.'

I dismiss my reservations about the movie. I don't want to be in Kevin's camp on this. 'They're really deep.'

Kevin snickers. 'So deep you've got no idea what's going on.'

'They make you think. Not everything's on the surface. You have to work for it. It's all about the meta-analysis.' Meta-analysis was something my English teacher was keen on. To be honest, I'm not sure what it is, but it seems right for this occasion.

Kevin gives me a long look and I'm worried for a moment he's going to call me out about meta-analysis, but he sniffs. 'What was with that sugar cube dissolving for about five minutes? Meta-analyse that.'

'I liked that scene. It showed how she was in such a trance, locked away from the world.'

Kevin snorts. 'I'd have left that one on the cutting room floor myself. Riveting, not.' He pulls open one door and gestures to me to get the other. Then he winks. 'It's all right, you can admit you don't understand it.'

'I do understand it.'

He rolls his eyes. 'I reckon it's like the Emperor's New Clothes. No one wants to be the first to say it's crap.'

If Kevin has a point, I'm not going to concede it. I pull open the other door. 'It's subtle.'

'*The Hunger Games*, now that was a good movie.'

I sniff. Kevin is a philistine who doesn't enjoy the intellectual challenge of French cinema.

Kevin's attention wanders and he gestures with his chin. 'Did I say you could put that up?'

I follow his gaze and see the *Amélie* poster behind the counter. 'Sorry. I know you're not showing *Amélie*, but it was the only French film poster I found. Don't you like it?'

Kevin eyes Amélie's mischievous grin. 'She looks like she's up to no good.'

'Oh no. She's like a guardian angel. She does good deeds.'

Kevin looks suspicious. 'She'd better not try it round here. I'm fine the way I am.'

As the crowd files out I see Alex. She seems to be in a trance. I hope the blue-lit images of Juliette Binoche haven't triggered a bout of Paris Syndrome. I wave my hand in front of her face and finally she focuses on me.

'Oh, hi. Didn't see you there.'

'I'll see you in the milk bar next door in half an hour, okay? I need to clean up here.'

She nods in a dreamy way and drifts off in that direction.

I watch her go. I know daytime movies are disorienting, but she seems more out of it than the other customers. It's lucky I'm going to check on her.

'Going outside for a smoke – can you clean the counter?' Kevin heads for the door.

I frown as I wipe the counter. I have never met anyone who smokes as much as Kevin. Imagine the tongue-lashing Mum would give him. As I head for the popcorn machine – alert for any stray popcorn on the floor, who knew it was so dangerous? – my gaze comes up and I see the *Amélie* poster. Her dark brown eyes meet mine. She smiles at me in an encouraging way and a fizzing sensation fills my chest. She is trying to tell me something.

The cinema is quiet and I feel like it is just the two of us here.

I decided to devote my life to good deeds, I hear her say.

A light bulb flashes on inside my head. The Regal Cinema may not be Amélie's Café des 2 Moulins in Montmartre, but there are some similarities.

Both places have people who could do with some help.

Chapter Twelve

When I get to the milk bar, Alex is at a table with a milkshake in front of her, scribbling madly in a large notebook. I get a chocolate milkshake for myself and join her.

She looks up. 'How good was that swimming pool scene?' She sounds like she is talking about an appearance by the Virgin Mary – completely awestruck.

It's true the swimming pool scene was a standout. Firstly, it was blue-lit, which made it eerie and atmospheric. Secondly, it featured Juliette Binoche swimming laps in a mysterious way. Only the French can swim mysteriously. 'Yeah, it blew me away too.'

'Is that a pun?'

'Huh? Oh I get it. Blue. Ha ha. No. It was such a fantastic metaphor.'

Alex sighs and gazes into her milkshake as if Juliette Binoche is swimming up and down in there. 'The way she immersed herself in the water, cutting herself off from everything … It makes you think, what is the meaning of liberty really?' She sucks on her straw, rather as a French philosopher might suck on his pipe while pondering existentialism in the Cafe Les Deux Magots.

I am pleased with the direction this conversation is heading. I might not be on the left bank of the Seine, but it's not too bad for Brisbane. 'I thought the symbolism of the chandelier was amazing, didn't you?'

Alex frowns. 'I didn't notice the chandelier.'

'Oh. Well, how about the old woman doing the recycling? She looked so lonely.'

'I didn't notice her either.'

'That's strange. She was in and out all the time.'

Alex studies my face. 'Are you sure we were watching the same movie?'

I shrug. 'Maybe that's the mystery of French filmmaking.'

'Do you think it was about the juxtaposition of liberty and isolation?'

I smile. 'Yes, exactly.' I slurp on my milkshake. 'Hey, if there was an Australian version of *Three Colours*, what would the colours stand for?'

Alex ponders. 'That's a good question. What are our three central values? Well, you'd have to have good old Aussie mateship, wouldn't you?'

'Got that one.'

'Holidays.'

'Got it.'

'So what's your third one?'

'I don't have one. That's why I'm asking you.'

She takes a sip of her milkshake. 'A fair go.'

'Mateship, holidays and a fair go. It doesn't have the ring of Liberty, Equality and Fraternity, does it?'

'I don't know. It gives us something to fight for. I'm prepared to go to the wall for mateship, holidays and a fair go.'

'I suppose so. As long as mateship includes us women.'

'It totally includes us women, mate.' Alex smiles.

'I'll take your word for it.' I glance at her notebook. It looks like she's working on some sort of formula. 'Got it all worked out?'

She shakes her head.

I study her notebook, reading upside down. At the top is a heading – *Three Colours: Blue* and below are a lot of words and numbers. I can only make out a couple.

Aesthetics: 9/10

Intellectualism: 9/10

I look up at her. 'What is it?'

'I'm trying to work out what it is about the images or culture of France, and in particular Paris, that sets off this ...' She waves her fingers in circles around the sides of her head.

'Syndrome?'

She nods. 'If I isolated it, maybe I could develop a way to immunise against it. Think how much suffering that would save.'

'A cure for malaria hardly rates in comparison.'

Alex laughs. 'First World problem, right? Still, it is relevant to our situation.'

'Is this something you're going to work on at uni?'

'Yes. There's a big self-directed project in first year. In Professor Tanaka's class, actually. I thought I'd get a head start.'

I look at her notebook. 'So you're scoring movies?'

'Well, I've started. I'm still developing my system. I'm considering criteria like aesthetics, intellectualism, stereotypical or idealised images of Paris ... That sort of thing.' She takes a noisy slurp of her milkshake.

'What about sex?'

'Pardon?' she looks up. 'Sorry, my milkshake ...'

'Sex.' I raise my volume.

The woman at the counter gives me a disapproving look.

I roll my eyes at Alex. 'You're not telling me you didn't notice how beautiful Juliette Binoche is?'

She meets my eyes, flushes, picks up her pen, writes *sex* at the bottom of the page and gnaws at her lip.

'Eight out of ten?' I suggest.

'Mm, though that doesn't leave much room for movement.'

'You planning on watching lots of sexy French movies?'

'No, it's just–'

'I know. Audrey Tautou and Marion Cotillard. Make it seven then.'

She scrawls a number seven on the page. 'It's still a work in progress, as you can see.'

'So, do you have a hypothesis?'

Alex hoovers the last of her milkshake. 'My theory is that we are insidiously exposed to a form of brainwashing. A particular type of person becomes overpowered by the notion that Paris is paradise. I think this brainwashing works on different levels – the intellectual, the romantic, the sensory, the aesthetic and, as you've pointed out to me, the sexual.'

My mind drifts to sexy Alex One and I adjust my beret. This probably proves her point.

'You, Happy, are a classic example of a person who for some reason believes a meaningful life can only be lived in Paris.'

'But it's true, life would be more fun in Paris.' I wave my arm around, taking in the café, the suburb beyond and the city itself. 'You call this living?'

'I rest my case. What makes you so sure life would be better in Paris?'

'But you think so too, don't you?'

'Yeah, I'm crazy about Paris. I'm playing devil's advocate here.'

'You don't really think I'd get Paris Syndrome if I went to Paris, do you?' I still find the idea absurd.

She points her straw at my chest. 'I'd have to say the odds are good.'

I narrow my eyes. 'So, you said brainwashing. Do you mean intentionally?'

Alex stares back at me. 'It's not beyond the bounds of possibility.'

I glance at her notes. 'Isn't that a little … paranoid?'

'The Film Festival's sponsored by the French Tourism Board, you know. That's kind of sinister, isn't it?'

'Maybe, but brainwashing … What if we're all just incredibly susceptible to the romance of Paris? Perhaps it really is the most wonderful city in the world.'

'Maybe.' Alex sounds unconvinced. 'That movie … How did it really make you feel?' She looks into my eyes. 'Be honest.'

'Um, well, I felt conflicted.'

'Aha. You wanted to love it but in fact you didn't, but you told yourself you did because you didn't want to admit you weren't clever enough or French enough to understand.'

My mouth quivers.

'I knew it. Happy, that is exactly what Paris Syndrome is. It's the confusion between expectation and reality which sends you crazy.'

I stare at her. Is she right? Was what I'd felt in the cinema the stirrings of Paris Syndrome?

'All these people,' Alex gestures at the queue forming for the next session, 'unwittingly trapped by Gallic propaganda.'

I look out at the street. At all the innocent Brisbane folk dreaming of a French paradise. I suppose maybe it is a little disturbing. Even a little Stephen King if you look at it that way. 'Okay. You might be onto something.'

'Did you know France is the number one tourist destination in the world?'

I shake my head.

'And what's more, when Australians are asked where they would most like to travel overseas, Paris tops the list. Isn't that strange?'

'Why? Paris is great.'

'Yes, it's great. But is it *that* great? What about Florence? What about Cape Town? What about New York? Or Berlin? Why Paris?'

'You obviously have a theory.'

Alex looks around, mock-secretively. 'I already told you. Brainwashing,' she whispers.

'You're serious, aren't you?'

Alex smiles. 'I am. It's like *The Bourne Identity*. If I vanish and there's a scent of garlic and some baguette crumbs left in my room, you'll know where to look.' She sounds like she's joking, but I can tell she's half-serious.

We are silent for a few moments as I consider her theory. 'It's more like *Zoolander*.'

Alex frowns. 'Because I'm a male model?'

'No, because Zoolander was brainwashed to make him assassinate the Malaysian Prime Minister when the song "Relax" came on.'

'Right.' Alex sounds unconvinced. 'So anyway, do you want to help me out with my project?' she asks.

I am about to say I'm too busy, but then I catch sight of Amélie's poster through the glass dividing door. That fizzing sensation fills my chest again. *What would Amélie do?* It is a little paradoxical to evoke Amélie in the fight against Paris Syndrome, but Alex needs some help with her project. She's set herself a pretty big task. 'Okay, sure. What do you want me to do?'

'You can be my undercover agent at the French Film Festival. Chat to people about the movies. Try to work on the scoring system. Add some new categories.'

'Mm, okay. And meanwhile, you will be …?'

'I've got a new job as a waitress at a French restaurant, so I've got the food side covered.' She pauses. 'You know there's a French Food Festival coming up too?'

'Sponsored by the French Tourism Board?'

'Uh huh.'

'The plot thickens. So, how does Professor Tanaka fit into this conspiracy?'

'You know in the Bond films, how Bond gets his briefings from M?'

'Professor Tanaka is M?'

'Yep.'

'And the essay competition is how she recruits new agents?'

She smiles. 'I know you two didn't get off to a good start, but she's cool once you get to know her.'

'Okay, I'm now a Paris Syndrome undercover agent. The name's Glass. Happy Glass. So, when will we meet again to talk tactics?'

'Professor Tanaka's next Tuesday? I've got work now.' Alex gets to her feet.

'Roger that. So do I.' Alex and I enter each other's numbers into our phones.

'Bye then,' says Alex. 'Good luck.'

'Au revoir. Bonne chance.'

She shakes her head and leans closer to adjust my beret. 'You're lucky I got to you before they did, kid.'

I decide not to tell her about Alex One. It is possible the enemy may have recruited me first.

Chapter Thirteen

My life as a Paris Syndrome undercover agent commences. It is not as exciting as I had hoped.

Over the next few days, I do a shift a day at the Film Festival, taking in, in the process, *Three Colours: White* and *Three Colours: Red*. *White* is about a man who has lost all his money and seeks to regain equality through revenge, while *Red* is about a university student and model whose lives become interconnected with others in the spirit of fraternity.

I keep a notebook under the counter and record my observations of moviegoers. I note how many of them look confused as they exit the cinema, but it is possible people always look like that after sitting in the dark for two hours. I will have to discuss my research design with Alex Two. Perhaps I need a control group who are watching Hollywood movies if I am to draw accurate conclusions.

On my way home on Wednesday, I continue my life of good deeds by ducking into a bookshop, cruising the health section and buying a copy of *Quit Smoking Instantly*. I now have seventy-five dollars left from my essay win, which should still be enough to get a tattoo. I don't want to wait a whole two weeks for my first pay packet. I will get a disguise sorted and give it another go.

On Thursday I surreptitiously leave *Quit Smoking Instantly* on one of the cinema seats. Kevin picks it up while he is cleaning and I see him flicking through it while he's waiting for the next session.

Amélie gives me a wink of approval, but my work is not yet done.

'Kevin, how about we jazz things up around here for the weekend?'

He looks up from the book. 'What do you mean? You've already put up that poster.'

I gesture around the cinema. 'We should get a bit of French ambience happening. It would bring the crowds in.'

Kevin looks sceptical. 'Nah.'

'Oh come on, Kevin. It's a French Film Festival. People need to believe they've stepped out of Toowong and into Paris.'

'Why would you want to do that?' Kevin rolls his eyes. 'What've you got in mind anyway?'

I smile at him. I have been giving this some thought. 'An accordion player on the street outside. Some French-themed snacks – we can sell little plates of them. And decorations – lots of red, white and blue.'

'And who's paying for all that?'

'You'll recoup your costs in increased custom.'

Kevin narrows his eyes. 'I advertised for an assistant not a marketing manager.'

'Well, you're getting my advice for free then, aren't you?'

'I hope I'm not going to regret this.' Kevin hits a button on the till and pulls out one hundred dollars. 'That's your ambience budget for the rest of the festival. I'll need receipts.'

I take the money. 'You won't be disappointed.'

On Friday evening I debut my main budget item – the accordion player. A quick Google search has led me to *Tony – Birthdays and Weddings a Speciality*. Tony arrives at six pm, dressed in a white shirt, red waistcoat and black trousers. I can only afford to pay him for a half-hour 'preview', but people throw money in his accordion case so he stays for almost three hours. It is extraordinary what an ambience boost accordion music gives. Lots of passers-by stop on the street to watch and come in to pick up a program.

I have made about ten little French flags out of coloured paper and stuck them up around the place, and prepared tasting plates of French cheese and slices of baguette, which we sell for ten dollars.

The customers are complimentary and though he doesn't say much Kevin seems pleased with our takings. Tonight is unusual as we are screening a double. First up is a short movie from 1956, *The Red Balloon*, about a boy wandering through Paris followed by a magic balloon. I like that one, especially the ending when he is gathered up by all the balloons in Paris and taken on a ride over the city. It's uplifting (no pun intended) and you get fantastic views of the city, which is a bonus. Paris looks amazing from the air. I don't know how many cathedrals there are, but pointed spires were everywhere.

Kevin's review is concise. 'Can't believe they made a movie about a psycho balloon.'

I can't believe he is not charmed by the magic of Paris.

We follow *The Red Balloon* with *Cafe de Flore*, which the blurb says is a love story about people separated by time and place but connected in profound and mysterious ways. This one is a little baffling, but I don't admit as much to Kevin.

'I didn't see what was so special about that café,' he says as we clean out the ice-cream trays. 'May as well make a movie about the milk bar next door.'

'The Cafe de Flore is one of the oldest coffee houses in Paris. Lots of artists and intellectuals like Picasso and Jean-Paul Sartre used to hang out there. Many people say it's the most famous café in the world.'

Kevin looks at me as if I've sprouted an extra head. 'Geez, you've got a lot of excess baggage in that head of yours. How do you know all this stuff? Are you studying cafés of the world at school or something?'

I shrug. 'It's common knowledge.'

'Not to me. So why was part of the movie set in Canada? I didn't get that part.'

'It was metaphysical.'

'The other day it was meta-analysis and today it's metaphysics. I'm worried about you.' He gives me a long look, frowns, shakes his head and walks outside for a cigarette.

On Saturday we screen *The Women on the 6th Floor*, about a Parisian man who regains his joie de vivre through a friendship with some Spanish cleaning women. It is easy viewing and the moviegoers enjoy it. Even Kevin admits it wasn't too bad.

Using my own unique sampling method, I have discerned that there are two distinct types of filmgoers – those who get it and those who don't.

'Fantastic movie, isn't it?' I say to a random selection as they come out of the cinema.

As you would expect in this self-selecting group of French Film Festival attendees, those who respond positively outnumber those who don't by about two to one. Women are also more likely to respond positively than men. I note my results in order to pass them on to Alex at our meeting. Hopefully she will have some good ideas on how to improve the validity of my research.

As I slide my notebook in my pocket, I have a brilliant idea. I will use Kevin as a control subject. I already know he is immune to the charms of French movies so I decide to test him out in some other areas. First, I quickly Google Jean-Paul Sartre quotes on my phone.

'Kevin,' I say, as we are making our way through the empty theatre, picking up popcorn containers and ice-cream wrappers. 'What do you think about Jean-Paul Sartre's idea that passion can never be used as an excuse to justify an action?'

'Music stopped with the Rolling Stones as far as I'm concerned,' he grunts without turning his head.

I pull out my notebook and put a cross next to French Intellectuals.

'I'm having boeuf bourguignon tonight, can't wait,' I say as I clean out the ice-cream dispenser and Kevin tallies the till.

'I prefer Hawaiian myself. Have you tried the one at Bennie's Pizzas? I go there every Tuesday. It's their cheap night.'

I put a cross next to French Food.

I take one last stab with something I think can't fail. 'Juliette Binoche is so beautiful, isn't she?' I murmur as I sweep the tiled floor of the lobby.

'Who?'

'The star of *Three Colours: Blue*, Juliette Binoche.'

'Oh, you mean Juliette Binochay. She's all right I suppose. Needs to liven up a bit. And, you know, wear something more sexy. How about Angelina Jolie in *Mr and Mrs Smith*? Phwoar, hey?'

So that's a cross for French Women. Kevin, clearly, would be safe to visit Paris. His expectations are at rock bottom.

I am looking forward to Sunday, which will bring me an opportunity to extend my research. Kevin will be going ten-pin bowling, he tells me. 'I'm going to leave you in charge.' He makes it clear I am being entrusted with a tremendous responsibility.

'I won't let you down, Kevin. I'm psyched.' I am, but not in the way he probably assumes.

On Saturday evening, I stay up late developing a questionnaire.

> In general I like/don't like French movies.
> If the answer to the above is 'like' please continue.
> On a scale of one to five from not important to highly important,
> please rank your reasons for liking French films.
> The locations are always beautiful.
> The actors are always beautiful.
> The characters are always intelligent.

They are so deep and profound.

They are romantic.

The food always looks delicious.

They make me feel like I am someone else.

They make me want to go and live in Paris.

After some consideration, I add a male/female, age and nationality question up the top. I print out multiple copies and tuck them in my backpack ready for the morning.

Then I check my phone again, in case I have missed a text, but Alex One still hasn't called. This is driving me crazy.

Sexuality still not activated, I message Rosie.

Must put in passcode. Beep, beep.

She sounds like her old self.

Passcode entered. Activation in progress, I message.

Full account must be submitted once activation is complete.

Account will be provided. G'night, Rose.

G'night, Happ. You and me and gay Paree.

Despite Rosie's messages, I still feel lonely. I miss her so much it hurts. No one else knows me the way she does. *You and me and gay Paree.*

I think of her lying on my bed, flicking through a *Paris Match*. How long ago was that? Just over a year?

Check this out, Happy, those girls on the scooter look like us. She hands me the magazine.

There is a full-page photo of two girls in summer frocks riding a scooter past the Arc de Triomphe. One has red hair and the other a wild mop of brown curls. *That's totally us*, I say.

She takes the magazine back from me and gazes at the photo. *Only seven hundred and ninety-five days to go, babe. You and me and gay Paree.*

Now, I lie back on my bed. 'Only three hundred and fifty days to go now, Rosie. That's not long.'

I pick up her copy of *The Great Gatsby* and flick through it. It falls open at a page with a dog-eared corner and a section underlined in pencil. *There are all kinds of love in this world, but never the same love twice.*

I imagine Rosie reading the line and I wonder if it's true.

On Sunday afternoon, we are screening an old movie, *Monsieur Hulot's Holiday*. Given the age and obscurity of the movie I anticipate a hard-core audience and this proves to be the case. The crowd is now closer to inner-city trendy than suburban yuppie. Large-framed black glasses, trilby hats and super-short fringes are the costume de jour. This gives me an idea for my next tattoo-parlour excursion.

I check for messages at every opportunity. It has been ten days since I gave Alex One my number. He has definitely lost his phone. I sigh deeply. It will probably be ten years before we are reunited in Paris.

With each ticket I sell, I hand out a questionnaire. 'Fill out the questionnaire and go into the draw to win dinner for two at Le Petit Escargot.' I feel guilty as there isn't really a prize on offer, but it is for a greater good – a world free of Paris Syndrome.

The queue is nearly at the end when my heart leaps into my throat like a startled frog.

"Ello 'Appy.'

It is Alex One. I stare into his dark brown eyes, mesmerised. Thank goodness I have taken this job at the cinema or we might never have met again. But what's that on his shoulder – a slender white hand? My vision expands to take in the owner of the hand – a tall blonde girl.

I swallow the frog with difficulty. 'Did you lose your phone?'

He raises his eyebrows.

The blonde smiles nervously.

Perhaps I have not been subtle.

"Appy, this is Amelia.'

'Hi.' My mouth does something that might pass as a smile if you had difficulty reading emotional cues.

'Hello.' Amelia also does a lame smile-thing and fiddles with a curl that hangs over her shoulder. Amelia's curls are civilised and tamed, unlike mine. I detest them.

'Two for *Monsieur Hulot's Holiday*?' I ask.

Alex pulls out his wallet.

'See you in a minute. I'm …' Amelia waves her hand in the direction of the toilet.

Alex smiles at me when she's gone and hands over some cash. 'I still 'ave your number, 'Appy. I was going to ring this week. But maybe you 'ave 'ad enough of French movies? Perhaps you would like to eat snails with me instead?'

I hesitate. I should say no, but he's awfully cute and he makes my heart pound and there's most likely a good reason why he has turned up at the Film Festival with lame-smiling, neat-curled girl. She might be his long-lost cousin, or maybe she's severely depressed and he's trying to cheer her up, or maybe–

''Appy?' Alex looks into my eyes.

My stomach feels like a thousand moths are having a party in there but I act casual as I hand over his tickets. 'I haven't had snails before.'

'Then you must try.' He holds his hand up to his ear with the thumb extended. 'I will call.'

I watch him stroll away with languid grace, and despite the fact he has failed to call and brought another girl to the movies, my heart goes pit-a-pat, pit-a-pat. Rosie is right. Once the passcode is entered, that's it. *Beep, beep. Activating.*

'Two for *Monsieur Hulot's Holiday*?' I smile so broadly at the next customers that they look a little startled. An appointment to eat snails with a French Love God does wonders for one's customer service.

Chapter Fourteen

On Monday, inspired by the hipsters at *Monsieur Hulot's Holiday*, I call into a two-dollar shop and buy myself a pair of large, black-framed glasses with clear lenses and a trilby hat. I try on a short-fringed black wig but it looks ridiculous on top of my hair. At home, I put on tight jeans and a pair of Mum's high-heeled black boots. With the addition of the glasses and hat, and with my hair pulled back tightly, I look rather rock star, if I say so myself. And obviously eighteen.

My third tattoo parlour is down the road in Toowong. There's a young guy behind the counter with a three-day growth and a faded, black T-shirt. Things go swimmingly. He doesn't ask for ID, just beckons me into a cubicle out the back. My heart prances as I follow him and I almost skip. At last!

I tell him what I want and he shows me a book with lots of different font styles. I choose one that's stylish and not too gothic. Rosie is going to be super-impressed.

'Okay. That'll be one hundred dollars,' he says.

I am pulling out my purse when I realise what he's said. *Damn.* *Damn. Damn.* If only I hadn't bought that book for Kevin. 'What can I get for seventy-five?'

'That'll get you *je suis une*,' he says, without a trace of irony. 'You can come back and do the rest when you've got the cash.'

'Do I seem like someone who wants to look like they changed their mind in the middle of making a statement?'

He shrugs. 'Lots of people do it in instalments. Guy last week got *There is nothing to fear but*.'

I stare at him. 'Wouldn't it be better if you left off *but*?'

'He had the cash for *but*. It was his call.'

I frown. 'Well, I'm not into indecisive half-statements. I'll come back.' I get to my feet. I'll have to wait until Kevin pays me, but at least I've got a friendly tattooist lined up now.

That evening Kevin returns, energised by his night off. He inspects the flyer for the night's movie, *Yves Saint Laurent*, which is about the famous fashion designer. 'Bor-ing. I can't believe I agreed to two weeks of this.'

'Why did you?'

'Because I get them cheap from the French Tourism Board. I told you that.'

'Oh yes.' Alex Two is right: the reach of the French Tourism Board is vast and slightly sinister.

Dad calls me on my mobile when I'm having a break – I emailed him to let him know I wouldn't be at home for my regular Monday night phone call.

'What's going on in your life, Happy?' he asks.

I have a dinner date with a French Love God, I want to scream, but I don't. Instead I give him a run-down on the movies we've been showing.

'I watched all of the *Three Colours* movies with your mother. Back when we were at university.'

I grind my teeth. 'Why do you have to say "your mother"? She has a name. You used to use it.'

'Oh, sorry, I'll call her Rhonda if you prefer that.'

'I don't want you to call her Rhonda because I prefer it, I want you to call her Rhonda because that's her name.' I snort into the phone. 'I've got to go; the movie's finished.' I hang up even though I've still got ten minutes of my break left and take out my irritation on polishing the counter.

'Ease up, Happy,' says Kevin. 'You'll rub the whole surface away at that rate.'

On Tuesday Kevin runs the cinema by himself so it is my day off. I catch the ferry to St Lucia and walk to Professor Tanaka's house for our scheduled meeting.

Alex is in the garden cutting flowers. She stands when she sees me and holds out the bunch of roses in her hands. 'For you, mademoiselle.' She gives me an impish smile.

I smile back and take the flowers with an exaggerated eye-flutter. 'Pour moi? Oh, you shouldn't have.'

Alex places her secateurs in the wheelbarrow. 'Shall we go in?'

The front door opens, as if by magic, and there is Professor Tanaka. She is even tinier than I remember.

I hand her the flowers.

'Thank you, Veronica. That's kind of you.'

'Actually, I didn't–'

But she is already trotting towards the lounge room and I don't think she hears me.

Croissants, jam and coffee are laid out on the coffee table again. A copy of *Paris Match* has been pushed aside. She must order it in. Maybe she's got the edition with the Rosie-and-me lookalikes on the scooter. I'd like to see that again. A vinyl disc is spinning on the old turntable and a woman is singing a French song I don't recognise. The beauty of her voice transcends the scratchy record.

'"Tous les Garcons et les Filles". "All the Boys and Girls".' Professor Tanaka moves her head to the melody. 'This was playing everywhere when I was in Paris. It came out a few years before, but it was still popular.'

Alex sits next to me on the couch. She has left her work boots by the door, exposing a pair of snazzy rainbow-coloured toe-socks. Her eyes flicker to the roses in Professor Tanaka's hands and she looks disappointed for some reason.

Professor Tanaka places the roses in a vase then serves coffee, which I decline, and passes around the croissants. They are as delicious as last time. Her bright, dark gaze turns from Alex to me. 'Alex says you are helping with her research?'

We both nod.

Professor Tanaka cocks her head. 'So you accept the reality of Paris Syndrome, Veronica?'

I swallow my croissant before replying. 'I guess you could say I'm agnostic on the subject. But it's an interesting project.'

Professor Tanaka smiles. 'A scientific approach. Excellent. I knew you were a clever girl.'

'And it will fill in the time until I go to Paris in November,' I add. 'With my friend Rosie.'

Professor Tanaka's smile quavers and she seems about to speak, but Alex jumps in.

'I thought,' says Alex, 'if we pinpoint the underlying factors that lead to Paris Syndrome, we can work out how to inoculate against it. And then people like us ... We can go to Paris without worrying.'

Professor Tanaka blinks. 'That is sweet of you to include me. I can imagine nothing more delightful than to go to Paris again, but I doubt it is possible. My wish is only that others do not suffer as I did.' She straightens her shoulders. 'So what have you found out so far?'

'I've been working at a French restaurant.' Alex pulls a notebook out of her pocket and flips it open. 'I have discovered approximately seventy per cent of customers have no particular interest in French food. Convenience and price are more important to them. Out of the thirty per cent who are French food enthusiasts, one third are what I would classify as "at risk".'

Professor Tanaka steeples her fingers. 'Interesting. So ten per cent in total?'

Alex nods.

'And how did you work that out?'

'I presented them with a number of increasingly obsessive statements about French food and noted at what stage they stopped agreeing with me.' She turns the page in her notebook and clears her throat. 'These were my statements: *French food is the best, isn't it? I'll only eat out at French restaurants myself. You may as well not be eating if you're not eating French food. The only true chef is a French chef; the rest are just cooks. If I didn't have haute cuisine three nights a week, life wouldn't be worth living.*'

'Goodness,' says Professor Tanaka. 'How many agreed to the last statement?'

Alex consults her notes. 'A total of ten per cent. My sample size is pretty small so far so that's just one person.'

'And how would you describe this person?' asks Professor Tanaka.

'Female, Anglo, late twenties.'

'As I suspected,' says Professor Tanaka.

The record on the turntable is emitting a dull scratching sound. I get up and lift the needle back to the beginning and the sweet warble of 'All the Boys and Girls' starts again.

Professor Tanaka nods her head appreciatively. 'So beautiful. And you, Veronica? What have you been doing?'

I pull out my sheaf of questionnaires. 'I issued a questionnaire to people attending the French Film Festival. About twenty people responded. Four of them said they don't like French movies, so I guess they were dragged along. Of those who liked French movies, four scored higher than thirty out of forty and one scored a perfect forty out of forty.'

'And the characteristics of the high scorers?' asks Professor Tanaka.

I flick through my questionnaires. 'Three females under thirty, one male under thirty.'

'And the perfect score?'

I find the questionnaire and a hot tide creeps up my face. 'Oh, sorry, that one was me.'

Professor Tanaka smiles and kindly refrains from comment.

'Can I keep your surveys?' asks Alex. 'I'd like to have all the data together in case we need to do some meta-analysis.'

'Sure.' I hand her my wad of papers, noting her excellent use of the term meta-analysis.

'Professor Tanaka,' says Alex, 'did you know the French Film Festival is sponsored by the French Tourism Board? And next week there's a French Food Festival, also sponsored by the Tourism Board? Le Petit Escargot is running a stall there.'

'Hm.' Professor Tanaka steeples her fingers again and gazes at Alex over the top of them – just like a Japanese version of M.

'Do you find that disturbing?' asks Alex.

'Disturbing? What do you mean, Alex?' asks Professor Tanaka.

'It's like they're trying to brainwash people.'

Alex's theory sounded plausible last time I heard it, but in the face of Professor Tanaka's questioning, I now have my doubts. The French Tourism Board isn't a strange cult. Surely they are a reputable organisation just going about their business?

Professor Tanaka smiles. 'You could say that about any tourism campaign, Alex. Like the poster in Tokyo that made me long for France – *Find Yourself in Paris.*' A dreamy look comes over her face.

'But that's exactly what I mean.' Alex sits forward on the edge of her chair. Her eyes are bright. 'Find yourself in Paris. Why do you need to go to Paris to find yourself? No one has to go to America to find themselves, or England, or New Zealand, do they?

Why France? Why do you need to find yourself at all, especially in another country? Why aren't you okay just the way you are? Why do you need to be something different?'

Alex is very persuasive and impassioned on this topic and I wonder for a moment if she is only talking about Paris.

'They're running a sophisticated campaign to convince susceptible people their life isn't worth living unless they're in Paris,' she says.

'Another croissant?' Professor Tanaka hands Alex the plate.

She takes one and bites into it. 'These are so good,' she murmurs through a mouthful of flaky crumbs.

Professor Tanaka sips her tea. 'Maybe you are onto something, Alex. We should investigate the French Tourism Board further. Find out what they're up to. It will add to your study.' Professor Tanaka cocks her ear and sways to the music. 'Ah, this is my favourite song. No one does love like the French, do they?' A faraway look comes over her.

Alex and I take advantage of her distraction to polish off the croissants.

As the song finishes, Professor Tanaka blinks and seems surprised to see us still here. 'One thing we have not yet discussed is literature.'

Alex and I wipe the crumbs from our faces.

'Literature is so influential in psychology. If we are looking at how Paris Syndrome begins, we need to talk about literature.'

'Of course,' says Alex. 'There are so many aspects. We should explore them all.' She takes out her notebook and makes a note. 'Is there a French Literature Festival?'

'There is,' says Professor Tanaka, 'but not in Brisbane. We will have our own study group on French literature. Next time we get together I want you to bring your favourite book about Paris for discussion. We will tease out the magic of Paris and how it gets under our skin.'

'Good idea,' Alex says, but she looks a little worried.

I nod enthusiastically. I already know what my favourite book is. And talking about *Madeline* is the next best thing to talking about *Amélie*.

Chapter Fifteen

Alex and I walk to the ferry wharf together and sit on the bench to wait. I look out at the river, visualising my future as a Paris Syndrome covert agent …

> *Rosie and I alight from the Metro in Montmartre. We walk up the steep, winding stairs to the street. A winter market is in progress and the footpath is crowded with people eating roasted chestnuts and toffee apples. On the other side of the carousel, a man in a black pork-pie hat and a coat with an upturned collar emerges from behind a painted horse. It is the infamous French marketing agent, Rene Blanc …*

'What's up, Happy? You're miles away.'

I look at her. 'I was just wondering … If Professor Tanaka is M and we're secret agents, where are our special weapons?'

Alex taps her head. 'Up here. We have to outsmart them.'

'No umbrella-mounted French propaganda detectors?'

Alex smiles. 'No, but I have a secret compartment in my shoe full of garlic in case rapid olfactory camouflage is required.'

'And,' I adopt a fake French accent, 'I am able to sound French at a moment's notice should I need to infiltrate in a 'urry.'

Alex laughs. 'If I was a French brainwasher, I'd be afraid. Very afraid.' She pauses. 'What we need, Happy, is a mole on the inside of the Tourism Board to uncover their tactics.'

'Um, I might have that angle covered …' I murmur.

Alex looks at me sharply. 'What do you mean?'

I fiddle with my phone. 'I met this guy who's an intern at the Tourism Board. We might be going out to dinner.' I try to make this sound like boring secret-agent business but the heat in my cheeks is probably a giveaway.

Alex doesn't look as pleased by this infiltration opportunity as she should be. 'Oh. Right.' She stares out at the river. 'That's good.'

A pall of silence descends.

I tap my fingers on the bench and hum. As we board the ferry, something occurs to me. 'How did you manage to survey all those customers in your restaurant? Didn't it interfere with your waitressing?'

Alex glances at me. 'It's not like I shone a light in their face and yelled "Answer ze question!" My questions were cunningly delivered in the guise of pleasant chit-chat.'

'Ah. Good strategy.' I tap my nose. 'Advanced-level sleuthing.'

'I got better tips than any of the other waiters, so the customers must have enjoyed it. They just thought I was really into French food.'

We sit on a bench out the front of the ferry.

'So, what about you, Happy? Is your life incomplete if you can't eat haute cuisine three times a week?'

I laugh.

'Answer ze question.'

'Get real. How would I afford haute cuisine three times a week?'

Alex looks relieved. 'That's good to hear.'

'I do have a baguette with Camembert cheese for lunch practically every day though.'

'That's just as bad.' She frowns. 'There are so many different facets to it all. You have the cut-price version of French food obsession.' She pulls out her notebook and scribbles something. 'This is my stop.' She stands as the West End wharf approaches. 'Would you like to see my chickens?'

'Pardon?' I thought I heard her right, but it seems unlikely. 'Did you say chickens?'

She grimaces. 'I know, it's not that exciting. You probably have a better offer. It's okay.' She turns to go.

'No, wait, I was just clarifying.'

Alex turns back. 'They're French chickens if that helps.'

'Well, in that case … Absolument.' I get to my feet. 'Take me to your chickens.'

We climb a steep street from the ferry wharf. My thighs start to burn.

'You ever been to West End before?' asks Alex.

'No.'

'I'll take you on a tour through the main part then.'

We turn a corner and walk up a street lined with vegetarian restaurants and esoteric bookshops. A couple of girls in tight black

103

jeans walk up the footpath in front of us holding hands, and a curvaceous woman with tattoos down her arms sorts through a stack of books on the footpath. An Aboriginal man is playing Jimmy Little on guitar next to a colourful goanna statue. Alex pulls a couple of gold coins out of her bag and drops them in his guitar case. He nods and keeps playing.

'Cool street,' I say. 'I haven't seen anywhere else in Brisbane like this.'

'Yeah.' Alex smiles. 'West End is hipster heaven.'

We turn another corner and climb yet another hill, and eventually Alex stops in front of a wooden house with a roof smothered in ivy and a garden that definitely hasn't been touched in at least ten years. From the gate a narrow tunnel leads through the undergrowth to the door.

'Is this your place?' I look at Alex out of the corner of my eye. The house looks abandoned.

She laughs. 'No, just tricking. I call this the haunted house. Now, when I show you mine it's going to look really well maintained by contrast.' Alex waves an expansive hand towards the house next door, a run-down old Queenslander with a peeling picket fence and a front yard badly in need of a mow. 'Chez moi.' She opens the gate. 'Look, you can even get to the front door without a machete.'

'Impressive. I love these traditional old houses. Who else lives here?'

'At the moment it's just me. The house belongs to the family of a uni student who's taken off for the summer. I'm still only paying rent for one room though, so it's a sweet deal. Once uni starts we'll get a couple more people in to share. Come on.' She gestures towards the backyard. 'Come and meet the gang. Ah, here they are.'

A group of ten or so chickens is clustered together in the shade of a large fig tree.

'Wow, they're stunning.' The chickens are not your average brown variety. Some sprout topknots, some have little red fleshy horns and some are black with white speckles. 'I didn't realise chickens came in assorted colours.'

Alex squats and points at the chickens. 'This is Juliette; she's a Crèvecoeur. This is Marie-Antoinette, who is a La Flèche. And this is Amélie. She's a cuckoo Marans. They lay chocolate-coloured eggs.'

'I can't believe you've got a chicken called Amélie and you haven't even seen the movie.'

Alex shrugs. 'She used to be called Marie-Claire but I renamed her.'

'Because I told you about Amélie?'

She stands. 'It's not like it makes any difference to her.' She lowers her voice. 'Between you and me, she's not the smartest chicken in the flock.'

'Hi, chickens.' The chickens ignore me.

'They understand English, but they pretend not to. You know how it is with the French.'

'Of course, how silly of me. Bonjour, poulets.' This time the chickens do glance my way before continuing with their pecking. 'Well, meeting these chickens is a real eye-opener. I didn't even know chickens were big in France.'

Alex shakes her head. 'I'm disappointed to hear that, Happy. There's a lot more to France than *Amélie* and *Before Sunset*. France has more chicken breeds than any other country in the world. You must have heard of the Gallic rooster, Chanteclair?'

'I have, now you mention it. It's pretty weird for a country to have a rooster as its national symbol.'

'Some would argue a kangaroo and an emu are stranger.'

'True. Have you got a category for attraction to French poultry in your questionnaire?'

'Good thought.' Alex pulls her notebook out of her backpack and scribbles. 'So, how would you rate your attraction to French poultry on a scale of one to ten?'

'Seven.'

'Seven? That's what people always say when they're not sure. We'll have to see if we can improve upon that.'

I watch the chickens strutting around the yard. 'So, you let them roam all around, huh?'

'I let them out of their coop in the morning and they go back in the evening.'

The chickens stalk off towards the corner of the garden.

'Those chickens look super-pleased with themselves,' I say.

Alex eyes the chickens fondly. 'They have a right to be.'

'True, they're pretty damn gorgeous. Make that an eight.'

Alex scribbles in her notebook. 'Has anyone ever told you you're easily influenced?'

I shake my head. 'Only in relation to French things. Otherwise I'm unswayable.'

'Cup of tea?' She gestures towards the house.

'Sure.'

We climb the stairs to the back door. Alex extracts a key from under the mat and lets us in. Inside, the house is decidedly un-renovated – the kitchen is notable mainly for the faded black and white checked lino, which curls up at the edges.

'Black and white lino. Wow. My grandparents used to have that in their kitchen. This is a trip down memory lane.'

Alex smiles. 'Maybe I should sell tickets.' She puts the kettle on the stove and lights the gas.

I settle at the scratched wooden table. 'So, what do you do with the chickens? Are they just for eggs?'

Alex leans against the bench. She has left her boots at the door and her long legs rise from rainbow socks again. 'I show them.'

'You show them? Really? That's so quaint.'

'They're pretty smart. I've trained them to do tricks.'

'What sort of tricks?'

'Playing the xylophone. Running through a hoop.'

'No way. Can I see?'

'Maybe next time. I need to get them warmed up. They're temperamental otherwise.'

'I understand. Stage fright.'

She nods. 'They're sensitive to strangers. They're more intelligent than children, you know.'

'Yeah? I always figured chickens were kind of dumb.'

'I guess there's a lot you don't know about chickens.'

I lean my elbows on the table. 'You're a surprising person, Alex. If I'd had to take a guess at your interests, I would have said street theatre or acrobatics, but no, chickens.'

'Why street theatre or acrobatics?'

107

'You look really strong and fit. Do you do hula-hooping?'

Alex shakes her head; she looks amused.

'I've never met anyone who trains chickens before.'

'You haven't been mixing in the right circles.' She gets the milk from the fridge and sets it on the table. 'You're right though, I did do circus stuff this year at school.'

'I knew it. What sort?'

'Acrobatics. Clowning. Our troupe even did a performance at the Ekka.'

'Ekka?'

'The Exhibition, you know, like the Easter Show.'

'Oh, right. Can you show me? I'm such a klutz – I love watching people do gymnastic stuff.'

She smiles and shakes her head. 'I only bring it out for special occasions. Chickens are my everyday thing. You should come along and meet the poultry club some time.'

'The poultry club – that's not a band, is it?'

Alex shakes her head. 'The poultry club is way cooler than that.'

'What sort of people are they, these poultry club members?'

'All sorts.' She measures the tea into the pot.

'Real tea?'

'We're into traditional tea making here.'

'We?'

'Me and the chickens. Look.' Alex ferrets around in a drawer and produces a red, white and blue knitted object, which she places over the teapot.

'That's cute. Did you knit a beanie for your teapot?'

'It's a tea cosy. Haven't you seen one before?'

'Never, we use teabags at my place. It's way cool. And French themed.' I point at the stripes. 'Don't tell me you knitted it yourself.'

Alex shakes her head. 'No. That would be pretty sad.'

'It would complement the chicken training.'

'Giving me a well-rounded psychotic personality?'

'I didn't mean to imply that. Chicken training is hip. Or if it isn't, it should be. So who knitted the tea cosy?'

'My mother. She keeps sending them to me.' Alex grimaces. 'I'm not quite sure why.'

'That's nice of her.'

'Mm.' Alex sounds doubtful. 'You can also wear it as a hat.' She pulls it off the teapot and places it on my head. 'And look.' She reaches in and pulls bunches of my hair out through the two openings. 'Perfect for pigtails.'

I swish my hair around. 'Awesome. It's like a Viking helmet.'

'Keep it. Present from Alex's old-time tea house. I've got more, they arrive from Toowoomba every few months or so.'

'I love it.' I gaze around the kitchen. 'How long have you been living here?'

'About a year.'

'But you're from the country?'

Alex nods.

'And you went to school in Brisbane?'

'Just the last year. I had a bit of a falling out with the school in Toowoomba.'

The kettle whistles and she turns off the gas.

I'm about to ask more but she frowns. 'Long story. I'd rather not go into it all right now.'

I'm dying to know how she ended up spending Year Twelve in a share house in Brisbane, but it seems to be a sensitive topic, so I move on. 'So, the poultry club – you get all sorts of people, hey?'

'Yep.'

'Inner-city trendies, Goths, corporate execs, that sort of thing?'

'Well, no.' Alex pours water into the teapot. 'They tend to be more your lost-in-time types. Most of them haven't noticed they're in the twenty-first century.'

'As I suspected. And you? Where do you fit in?'

'I'm the hippest member of the group.' Alex joins me at the table and pours the tea. 'I raise their hipster rating by, like, two hundred per cent.'

'That doesn't surprise me at all.'

She smiles. 'I made a Facebook page for them and they thought I was Bill Gates.'

'Ooh.' I pull out my phone. 'What's the name of your page?'

'The Brisbane Unique Chicken Collective.'

'BUCC?'

Alex nods. 'Buc buc.'

I smile. 'That's clever.' I tap on my phone. 'There. I've liked them. Now you've got five fans. Are there only four of you?'

Alex grimaces. 'No, there's a lot more, but most of them think they're going to have their identity stolen by a Russian mafioso if they go on Facebook. It would be nice if I had a few more fans for the page. My social media failure gets me down, to be honest.'

'I expect all the best chicken enthusiasts were undervalued in their lifetime.'

'True. I'm the Vincent van Gogh of chickens.'

'The world doesn't know what it's missing out on. Personally, I can't wait for my chicken updates.'

'Don't worry, I'll keep 'em coming. Just because no one's listening doesn't mean I'm going to stop spreading the word.' Alex places a plate of biscuits coated in pink icing and coconut on the table.

'Oh my God. Those aren't …?'

She smiles. 'Yep.'

I sigh and hold one up to inspect it more closely. 'Lino, tea cosy, tea leaves and now Iced VoVos. You have amazing attention to detail here in your old-fashioned tea house.'

'That's why they pay me the big bucks.'

We sip our tea, dunking our biscuits in it. It's nice here with Alex and I am as close to contentment as I've been in a long time. 'So what made you get into chickens? Do you really like eggs, or what?'

'It's hard to say what came first, the chicken or the egg.'

'Ha ha. But seriously, it's an unusual interest for someone our age, isn't it?'

'I'm from the country. I've never known a time before chickens.'

'BC?'

Alex smiles. 'Right. You have a house, you have chickens. That's the way it is.'

'Well, it beats *Glamour in the Wild*. That's what most of the girls around here are into.'

'What makes you think I'm not into *Glamour in the Wild*?'

I glance around the kitchen. 'I'm pretty sure it'd be making its presence felt by now. I don't see any promotional posters.'

Alex raises her eyebrows. 'You are yet to see my bedroom.'

Then she flushes and for some reason we seem to be on the verge of an awkward moment so I change the subject. 'So what's next on the Paris Syndrome front, Agent Alex?'

Alex pulls out her notebook and flicks through the pages. 'It's very suspicious that the French Tourism Board is sponsoring both the Film Festival and the Food Festival. What are they going to get their fingers into next?'

'They don't sponsor your French Poultry Club, do they?'

Alex shakes her head. 'That's chickenfeed to them.'

'Very funny. Well, I'll try to find out.'

'Oh yes that's right, you can ask your *date*.' She emphasises the last word in an ironic manner and raises her eyebrows.

I drain my teacup. 'He's not a date, he's um … a job. I'm going undercover.'

Alex looks unconvinced.

We run out of things to say after this, so I put down my teacup and bid my farewells. 'Thanks for the tea cosy.' I touch my head.

'No problem.' Alex shuts the door behind me before I've even made it to the bottom of the stairs.

I wonder if it was something I said.

Chapter Sixteen

I am on the ferry heading for Toowong when my phone beeps. My heart hops and gambols as I see a text from Alex One.

Want to meet up at the French Food Festival tomorrow evening?

I reply straight away, *Love to. Where do you want to meet?* As I press send I realise it would have been cooler to wait at least an hour and sound a little less enthusiastic, but it's too late now. Annoyingly, he fails to respond, reinforcing my faux pas. And by the time the ferry pulls in at my wharf he still hasn't replied. Guys! They're such an energy suck.

No wonder Joan of Arc remained sexually inactive. I'm sure she felt interacting with boys would use emotional energy that was better spent freeing France from English tyranny. I'm not sure I disagree, but as I don't have a calling from God to save my country, I can expend my energy as I please.

As I walk up the street to our apartment block I give a little skip. The mixture of a French Food Festival and French Love God has to be a winner.

Mum is home late, as usual. It's my turn to make dinner, but when I'm in my bedroom getting changed, I see my *Amélie* poster. I get that strange fizzing sensation in my chest again as I remember Kevin's words from the other day. *I go there every Tuesday ...* Today is Tuesday. The door bangs – Mum's home.

I come out and see that she has a small pine tree under her arm. 'I thought I'd get us a Christmas tree.' She places it in the corner of the lounge room where it leans against the wall looking wonky and dispirited.

I'd almost managed to forget that Christmas is less than two weeks away. It's going to be different this year without Dad and Rosie.

Mum opens her handbag and pulls out a plastic bag. 'I've got some tinsel and stuff here.'

'Great. I'll decorate it tomorrow.' I have zero enthusiasm for this task but I try not to let it show. Tree decoration is usually my forte.

'Are you okay with spaghetti again?' Mum yawns as she puts her bag down.

'Why don't we go get pizza at Bennie's? I've heard it's good. And tonight's their cheap night.'

Mum smiles. 'Great idea.'

My phone goes ting as I'm in my room grabbing my shoes. It is Alex One. *South Bank Ferry terminal six pm?* I am about to reply when my eyes roam to Amélie. *What would Amélie do?* I ask myself. *Make 'im prove 'is love for you by setting 'im a treasure 'unt*, she says. *Disguise yourself using a scarf and ...*

Let him know who's in charge, says Billy.

'Ide yourself behind the carousel and ring 'im from the public phone, says Amélie.

I resist the urge to reply immediately and slide the phone back into my pocket. I'm learning.

'What's that on your head, Happy?' asks Mum as we walk out to the car.

I pat the tea cosy. 'My new hat. Do you like it?'

'It's very practical, those holes in the side for your hair. It's funny, it looks a little like a tea cosy.'

'Well it's not – it's a fashion-forward hat.'

Mum looks relieved. 'That's good. Wearing a tea cosy on your head might be a bit strange.'

In the car park at the pizza restaurant we walk past an old Holden with a hula dancer stuck to the dashboard.

My phone has been burning a hole in my pocket the whole way here. Once we are seated I can't delay any longer. 'Excuse me a sec.' I pull out my phone, reply to Alex's text saying, *Cool, see you then*, and slide it back into my pocket again. Alex and I are not at the treasure hunt and disguises stage yet. When I look up, Mum is smiling.

'A boy?'

'Um, yeah. How'd you know?'

She waggles her head. 'Just a guess. Something about your face. Want to tell me about him?'

I shake my head. 'Not really.'

'Well, any time you do …'

'Oh look.' I point. 'There's Kevin, my boss from work.' I wave at him madly.

Kevin wanders over in our direction. He is wearing a Hawaiian shirt I haven't seen before and his floppy hair is neatly combed.

'Hi, Kevin. This is my mum, Rhonda. Mum, this is Kevin.'

Mum smiles politely.

Kevin, strangely, blushes. I've never seen him do that before. 'Hello, Rhonda.'

'Why don't you sit at our table, Kevin?' I pat the seat and Kevin obliges by sliding his bottom onto the vinyl next to me. 'Kevin's a smoker,' I say in the tone of a hostess letting her guests know they have lots in common. 'He goes through a pack a day, don't you, Kevin?'

Kevin's eyes flicker to me and he nods doubtfully.

'Really?' Mum couldn't have sounded more shocked if I'd told her he was a mass murderer. 'Do you have any idea what you're doing to yourself?'

Kevin mumbles something indistinct.

Mum leans forward over the table. 'How long have you been smoking for?'

Kevin slides a little lower in his seat. 'Twenty years.'

'Twenty years?' Mum does her usual chicken squawk. She pulls her phone out of her handbag. 'Your lungs must be coated in tar.'

'Sorry, I've got to go to the loo, excuse me a sec.' I take my time in the toilet, combing my hair – a lengthy process – and washing my face and hands.

Back at the table, Kevin is looking pale. Beads of sweat are standing out on his forehead and he is leaning backwards.

This isn't helping him any as Mum is leaning forward to compensate.

Mum scrolls through photos on her phone as if sharing holiday snaps, but I'm pretty sure she isn't showing Kevin our SeaWorld pictures.

'And these are the lungs of a man who smoked only ten cigarettes a day for ten years,' she says as I sit.

There's a mumbled announcement over the PA system.

'That's my order.' Kevin leaps to his feet. 'I forgot I'm getting takeaway.' He runs for the counter without even saying goodbye.

'You two looked like you were getting along well,' I say.

'He's quiet, isn't he?' Mum shakes her head. 'Doesn't have much to say for himself. Don't you ever smoke, Happy.'

I laugh. 'As if I would.'

A girl with long straight hair goes past our table. She flicks her hair back over her shoulder and it floats like silk across her back.

'I wish I had hair like that.' I pull at my pigtails. 'This fuzzy hair makes me feel like a second-class citizen.'

Mum watches her go past. She sniffs. 'She looks like she's straightened it. No one has hair like that naturally. Besides, your hair is beautiful the way it is, Happy.'

Straightened it. I have, of course, tried this before – what fuzzy-haired girl hasn't? It was a total disaster. Rosie did it for me one night before a birthday party but she burnt my hair and I ended up looking like a scarecrow. I haven't tried again since. Is it worth another shot? *Straight hair. Straight hair.* The thought is a siren call inside my head.

'I'm pretty sure Hannah straightens her hair,' Mum says in a dismissive way.

She does. Hannah has the most beautifully swishy hair. Mine can be like that too. This is what I need for my date with Alex.

'I hope that man gives up smoking. I gave him all the facts. He's got no excuses. I'll bring home some brochures from work for you to give to him.'

I nod, but I'm a little distracted. My head is full of swishy, flicky, French-style hair. My determination is bubbling inside and once that happens there's no stopping me. Hair straightening may have been a disaster three years ago, but that doesn't mean it needs to be a disaster now. Surely the technology has advanced?

I eat my pizza as quickly as possible, keen to get back and do some research.

Back home I Google *hair straightening* and watch a YouTube tutorial, getting a list of the necessary equipment. It is reassuring to find things have moved on since the scarecrow incident. I hold down the sides of my hair as I look in the mirror. Yes, tres glamorous. I smile as I check the list of hair care products. Once I have swishy hair, Alex will be under my spell.

I check my phone again several times before I go to bed, but Alex hasn't replied. I message Rosie to tell her about my date, but she doesn't reply either. She has teased me so often about my celibate state I'd have thought she'd be keen to hear I'm making progress. And with a French boy no less.

I sigh as I stare up at my Amélie poster.

Love is very 'ard, says Amélie. *When Dino came to Les Deux Moulins I was so shy I pretended I was someone else. And then I thought he was involved with one of the other waitresses in the café.*

When you meet the right person it all falls into place, says Billy. *It wasn't until I took the advice of Monsieur …*

Amélie is still telling me about the ups and downs of her romance as I fall asleep.

Chapter Seventeen

Rosie is riding a scooter down a Parisian laneway. I am close behind on my own scooter, but I can't seem to keep up. 'Slow down, Rosie,' I call.

She gets further and further ahead. The laneway leads into a long flight of stairs, but instead of stopping, Rosie accelerates. She flies into the air and by the time I reach the stairs she has vanished.

On Wednesday I wake, disoriented, with a wet pillow again, and it takes me a while to get my day into motion. I spend a lot of time decorating the tree, arranging the tinsel and baubles in various combinations. Whichever way I do it though, the tree still looks dejected. It is too small and the tinsel too new. I'm used to our old decorations, but who knows where they are now.

When I eventually get out of the house, sourcing the hair-straightening products takes longer than I expected. I have to try three different pharmacies before I get the right brand. Consequently, it is mid-afternoon before I find myself at the mirror with an array of potions, a blow-dryer and a hair straightener in front of me. I have a sudden flashback to the Great Hair-Straightening Disaster of 2014. Having hair like a broom at Rosie's birthday party was traumatic. But that won't happen again. That was an amateur job, and this time I know what I'm doing. I mentally run through what I learnt on the internet last night.

I have to admit it was slightly disturbing that half of the Google links led to lawyers specialising in hair-related injuries. Hair straightening is clearly the bungee jumping of the beauty world. But Joan of Arc wouldn't have been deterred by such things, had she wanted to straighten her hair, and neither will I be. A positive attitude is essential. 'Be afraid, curls, be very afraid,' I mutter.

The instructions outline a three-stage process. First I must wash with the special shampoo and conditioner. Then I need to blow dry. Then I have to divide it into sections and run the straightener over each bit.

I decide to skip stage two. Blow-drying is a disaster when you have as much hair as me. I end up with an out-of-control Afro, like a seventies rock star. Usually I let my hair drip dry. I glance at my watch as I step out of the shower. It's only three-thirty, should be plenty of time ...

By four o'clock I have made little headway with the straightening. How long will this take? When Rosie did it, it was only half an hour or so, but that's because she had the straightener super-hot, with catastrophic results. I decide to seek some advice.

How long does it take you to straighten your hair? I text Hannah. She doesn't reply and I immediately feel bad about bothering her with my trivial problems. I have probably interrupted an important refugee negotiation. *Never mind*, I text. *Sorry to bother you.*

At four-thirty I am still running the straightener over my hair, bit by bit. The part I have done looks amazing – silky and straight. I toss my head experimentally and am thrilled to the core at the way it swishes. I must persevere.

By five o'clock I am a little panicky. Only one hour before I meet Alex. I need to leave soon and I'm only half-done. What is better, to be late or to be only partly straightened? I'm not sure. I start to do every second section. It should be fine.

By five-thirty one side of my hair is beautifully silky and sleek, while the other side is only half-tamed. I squint and try to convince myself it's not noticeable, but I look like one side of my head has been zapped by static electricity. Why did I try this again? I'm such an idiot. That's what history is for – to teach you not to repeat the same mistakes.

There is only one thing to do – call Alex and tell him I've come down with a bout of something nasty. I decide on Taijin Kyofusho, a syndrome where you have a crippling fear of social interaction.

I ring him but he doesn't answer. I don't want to leave a message: it would be too confusing. It's time to seek help.

I've got a date with the French Love God in twenty minutes and my hair's a calamity, I message Rosie on Facebook.

I'm sure it's fine, flashes up on the screen.

Considering Rosie can't see my hair I'm not all that reassured. *I know, First World problem. With the world the way it is and all that it doesn't rate, but–*

122

Dude. Shut up. I'm sure your hair is ... NOT ... THAT ... BAD. Wear a bonnet.

A hat! Why didn't I think of that?

Well duh.

I quickly scan my cupboard – the tea cosy! I slide it on and pull my hair through the holes. One side hangs like a silken rope, while the other puffs out like a feather duster. Can I go out looking like this? I don't know.

I think I've got aboulomania, a condition causing crippling indecision. I'm not sure though, I can't decide.

Go, Happy. There's nothing wrong with you.

But what will I wear? *No time, no time.* I scrabble around in my cupboard and choose the blue-striped T-shirt I wore to the opening of the French Film Festival. It seems appropriate for a French Food Festival.

I inspect myself in the mirror and manage to convince myself that with the addition of the tea cosy my uneven hair is not all that noticeable. I can keep the left side of my face towards him. And anyway, it will be dark. It will be fine. I glance at my watch – aargh, I am seriously late. Grabbing my phone and my purse, I text Alex to let him know I'm running late and rush for the ferry terminal.

Once on board I calm down. I sit out the front of the ferry and my mind roams. Here I am on my way to meet a handsome Frenchman at a French food festival ...

A gentle accordion plays in the background. My hair has transformed into an elfin bob and a playful breeze lifts the skirt of my chic but quirky

123

dress that could only have been bought in a cobbled lane off the Boulevard
Saint-Germain. As I arrive Alex is standing beside the river holding a
handful of freshly picked poppies ...

I realise Alex hasn't replied to my text. Why hasn't he replied? Maybe he's pissed off that I'm late. Maybe he's forgotten he's invited me to the food festival and he's at the movies. Maybe I've got the wrong day.

The reason soon becomes clear. As the ferry pulls into South Bank I see him standing on the wharf. He is not looking eagerly out to the river holding a handful of poppies, but is deep in conversation with a small, dark-haired girl with an elfin bob. An elfin bob! My pulse quickens and I get a tinny taste in my mouth. I breathe deeply, trying to convince myself that she's waiting to catch the ferry and they're just making polite small talk.

I step off the ferry unnoticed and approach them. 'Hi, Alex.' I flick my sleek pigtail as he turns.

He smiles in a devastating way. ''I, 'Appy.'

I flick my hair again. It is satisfyingly swishy.

The girl's eyes move from one side of my head to the other. She is wearing an Amélie-esque red dress and, as she is petite with an elfin bob, looks way better in it than I would.

I flick my pigtail again to distract her from my lopsided hairdo.

''Appy, this is Juliette. She's from Paris too.'

Juliette. All of a sudden my life is filled with Juliettes – Juliette Binoche, Juliette the chicken, and now this one. Even though I hate her, I smile.

Juliette smiles at me. ''Ello.'

''Ello, I mean hello.' I wish I could get away with saying 'ello. It's so much sexier.

'That is an interesting 'at,' she says. 'I 'aven't seen one like this before.'

'No, um, it's a special Australian design.'

'But in the French colours?'

'They're the Australian colours too,' I say.

'Where can I get one?'

'Oh, they're hard to find ...' I could say at a Country Women's Association craft stall but that would mean admitting I'm wearing a tea cosy. 'I bought this one in Sydney.'

'Let's go get some food,' says Alex.

'Great,' I say. 'Bye, Juliette. Nice to meet you.'

'I am coming too.' Juliette smiles. 'I am missing French food already.'

A hyena-like laugh of surprise bursts from my mouth.

Chapter eighteen

My hyena laugh fades to a strangled chortle as I look from Juliette back to Alex. What kind of date is this? I realise I am grinding my teeth and stop with some effort.

'Juliette is working at the Tourism Board too.' Alex seems to have decided to ignore my hyena impersonation.

Juliette nods her elfin bob in confirmation.

I grind my teeth anew at this news. 'Are you over 'ere for long?' The shock of her date-crashing has given me Foreign Accent Syndrome. With any luck, she's about to fly back to gay Paree at any moment.

'I 'ave been 'ere for three days so far. Three months to go.'

So much for that.

As we walk towards the food tents I place myself to the right of Alex, so he gets the benefit of my silky pigtail. Juliette walks on the other side of him. Her presence strains my overwrought social skills but perhaps it's a French thing, the two girls/one guy date. A ménage à trois. I will have to rise to the occasion.

The festival is going off – hordes of people roam the South Bank Parklands in search of French delicacies. As a form of French propaganda, it's working well. We pause in front of the first tent we come to. It is serving nothing but sausages.

'Ah, andouillette,' gushes Juliette.

Not to be outdone, I gush too. 'Oh, I love andouillette.' In actual fact I've never had them before but I do love sausages.

Alex smiles at me. 'You 'ave 'ad them before?'

I nod. 'All the time.'

He pulls out his wallet. 'Let me pay for this one.'

A rapid-fire exchange in French follows with the stallholder, a dour middle-aged man whose stomach suggests he has eaten many of his own sausages. Juliette joins in. I can only understand the odd word as they speak so quickly. Year Eleven French has some limitations. As the stallholder prods at the sausages on a grill in front of him, a terrible smell drifts towards me. I examine my shoe to check I haven't stepped in any dog droppings. All clear. It seems the smell is coming from the sausages.

'For you.' Alex hands me a sausage on a paper plate.

I thrust down a queasy uprising and take the plate. As we stroll on Juliette and Alex bite into their sausages with gay abandon. I examine mine suspiciously. Up close, the sausage looks strange – pale, with lumpy bits inside it.

'You are not 'ungry, 'Appy?' asks Alex.

'Oh, yes. I'm just enjoying the anticipation.' I take a big bite, chew rapidly and force it down as my whole body screams resistance. The sausage is much lumpier and chewier than a normal

127

one and smells like faeces. 'Mm, delicious.' Sweat breaks out on my forehead. I hope I'm not going to throw up.

We stop in front of a busker in boater hat and waistcoat who is playing an accordion. It is Tony: he must be the only accordionist in Brisbane. He winks when he sees me and I wave back, like an accordion groupie. While Alex and Juliette are distracted, I take a stealthy step towards a nearby rubbish bin and thrust the sausage inside.

'Psst.'

I look around.

'Psst.'

The whisper comes from the right, in the darkness near the river.

'It's me, Alex.'

Alex Two is standing almost out of sight in the shadows. Her black T-shirt and black pants make her hard to spot.

I step towards her. 'What are you doing here?'

'I'm working for Le Petit Escargot. I'm on my break.' She looks towards Alex and Juliette. 'Is that the guy from the Tourism Board?'

'Ah, yes. I'm–'

'Who's the girl with him?'

I shrug. 'Some French girl. She works there too.'

'Are you getting some inside information?' she whispers.

I nod briskly. 'I will do. I haven't interrogated him yet; I'm lulling him into a false sense of security.'

'Good. I'd better get back.' She turns to go.

'Alex?'

'Yes?' She pauses and looks back.

'Have you ever eaten andouillette?'

'No way. I'm not into pig innards stuffed inside a colon.'

I put my hands to my mouth to stop a retch. *Pig innards. Colon.* That explains the smell.

'Are you okay?'

'Fine.' I open my mouth and throw up into the grass.

Alex steps back towards me, pulls a tissue out of her pocket and hands it to me. 'I've never seen anyone vomit like that before. It was like you turned on a tap.'

'I might have caught a touch of Paris Syndrome.'

'Andouillette?'

I nod as I wipe my face with the tissue.

'Brave move.' Alex smiles. 'Taking one for the cause, huh?' She touches my shoulder. 'Be careful – the French are into some strange shit. So to speak. Better go.' She vanishes into the darkness. A few moments later I see her walking past as we make our way through the crowd, but she disappears into the shadows in a secret agent-ish way. I'm rather impressed.

The rest of the evening follows a similar path. Alex and Juliette gaily tuck into cervelle, which looks like brains and probably is. When they're not looking I thrust mine at a scruffily dressed man who is sitting on the grass under a fig tree. 'Here, would you like some French food?'

'Hey,' he calls after me loudly as I walk away. 'What's this stuff? Did I ask for it?'

'Do you know that man?' asks Alex.

I shake my head and walk more briskly.

'You trying to poison me?' he yells.

I roll my eyes at Alex. 'He must think I'm someone else.'

We queue to buy something sludgy called manouls. I have to eat some because Alex is watching. 'Mm, delicious.' I smile through gritted teeth.

Juliette wanders off towards the next stall and for the first time tonight we are alone.

'You are an adventurous eater, 'Appy,' Alex says. 'Manouls can be an acquired taste.'

'No, I love it.' I point at a slithery white bit on my plate. 'What's that?'

'Sheep intestine,' says Alex. 'Do you like it?'

I give him a thumbs up as I can't trust my voice.

He takes my fork from me, stabs the intestine and holds it to my mouth. I hesitate, then open up. It is a romantic moment. I must rise to it.

He looks into my eyes and smiles as he inserts the intestine between my lips.

I call upon all of my determination and chew in a seductive way. 'Mm, mm,' I murmur. I suspect my eyes are bulging with the strain. It is without a doubt the most disgusting thing I have ever eaten. But it is worth it, because Alex hooks his arm through mine as we stroll past the frog leg stall without stopping – *hallelujah*. I feel like I have come through fire and conquered all.

But then Alex pauses at the next tent. 'Escargot?'

I look from him to the stall. Behind the counter, Alex Two gazes out at me. She looks different tonight, now that I see her in the light. Her long blue fringe is gelled back off her face and her black

130

waitressing outfit clings rather becomingly to her pale skin. Her eyes flicker to Alex's arm, which is still linked through mine and back to my face.

I flush, like an enemy collaborator.

'Escargot?' says Alex Two, echoing Alex One. Her mouth pulls up into a smile and I notice she is wearing red lipstick. I hadn't thought of her as a red lipstick sort of person. Alex is quite surprising.

I nod and she piles a paper plate high with plump, white snails. 'I've given you a few extra. On the house.'

'Merci,' says Alex One.

'Merci,' I repeat though this is more of a punishment than a reward.

Alex Two's mouth curls up at the side and I wonder if the extra snails are payback for consorting with the enemy. She holds out the plate to Alex One, but as he takes it she lets go too quickly and it collapses. An avalanche of escargot slides down his stomach.

'I'm so sorry.' She jumps out from behind the counter with a cloth. 'Let me clean you up.' She dabs ineffectually at Alex's shirt and jeans, smearing garlic sauce everywhere.

'Don't worry about it.' Alex One steps back, but Alex Two pursues with her dishcloth.

'Let me wipe that bit of sauce on your hip. Here wait, I'll get you some more escargot.' She darts back behind the counter and loads up another huge plate of escargot. 'No charge.' She thrusts the huge pile of escargot towards us.

Alex picks it up cautiously, holding the plate with two hands, and we retreat.

I glance back over my shoulder as we walk away.

Alex Two gives me an innocent smile and a little wave as she turns to the next customer.

Juliette has vanished, but Alex doesn't seem concerned, so I'm certainly not. We stroll along with our snails and find a seat looking out over the river. The lights from the skyscrapers shine on the water and this would be a perfect romantic moment if it wasn't for the overabundance of snails to contend with.

Alex holds the plate out to me. 'After you.'

I take one and, using the little fork, prise it out of its shell, insert it in my mouth and chew. Surprisingly, it is bearable. The snail tastes of nothing much at all except the garlic sauce which smothers it. I smile. 'Scrumptious.' An oily snail stain on Alex's jeans reminds me I'm supposed to be interrogating him. It must be the association with Alex Two. I pop in another snail and chew slowly while I try to think of a suitable opening question.

'So, what's Juliette's job in the Tourism Board?' I ask.

'She is 'elping out with a big campaign.'

I try not to look too interested. 'Oh yeah, what's that about?'

He waves a snail around airily on the end of his fork. 'This and that.' He inserts the snail into my mouth, puts down the fork, turns to me and strokes his hands down my pigtails.

A delicious shiver runs up my neck.

'Why is one side straight and one side curly?'

I had forgotten the strange state of my hair. My mind is a blank, I want him to touch me again. 'Garlic-Induced Hair Follicle Disorder.' It's all I can think of.

'It's unusual. Like you, 'Appy.' He makes this sound like a good thing.

My heart goes thump-a-thump.

We dispatch the remaining snails without too much difficulty and Alex walks me to the ferry terminal. Despite the crowd at the festival there is no one else around. The night is warm and the river water sloshes gently against the pier. It might not be Paris, but by Brisbane standards the ambience is excellent.

Alex puts his hand on my shoulder and leans closer.

Is he about to whisper a French Tourism Board secret into my ear? But no, he kisses me. His lips are soft and his hands touch my neck and … his breath is garlicky. This worries me, because mine must be too. I thought if two people both ate garlic then they cancelled each other out, but this doesn't seem to be the case. If I can smell him then he can probably smell me. I am so anxious about the garlic situation, I have trouble enjoying my first kiss from a French Love God. Although of course it is fabulous.

I would like to stay in this moment longer, so that I could get over the garlic, but a chugging sound from the river interrupts us.

''Ere's your ferry.' Alex steps back, running his hand down my arm. 'I will call you.'

He waves to me as the ferry pulls out and I lean against the ferry railing waving back, before he turns and walks away. I sit out the front, watching the giant Ferris wheel on the riverbank go round and round, its lights reflected in the water. Regardless of the garlic, my head is spinning from his kiss and right now I'm not sure if Paris could top this.

I message Rosie on Facebook. *Have kissed Gallic lips.* But she doesn't reply.

'I hate it when Rosie doesn't reply. Once, she would have been back to me in an instant. Unless we'd had a fight. That happened sometimes. Like the last time I saw her.

You're such a bore, Happy.

Am I? Maybe. I know it's hard for me to keep up with Rosie.

'I'm going as fast as I can, Rosie,' I whisper to the glittering river.

Chapter Nineteen

'Phew,' says Mum, when we intersect in the kitchen on Thursday morning. 'Who's been eating garlic?'

'I ate a lot of escargot last night.'

'That's adventurous of you.'

'They weren't too bad.' I yawn loudly. 'Do you know, if two people both eat a lot of garlic, can they smell each other?'

Mum gives me a funny look. 'Depends on how sensitive your nose is I guess.'

'Mm.' Perhaps Alex, being French, is de-sensitised to garlic. After all, the French would never get anywhere romantically if they worried about garlic breath. I decide to put this anxiety behind me.

After the excitement of the kiss, I hardly slept last night. All I did was toss and turn, remembering Alex's lips against mine. The river, the lights, the Ferris wheel ... If not for the escargot it would have been perfect.

'What's happened to your hair?'

I had forgotten my dysfunctional hairdo. I put my hands to my head. 'Nothing. Why? I must have slept on it funny.'

Mum picks up her bag. 'Never seen it look like that before.' She kisses my cheek and rushes from the house.

I brush my teeth and gargle after breakfast, but I suspect the garlic has infused itself into my body. My phone goes ting as I walk into my bedroom. And – oh joy – Alex's name is on the screen. I swoon as I read his text.

Want to have coffee at the Eiffel Tower at eleven o'clock?

This is so funny and romantic – he's pretending we are in Paris. *Maybe somewhere closer?* I add a little smiley face before I send it.

No, the Eiffel Tower in Milton. It's on top of a café, he replies immediately.

An Eiffel Tower in Brisbane? How did I not know this? *Oh, okay. See you there!* I smile as I press send. I hadn't expected to hear from him so soon, but it seems we are on the same page about the effects of last night's kiss.

In an excited frenzy I dress in my Number Two Amélie outfit – the dark blue polka dots – and slide my tea cosy on again as there is no time to wash my lopsided hair.

At ten am, I catch a ferry down the river to Milton. My heart is doing a crazy cancan at the thought of seeing him again. Was Joan of Arc ever kissed like that? Was she ever tempted to throw away her banner and jump into bed with some spunky peasant boy?

My body is a seething quagmire of desire, I message Rosie but she remains silent.

As I walk down Park Road, I can see the Eiffel Tower rising above the street. It is remarkable. If I squint a little I can pretend that rather than being close to a small replica of the Eiffel Tower, I am a long way away from the real thing. If I breathe deeply, I can smell croissants. I feel like I am practically in Paris.

There is a loud beep behind me. 'How ya goin', Bazza?' yells a guy in a passing car.

His blue-singleted mate on the footpath gives him a thumbs up.

The Parisian spell is broken. Deflated, I continue towards the tower, stop at the bottom and look up. It is not all that big, but bigger than expected. A sign is attached halfway up, saying *Savoir Faire*. This is a bit like wearing a T-shirt saying, *I'm cool*. If you have to announce it, you don't have it.

'It looks better at night when it's lit up.'

The voice makes me jump. Alex Two is standing right beside me in a loose white T-shirt and baggy jeans. Her blue fringe is again un-gelled and flopping over her blue eyes.

I stare at her. 'What are you doing here?'

'What do you mean, what am I doing here? We arranged to meet here.'

'We did?'

She frowns and speaks slowly. 'You replied to my text. That's why you're here.'

My mind flashes back to the text from Alex. Oh no – surely I haven't put the two Alexes' numbers into my phone without differentiating between them? I must have. My exuberant mood diminishes. Alex One and I are not on the same page about the effects of last night's kiss after all. Why hasn't he texted me? I must have been too garlicky.

Alex has a funny expression on her face. She flicks her fringe out of her eyes.

'Sorry, Alex. I think I might be suffering from Capgras Syndrome, which is a condition where you think the person you're with is an imposter and as a result–'

'Happy.' Alex points to a café table nearby. 'Never mind. Let's get a coffee, huh?'

'Yes, okay, sure.' I mentally readjust to coffee with Alex Two rather than a post-kiss debrief with Alex One.

Confusingly, the café is called La Dolce Vita, which means the sweet life in Italian, and it specialises in Italian food. 'Why is there an Italian Restaurant underneath an Eiffel Tower?' I ask Alex as we sit.

'Why not?'

'That's rather an existential question.'

'This is rather an existential place.' Alex smiles. 'Life is full of mystery.'

She doesn't seem to bear any grudges about last night's fraternisation, which is a relief. Following the escargot incident I wasn't sure if we were still on friendly terms. 'You're right, a French restaurant next to the Eiffel Tower would be way too obvious. It's better to subvert our expectations. Tiramisu,' I squeal as I spot the blackboard.

'Bless you.'

'Thank you. I love, love, love tiramisu.'

'The hot chocolate is good here too.'

We both order tiramisu and hot chocolate. After the culinary horrors of last night, I am in the mood for food I can enjoy. If

Alex One and I become an item will I have to eat andouillette and manouls regularly? Perhaps I can develop a taste for them ... Then I remember the slimy, slippery texture, and the pungent smell. My nose wrinkles. No, I will have to specify upfront that there will be no offal eating on my part.

'... what do you think?'

I stare at Alex blankly.

'Did you hear a word I said, Happy?'

Luckily our hot chocolate and tiramisu arrive, which provides a distraction. The hot chocolate is almost as thick as chocolate mousse and must be eaten with a spoon. 'Mm, this is so much better than snails.' I scrape up the last of my hot chocolate and lick my spoon.

'Listen to you. You haven't even made it to Paris and you're already disillusioned.'

'No I'm not. I'm still crazy about Paris. That food was weird. There's lots of French food that doesn't involve intestines or garden pests.'

'So how did it go?'

I stare at her. She wants an update on my romantic evening? I sigh. 'It was –'

'Did you get some good intel?' Alex cuts me off.

Oh that. I had almost forgotten my role as an undercover investigator. I scoop up some tiramisu and swallow it to give me time to consider my response. 'Mm, this is delicious.'

Alex taps her spoon on her saucer.

'I was gaining his confidence; I didn't want to get his guard up.'

Alex frowns. 'This is important, Happy. Did you even try?'

'You can't rush these things. Double agents are often implanted for years before they produce any useful information. Next time I see him I'll drill him about the French connection.'

Alex taps her fingers on the table. 'He probably doesn't know anything. I wouldn't bother if I were you.'

'No, he knows something. I can sense it. I need to prise it out of him.'

Alex pushes her half-eaten tiramisu away and waves to the waiter for the bill.

Things seem a little tense as we pool our gold coins to reach the total. I expect she is disappointed with my undercover investigations.

'Would you like to watch *Amélie* with me?' Alex asks as we stand.

I smile. 'Sure. I'd never pass up a chance to watch *Amélie*. Where's it showing?'

'My place. I've downloaded it.'

'Oh, cool. Just you and me?'

'And the chickens. They like to watch TV. Especially French movies.'

'They do? You guys all sit around watching TV together?'

She nods. 'I shouldn't have told you that.'

'No, that's cool. Unusual, and slightly creepy, but cool.'

She smiles. 'We have a similar taste in movies. Chickens dream, you know. They have a fantasy life.'

'What do they dream about?'

'Paris, of course. Same as everyone else.'

I laugh. 'Well, okay. I'm open to socialising with chickens. I'm not fowlist. Let's go.'

Alex's house is three stops away on the ferry. Unlike in Sydney, nowhere seems that far away in Brisbane. It's kind of nice.

'Do you want to play tennis?' I ask as we sit next to each other watching the river go by.

'What, right now? I thought you wanted to watch *Amélie*.'

'No, tennis the game where you choose a category and compete to think of as many things in that category as you can.'

'Oh, that tennis. Sure. You choose the category.'

'Paris streets.'

'Champs-Élysées,' says Alex before I can draw breath.

'Quai d'Orsay.'

'Boulevard Saint-Germain.'

'Avenue de la Republique.'

We are still going as the ferry pulls into West End and I strike a winning blow with Boulevard Voltaire. Alex ums and ahs before admitting defeat. 'You've been studying, haven't you?'

'No. Anyway we were pretty close. You did well.'

'Oh, damn me with faint praise,' she says as we climb the street. 'Next time I'm choosing the topic and it's breeds of French chickens.'

Chapter Twenty

As we open Alex's front gate, the chickens run up clucking madly.

'Aw, that's cute, they missed you,' I say.

'That's what's nice about chickens. Unconditional love. Well, maybe not totally unconditional; if I didn't feed them, they'd probably turn against me.'

'That would be scary.'

'It would be like a Hitchcock movie.' She falls to the ground dramatically and the chickens rush forward to inspect her at close range. 'Aargh, no – not the chickens!' The chickens cluck among themselves. 'They're the closest living relative to the T Rex, you know.' Alex looks up at them.

'You'd better get up before they tear you to shreds.' I notice a small ramp set up in the garden with a hoop at the top. 'Can I see them do their tricks?'

Alex gets to her feet. She looks bashful. 'Okay. Let me get some chicken food.' She wanders off to the shed in the corner of the yard and comes back with a handful of pellets. Squatting next to the hoop she makes clucking noises and holds out her hand. Amélie goes first, strutting up the ramp, walking through the hoop and fluttering to the ground. Alex holds out her hand and gives her a couple of pellets.

I clap. 'Well done, Amélie.'

The other chickens follow suit. Their gait is serious and measured as they concentrate on the task. They have a proud set to their heads as they stalk away, having completed their mission.

'Woohoo! Go chickens. That's so cool – you could charge admission for that.'

'Yeah, I'd like to get a busking act together, but it needs more work.' Alex stands and brushes her knees after the last chicken goes through. 'I'll get them to play the xylophone for you next time. I'm building up to "Chopsticks", but at the moment we're doing "Three Blind Mice".'

'No way.'

'Oh yeah.' She flashes her eyebrows at me. 'They're incredibly musical. They like to compose their own tunes but I'm trying to get them interested in the classics. Want to watch *Amélie* now, girls?'

They fluff their wings and wander off in search of more edible entertainment.

Alex shrugs. 'Guess it's just you and me.'

'Now I know what it's like to come second to a bunch of chickens.'

'I'm afraid that's the way it is, Happy. Take it or leave it.'

'Haven't got much choice, have I?' We head for the stairs. 'They don't really watch TV, do they?'

'No. I was trying to make my social life sound more exciting than it is.'

'That's sad.'

'I know. I lead a dull life unrelieved by watching TV with chickens.'

'It's okay. I don't have any friends from different species either. I thought I had an intimate relationship with a goldfish once but he turned out to be only in it for the fish food.'

'Typical.'

'Yeah, a good fish is hard to find.'

Inside the kitchen, Alex opens the fridge and inspects its contents with a disappointed air. 'I can offer you a refreshing glass of tap water fresh from a dam somewhere above Brisbane.'

'Sounds divine.'

We sit on her worn-out couch with a glass of water each.

'I need to warn you,' I say.

Alex glances at me.

'When I'm watching *Amélie* I don't like to be distracted.'

She salutes. 'Got it.'

I wriggle with delight as the opening credits roll and the familiar Paris scenes unfold – the cobbled streets, the chic Parisians, the Seine, the cafés … Oh, the romance of it all. I can hardly believe one day I'll get on a plane and be there. I hope my head doesn't explode with delight when that time comes.

Alex glances at me and smiles from time to time but she doesn't talk, which is good, because I would have to smother her with a pillow if she did. She makes all the right noises of appreciation in the right places and doesn't interrupt with stupid comments. Watching *Amélie* with Alex is almost as good as watching it with Rosie.

We are both smiling as Amélie and Dino ride a scooter through a narrow Montmartre laneway at the end. It is clear Dino is in love with her and she with him and they are going to live a quirky Parisian life together forever more.

'So tell me if that isn't the best movie you have ever watched?' I say.

Alex hesitates. She looks at me out of the corner of her eye. 'Have you ever seen *The Matrix*?'

'The what? I beg your pardon?'

Alex laughs. 'Just teasing. That was the best movie I have ever watched. Without a doubt.'

'Lucky for you. People who criticise *Amélie* in front of me have been known to vanish without trace.'

'I watched *Before Sunset* last night too.'

'Isn't it great?'

'Yeah, but ...' She looks wary.

'It's okay, I don't feel as strongly about *Before Sunset*. You may voice your opinion.'

'I can't believe they cut it right before the climax.'

'You prefer things all wrapped up, like an American rom-com?'

Alex drains her water. 'No, not totally wrapped up, but ... It felt like there was something missing.'

'That's why there's a third movie. It shows them as a married couple.'

'Oh, but that's not the same, you miss out on the passion.'

145

'Yeah true, I didn't like that one so much. What I love about *Before Sunset* is that it leaves them at the point where their whole life together is ahead of them.'

'Ah, you're a true romantic, Happy. You want the happily ever after.'

'Doesn't everyone?'

'Yes, I suppose so. But I don't know if it's achievable.' Alex leans her head on the back of the couch and stares at the ceiling.

Thinking about happily ever after makes me think about Mum and Dad. 'Are your parents still together?' My segue is a little abrupt, but Alex follows.

'Yes, but they're not exactly the world's most romantic couple. You wouldn't make a movie about them. How about yours?'

'No.' I tell her about Dad and Hannah. 'Hannah's cool, but ...'

'You're still pissed off?'

'Yeah. And Mum hasn't been the same since. She tries to act brave, but she's still really sad.' Silence falls and I hear the chickens cluck outside. 'How did we get onto this? We should be talking about Paris. So are any of the places in *Amélie* on your hit list for Paris now?'

'Oh yeah.' Alex smiles broadly. 'That cathedral on the hill looks stunning. Did you see the view it had over Paris?'

Alex and I are ensconced in a Parisian fantasy when a reminder message goes off on my phone.

I check it. 'Eek, I've got to go to work – I've got the afternoon shift.'

'What time do you finish?'

'Seven-thirty.'

'We're meeting at Professor Tanaka's, remember? For the book club. She's making us dinner too. We can debrief the French Food Festival with her and decide on a plan of attack.'

'Okay, sure. I'll see you there.' I meet her eyes. 'Thanks, that was fun.'

She holds my gaze and smiles and a warm glow spreads through me. She's the first person I've met in Brisbane who feels like she could be a friend.

The afternoon shift is busy. Thursday afternoon must be prime time for watching French films. Today's movie is *Gigi*, an old one from the 1950s about a wealthy Parisian who falls in love with a young courtesan-in-training. It's a bit like *Pretty Woman*, that one from the nineties where Julia Roberts plays a prostitute. I wouldn't call *Gigi* a French movie myself as it's in English, but it's set in Paris, so no one seems to care.

Mum's anti-smoking intervention with Kevin has produced results. His top pocket, for once, is empty of cigarettes. Amélie winks at me approvingly when I catch her eye.

'So you live with your mum and dad, huh?' Kevin asks casually as we shut the doors on *Gigi*.

This is a strange question, coming, as it does, out of the blue. 'No, they're separated. Dad's in Sydney. Why?'

'No reason.' Kevin hums cheerfully as he wanders off towards the counter.

The cinema is almost empty and I am wiping the counter when I hear an unmistakeable voice, ''Ello 'Appy.'

My heart does a wild flamenco as I stand. ''Ello. I mean, hello.'
My mouth is instantly dry. Just when I want to be at my best,
my body turns against me. I do a mental appearance check. I am
wearing my blue-striped T-shirt again, neck kerchief and French-
themed tea cosy. How many times has Alex seen me in this outfit?
Too many, I am sure. I should have stuck with the Number Two
Amélie outfit instead of getting changed for work.

Alex is wearing a black T-shirt and jeans and looks incredibly
sexy and French.

My lips tingle, remembering our kiss. I wonder if his garlic
breath has worn off now. I'd like to leap the counter and press
my mouth against his to check, but I am not athletic or impulsive
enough to achieve this. And there is my breath to consider too.

''Ave you finished work?'

'Yes, almost. I just need to close up.'

'Maybe we can 'ave a drink?'

I nod with forced calm. 'That would be nice.'

Alex waves his hand in the direction of the pub across the road.
'Beer is 'alf-price over there now. Do you like beer?'

I don't, but that's pretty much beside the point. 'Absolutely.
Um, I'm only seventeen though.'

Alex shrugs. 'I will buy.'

I shut up the cinema at full speed, while Alex waits outside,
leaning on a streetlamp light. I shoot glances his way, drinking
in his profile, the lines of his shoulders, his stomach. Deep sighs
well up inside me and burst forth like a whale blowing. I work
hard to bring this under control as I imagine how our drink
could go …

My hands are clumsy as I fumble to lock the door. Finally I succeed and walk towards him, trying to summon a little hauteur. Failing that, it would be good not to look like an over-eager puppy. It is going to happen tonight. I can feel it in my … everywhere. My insides feel like creme caramel. If only the garlic doesn't come between us.

Alex puts his hands on my hips when I reach him. He pulls me towards him, leans in and presses his lips to mine. There is the merest hint of garlic. It is hardly there at all. If I don't focus on it, I can completely ignore it.

I close my eyes, losing myself in the sensation, when I open them again he is looking at me. A wave of heat rushes up from my stomach.

He smiles. 'I like 'ow you are so tall, 'Appy. You are easy to kiss.'

'So are you.' I swallow.

'Do you want to 'ave a drink at my place instead? It is more comfortable there.'

My heart nearly leaps out through my throat. I know exactly what this means. *Activation sexuelle*. I nod, mutely.

He puts out his hand and takes mine. His fingers are warm, strong and confident.

Mine are sweaty and nervous. I am about to go to bed with a Frenchman who looks like a young Johnny Depp. It is a little overwhelming. I would like to stop and message Rosie for some last-minute advice, but that would be a bad look and, besides, she's been unreliable lately.

I'm going to have to do this on my own.

Chapter Twenty-one

Alex and I walk towards the train station hand in hand. My heart is thumping so hard it's a wonder he can't hear it. I study him from out of the corner of my eye, trying to find something witty to say. I am so nervous my ears are ringing.

Alex stops. 'Your phone?'

That explains the ringing. I pull it out. 'Hello?'

It is Alex Two. 'Happy? I'm at Professor Tanaka's – where are you?'

In my trance-like state, I had forgotten we were supposed to be meeting. Alex One looks at me and I imagine the length of his body against me. I bite my lip.

'A problem?' he asks.

I waggle my head in an indeterminate way. 'Happy?' says Alex Two in my ear. 'Are you coming? Professor Tanaka's keen to talk about the Food Festival.'

'Um …'

'She's made dinner,' Alex Two hisses.

Damn. This last bit is the clincher. I can't stand her up if she's made dinner. 'Yes,' I murmur. 'I'll be there soon.' I hang up.

'What is it?'

'I forgot, I have somewhere I need to be.'

Alex shrugs in an off-hand way.

Aargh. Maybe he thinks I've got a better offer. Now he's going to wander off and I'll never see him again. I try to clarify. 'There's this Japanese woman, you would have seen her at the essay ceremony.' I explain as much as I can, leaving out the part about Paris Syndrome and the fact we suspect the French Tourism Board of brainwashing people. That doesn't leave much. I can see Alex is perplexed about the nature of my relationship with Professor Tanaka.

'No problem,' he says.

The temperature on the street drops ten degrees. I can practically see icicles forming.

We walk to the train station together, but no longer holding hands. Alex's train comes before my bus so I wait with him on the platform. He gives me a cursory kiss on the cheek and as his train pulls out, holds his hand to his face in the universal sign for *I'll call you.*

I wave at him, cursing the fates.

Professor Tanaka opens the door and smiles. 'Ah, Veronica, come in, come in. I was beginning to wonder if you were coming. I am excited to hear about your visit to the French Food Festival. Was it wonderful?'

*

'Um.' I catch Alex's eye. 'It was interesting.'

'Happy has been working hard to infiltrate the French Tourism Board.'

Alex sounds vaguely ironic but Professor Tanaka doesn't seem to notice so maybe I'm imagining it.

'Have you, Veronica?' It is like Professor Tanaka doesn't notice that Alex calls me Happy.

'Yes, I, um ...' I blush madly as Alex and Professor Tanaka inspect me.

'Have you been doing some more infiltrating? Is that what held you up?' Alex's face isn't giving much away.

'No, it's not.' I meet her eyes, obscurely guilty, and look back to Professor Tanaka. 'I went to the French Food Festival with someone who works at the Tourism Board.'

She smiles. 'Is this someone a boy?'

'Ah,' I hesitate, 'yes, he is.' Even the tips of my ears are burning.

Alex finds something interesting outside the window.

'And what have you learnt by accompanying this boy to the French Food Festival?' Professor Tanaka's dark eyes are twinkling.

The French kiss. His French fingers in mine. His French legs in denim ...

Professor Tanaka gives me a quizzical look.

I pull myself together. 'I've learnt some French food is disgusting.' I fill her in on the manouls and andouillette.

'Oh yes, they are an acquired taste,' she says.

'You like them?'

She chuckles. 'They are a taste I am yet to acquire.' She exchanges a significant look with Alex.

'What?' I say.

'You are already disappointed,' says Professor Tanaka. 'Imagine the depths of your disappointment when you get there.'

I open and shut my mouth. 'But so much French food is wonderful.'

'It is, isn't it?' Professor Tanaka smiles in a sympathetic way. 'Come, let's see what you think of my cassoulet.' She gestures towards the table.

I approach cautiously but the pot on the table smells delicious.

Professor Tanaka ladles out a stew of meat and cream-coloured beans onto plates for us all.

I take a mouthful. It is warm and richly flavoured. 'Mm, this is fantastic.'

'I have made the Toulouse version. With pork sausage.'

'This stew has restored my confidence in French food.' I spoon up some more.

Professor Tanaka steeples her fingers together and looks at me eagerly. 'So, tell me what else you learnt at the French Food Festival.'

I chew thoughtfully, considering my options.

Luckily Alex jumps in. 'It was interesting how many people wanted snails, I guess because they're the iconic French food. But I did a survey of the rubbish bins in the vicinity and there were a lot of discarded snails.'

A rubbish bin survey. Alex is such an over-achiever.

Professor Tanaka nods. 'It is a conundrum: we can desire something so much that it can only disappoint when it is acquired.' She points her finger at Alex. 'This is the heart of Paris Syndrome. Well done.'

Alex glows with the praise. She pulls out her notebook and writes, *Why do we desire something that can only disappoint when it is acquired?* She underlines it.

Professor Tanaka turns back to me. 'And you, Veronica? What else have you learnt from this boy?'

His kiss outside the cinema tonight ... His hands on my hips ... I could be at his house now. I could be–

'Veronica?'

I extract the single item of intelligence I gleaned from Alex One at the Food Festival. 'They're working on a big campaign.'

'What sort of campaign?' asks Alex.

'I don't know.'

'Why didn't you ask?' Alex frowns at me.

Why didn't I? I remember Alex One stroking my pigtails. 'I got distracted.'

Alex's expression suggests that I am a bad secret agent. She is right. I am too easily led astray.

'You should try to find out more about this, Veronica. It is intriguing,' says Professor Tanaka.

'It's probably nothing.' Alex puts down her spoon with a clatter.

Professor Tanaka raises her eyebrows. 'On the contrary, it may be important.'

'I'll follow it up,' I say.

Professor Tanaka offers Alex and me the bread basket. We both take a second roll. 'Now we will talk about literature,' she says. 'What book have you brought, Veronica?'

I am a little shy about my choice, but pull my book out. '*Madeline*.'

'Snap.' Alex pulls a copy of *Madeline* out of her bag too.

We smile at each other. 'What a coincidence,' I say.

'I was a bit worried about my choice,' says Alex.

'Me too. I thought you'd have something really intellectual.'

Professor Tanaka smiles. 'And what do you both love about Madeline?'

'She has such an adventurous approach to exploring Paris. She ignores the weather, plays whenever possible and stays out of the Metro,' says Alex.

'They are good rules for life, aren't they?' says Professor Tanaka. 'Why go underground when you can travel above?'

'I love the pictures too,' I say, 'the little girls in front of the Eiffel Tower,' I hold up the book, 'and the rain on Notre Dame. When I look at them I feel like I'm there. When I was in Year Six my friend Rosie and I organised for all the girls in our class to come to the book parade dressed in little straw hats and blue dresses.'

Professor Tanaka smiles. 'That sounds lovely.'

'How about you, Professor Tanaka, what's your favourite?' asks Alex.

Professor Tanaka looks around at her shelves. Her eyes seem to rest on *The Great Gatsby* for a moment, but then they move on. 'It's hard to choose a favourite. Should I choose the world's longest novel, *Remembrance of Things Past*, by Marcel Proust, or the also lengthy *Life, a User's Manual* by Georges Perec? Or ...' She smiles and raises her palms to us. 'I can't choose.'

'That's not fair, you have to,' I say.

'Very well. *Zizi* then.'

'*Zizi*?' I echo.

'It is a story by Colette about a romance between a young woman who is being groomed as a courtesan and a wealthy Parisian.'

'Oh, you mean *Gigi*. We were showing it at the cinema. I didn't know it was a book.'

'Yes, *Zizi*. Colette's husband forced her to write books under his name for many years. At last she divorced him and started writing for herself. Ah, there are so many superb French authors.'

'Are French books like French films?' I ask. 'Kind of philosophical and deep?'

'Absolutely. Art must strive to get to the essence of life.'

Alex and I exchange a glance. We might both be thinking the same thing – there's room for entertainment as well.

'Ah, you two are young. When you get to my age you want to know the answers to the big questions, not the small ones.' Professor Tanaka smiles. 'Literature can help us to discern what's important in life.'

'*The Great Gatsby*,' I say. 'Why is that on your shelf?'

Professor Tanaka puts a hand to her chest.

I feel like I've said something wrong. 'It's the only book that isn't about France,' I murmur.

'Oh. Yes.' Professor Tanaka gazes past me out the window for some time.

I'd thought it was a straightforward question, but clearly it is not.

At last Professor Tanaka returns her gaze to me. 'I was reading it when I was in Paris.' Her tone does not encourage further questions.

Alex and I catch the ferry home together.

I fold my legs up on the seat. 'It was strange, the way Professor Tanaka reacted when I mentioned *Gatsby*, wasn't it?'

'Yeah, she looked kind of freaked out.'

'Have you ever talked to her about *The Great Gatsby* before?'

Alex gives me a lopsided smile. 'Believe it or not, throughout my period of employment as Professor Tanaka's gardener, the subject of *The Great Gatsby* has never been raised.'

'Very suspicious. It's almost like–'

'She's been avoiding it.' Alex flashes her eyebrows.

'Right. She can't go to Paris and she can't talk about *The Great Gatsby*.' I point at her. 'There may be a link. Write that in your notebook. It could be important.'

Alex rolls her eyes, but she pulls out her notebook and makes a note – *Gatsby?*

'What would you do if you had only one day in Paris?' I ask.

'The gardens next to the Louvre, the windmills in Montmartre, a rotisserie chicken from the market …'

'You've really looked into this, haven't you?'

'Don't tell me you haven't.'

I smile. 'Mais oui, but of course.'

'And what would you do?'

'For a start, I would climb the Eiffel Tower.'

'In the morning? Wouldn't it be better to wait until evening?'

'Whose itinerary is this?' I say.

'Sorry.'

157

'After I climb the Eiffel Tower I will go and have breakfast at the Cafe de Flore.'

'Ah, the old Cafe de Flore. So, what's for breakfast?'

'Croissant, jam, butter, café au lait.'

'Perfect.' Alex stands. 'Here's my stop.'

'But I haven't finished yet.'

'I'll have to catch up on the rest of your Parisian day another time.' She gives me a crooked smile and walks over the ramp to the wharf.

'I'd climb the Eiffel Tower again in the evening,' I call to her as the ferry leaves the wharf. 'And go ice-skating in the park next to it.'

She calls something back, but we are too far away and I only catch the words, '… underestimated you.'

'Don't underestimate me,' I murmur, though I know she can't hear. I hug my knees to my chest and rest my chin on them. Bantering with Alex is bittersweet. It reminds me of Rosie.

I check Facebook when I get home but Rosie remains quiet. I suppose she's out partying with Luke again. She's been doing a lot of that lately.

Alex, however, has posted a new picture of Juliette the chicken going through a hoop to the Buc Buc page. *Juliette the chicken is the Gatsby of poultry – she never lets go of her dreams.*

Someone called Sarita has commented on her post. *I have such happy memories of your chickens, Alex xx*

Perhaps Sarita is one of the poultry club members. I add another comment. *Most talented chicken I've ever met.* I look at the number of 'likes' on her page. There are still only five. I glance up at the wall and Amélie's poster winks at me. *What would Amélie do?*

I have an idea. I check my tattoo fund bank account and do a quick calculation. Once Kevin pays me there'll still be enough for a tattoo. My chest fizzes as I tap my fingers on the keyboard.

The next day I do an afternoon shift at the cinema. We are screening *Joan of Arc*, a film from 1999, which is of course relevant to my situation as it reminds me of my mission to sexually activate. Although, watching Joan at the helm of her army, I expect she had other things on her mind.

'How crazy were those French, following a seventeen-year-old girl into battle?' says Kevin as we clean up after the movie.

'As a seventeen-year-old girl I take offence at that, Kevin. It went pretty well for them from what I saw in there. Maybe more people should appreciate the leadership qualities of seventeen-year-old girls.'

'Didn't go so well for her in the end though, did it?' Kevin stuffs the dregs from the popcorn machine into his mouth. He's been eating a lot since he gave up smoking. I hope he isn't replacing one vice with another. 'Never got to, you know, be with a bloke either.'

'I'd say leading the French army to victory was enough satisfaction for her. She had more important things to do.'

Kevin looks unconvinced.

'Not everyone needs a man in their life.'

'What about your mum?'

If there was a connection there, it slipped past me at the speed of light. 'What do you mean?'

'Has she got herself another bloke? Now she and your dad are separated?'

'No.' I stare at Kevin. 'Why?'

'No reason.' Kevin blushes slightly.

I study his face with a sinking feeling. Don't tell me he's developed a crush on Mum after her smoking lecture? That would be bizarre. Talk about Stockholm Syndrome. Perhaps he has masochistic tendencies. My phone goes ting at that moment and my mind jumps to Alex One. Unlike Joan of Arc, *my* mind is not on more important things.

I pull my phone out. The name on the screen is Alex, but which one? As I read the text the sender becomes clear.

Professor Tanaka has collapsed. I'm at the hospital. Can you come?

I stare at the phone, the words blurring in front of me.

'You right?' Kevin has an unexpected show of sensitivity.

I shake my head. 'A friend of mine's gone into hospital.' My voice comes out strangely calm.

'Off you go. We're finished here.' Kevin waves his hands at me. 'Scoot.'

Chapter Twenty-two

On the train to the city, I text Mum to tell her I'm going to be home late. It is getting dark outside and when I look up I see my face in the train window – a pale moon with a fuzzy aura of hair. Professor Tanaka was so exuberant at our meeting last night. What happened? Did she overdo things? I hope it wasn't my mention of *The Great Gatsby*. She did look startled …

I press my nose to the window and breathe steam on the glass, my mind returning to Joan of Arc. She was just two years older than me when she was burnt at the stake. Did she feel it was all worth it? I suppose she did.

But Joan of Arc doesn't fill my head for nearly long enough. I don't want to think about the last time I was in a hospital, so I scroll through Facebook, reading Rosie's old posts. I should stop doing this. It doesn't help. There is nothing that can help to prepare me for this.

I change to a bus in the city and when it pulls up at Princess Alexandra Hospital I walk along an elevated tunnel and into the foyer.

Hospitals are my least favourite places. They suck something out of me. I feel too full of life here, as if I should be talking more softly, walking more slowly. A pent-up heat fills my head but I catch the lift to the third floor and find my way to room 303 as Alex instructed.

A sign on the nurse's desk out the front tells me to turn off my mobile phone, so I do. I peer in through the little window in the door. Alex is sitting beside the bed holding Professor Tanaka's hand. I watch her, summoning the strength to go in. I can see Alex is talking, but it doesn't look like Professor Tanaka is talking back.

Alex looks up and sees me. She raises her spare hand in a subdued wave and it is too late to run away.

The door is heavy and creaks loudly as I push it open.

Alex's face lifts. 'Hi, Happy.'

I walk over and stand beside the bed. There is only one chair. Professor Tanaka's eyes are closed and her face is pale. She seems even tinier than before – her body is the size of a child's beneath the white sheet. 'What happened?'

'When I got there to do the gardening this morning the house was all shut up. I had to climb in through a window.' Alex takes a deep breath. 'I found her lying on the floor in her lounge room. She'd been playing that record, "All the Girls and Boys". It was stuck on the turntable, making a scratching noise.'

'I'm sorry I wasn't there.'

'It wouldn't have made any difference.'

'Is she unconscious?'

'I don't know. She might be sleeping. She's been like this ever since I got here.'

162

'Do you know what happened?'

'They won't tell me much because I'm not family, but the nurse said there's something wrong with her heart.'

I perch on the edge of the bed. My pulse is thumping hard and I have a tinny taste in my mouth.

'Are you okay?' asks Alex. 'You look a bit …'

'Hospitals and me don't mix.' I gnaw on the inside of my lips.

Professor Tanaka is breathing in shallow, rapid gasps.

The door opens and a nurse comes in. She is plump, with round arms and a pink, flushed face. *Debbie Simpson* says the identity card that dangles from her bosom. Bosom is not a word I had ever imagined using, not even in my head, but in this case no other word will suffice. She frowns when she sees us. 'Are you two family?'

'Not exactly,' says Alex, 'but–'

'Visiting hours are over.' She jerks her chin towards the door.

'But I just got here,' I say.

Nurse Debbie folds her arms. 'The rules are here for a reason. Ten o'clock tomorrow.'

Alex grimaces at me. 'Oh well. Bye, Professor Tanaka.' She moves to the head of the bed and touches her arm. 'I'll come and see you tomorrow.'

'Bye, Professor Tanaka.' My voice comes out croaky. I touch her shoulder. It is birdlike and fragile. 'Sleep well.'

Alex and I are quiet as we leave the hospital and make our way through the tunnel to the bus stop. Everyone we pass looks tired and sad in the fluorescent lighting, like zombies in an apocalyptic movie.

Our bus takes off from the kerb with a swoosh. A light rain is falling and the streets glisten in the glow of the red taillights ahead.

The bus is almost empty; just a few solitary figures lean against the windows.

'Hospitals are strange places, aren't they?' I say.

Alex's face is pale in the dim glow from the streetlights. 'Yeah, they're intense. Everything is so close to the bone.'

'It's like birth and death are commonplace there. There's no room for everyday things.'

'Like what?'

'I don't know. Laughter. Music.'

'They're kind of otherworldly, aren't they?'

I nod. 'They make me want to …'

'Scream?'

'Yeah that, and open the windows to let some wind blow in.'

'I know what you mean.'

I lean my head against the window.

'Thanks for coming. I know you don't … but I didn't know who else to call,' Alex says.

'I don't what?'

'Well, you don't really know her. Not like I do.'

'You've got an extra year on me, that's all.'

'Yeah.' A car light flashes across her face.

'Did you meet her through the job?'

Alex nods then rests her head against the seat. 'She put an ad in one of those free papers. I needed some money and I figured it couldn't be any worse than stacking supermarket shelves.'

'You seem like you're pretty close to her.'

'Yeah, I am I suppose. We've got to know each other. She's eccentric, but I like her. She got me interested in doing psychology so I worked really hard to get the grades. Sometimes she feels more like my mum than my mum does.'

I look at her. 'How come?'

Alex looks past me out the window. 'Mum and I don't get on.'

It's clear that she doesn't want to talk about it, so I restrain myself from probing further. 'Has Professor Tanaka got any children?'

Alex shakes her head. 'The only family she's mentioned is a brother in Tokyo. She has a good friend, another professor. They do things together – art galleries and stuff. She's away on a hiking holiday in New Zealand at the moment though.'

'So have you been looking for a cure for Paris Syndrome ever since you met her?'

'Not really. It's not like I'm about to jet off to Paris any time soon. I suppose it didn't seem that important. Then I figured it would make a good project and Professor Tanaka agreed. I'm hoping I'll pick up a scholarship if I do really well in the first semester.'

I look out the window at the street. It is drizzling outside and the air is heavy and humid. I put out a finger and draw a question mark in the mist that's forming on the inside of the window. It feels like a day for big questions. 'Why do you think Professor Tanaka loves Paris so much?'

Alex's hair is damp and she runs her fingers through it so it sticks up at odd angles like a blue-crested cockatoo. 'I don't know, Happy. Why do *you* love Paris so much?'

I think for a minute. 'I suppose she's right – it's a fantasy. I feel like I might be able to become someone different there. Someone better.'

Alex gives a faint smile. 'What's wrong with who you are now?'

'I don't know. Sometimes I feel ...' I turn back to the window and draw a few lines radiating out from my question mark '... like I don't know who I am.'

Alex touches my shoulder. 'I know what you mean, Happy. Like maybe there's someone else more fabulous inside, trying to get out.'

I turn to her. 'Yeah, and if I was in Paris ...'

'That person would emerge?'

I nod.

'Maybe you don't need to be in Paris to be that person?'

'Maybe I don't. It couldn't hurt though, right?'

Alex looks into my eyes with a quizzical expression. Her blue eyes look almost black in this light. She smiles, then she leans over and touches her lips to mine.

This is so unexpected that I jump.

She flushes. 'Sorry, I–'

'No, that's okay. It's fine. It was nice.' I sound fake and breezy and I don't know what to do about it. But neither do I know what to do about Alex's kiss. I need to freeze time. Then I can respond appropriately. But time keeps moving on and the kiss gets bigger and bigger the further we get away from it.

Alex shifts a little away from me on the seat and it's too late to put things right. I gnaw my lip. It was just a kiss. I shouldn't have jumped like that. I look out the window, my heart thumping, trying to make sense of it. I wish I hadn't acted like I hated it.

Because part of what is making my head spin is that I didn't hate it at all. It sent a jolt right through me that I've never felt before. And that's the most confusing part.

We finish the bus ride to the city in silence. My pulse is still racing as we get out of the bus and walk around to the train station. Alex's platform is first.

My throat is tight. I cough. I run various sentences through my head, but none of them are right. 'Bye. See you soon.'

'Bye.' Alex sounds casual. She avoids my eyes. Then she climbs the stairs and she doesn't look back.

I want to call out to her to stop, but I don't know what would happen after that. So I keep quiet and I let her go. Inside me, something curls up and dies.

It is almost eleven o'clock when I get home, but Mum is still up. 'Have you had dinner?' she asks.

I realise I forgot to eat, but I think I am too sad anyway.

'Would you like me to warm you up some shepherd's pie?'

Surprisingly, my stomach rumbles out loud at her question. 'Thanks, Mum.'

We sit at the table together and Mum nibbles on some dark chocolate while I consume a large serving of shepherd's pie. 'This is great.' For once I'm not lying. The warm food revives me. It fills the hollows.

'So where have you been? I tried to ring back after you texted, but I couldn't get through.'

'I had to turn my phone off. I've been visiting someone in hospital.'

Mum puts down her chocolate. 'Who?'

I place my fork on my empty plate and take a drink of water. Then I tell Mum about Professor Tanaka, which leads me on to Alex One and Alex Two. I leave out both the kissing parts. There is still a lot to process.

'I had no idea there was so much going on in your life. Why haven't you told me about all this before?'

I shrug. 'I don't know. You've been busy, I guess.'

'I haven't been that busy.' Mum's brow is furrowed. 'You've been having a pretty full-on time, haven't you?'

I nod. I feel like my head might explode, I have so much to think about. Alex One, Alex Two, Professor Tanaka, Rosie.

'Are you okay?'

'I'm kind of wound up.'

'I can see that.' She puts out her hand and squeezes mine. 'You know you can talk to me about anything, don't you?'

I nod, but I don't want to worry her any more than I have. Mum's done enough worrying about me, and she has her own problems to contend with. 'When you and Dad met, did you know he was the one for you straight away?'

Mum gives me a crooked smile. 'Yeah, but I guess I was wrong, huh?'

At that moment my phone rings. This is an unusual event – Dad's the only one who rings instead of texting and it's so late. My pulse thumps as I see the name on the screen. 'Hello?'

''Ello.'

I move into the other room for some privacy. ''Ello,' I murmur back.

''Ow are you, 'Appy?' asks Alex One.

'Tres bon, merci.' My hand finds my hair and twirls it. I've never done this before. It must be my hormones playing up. Or the moon cycle. Or both.

'I am sorry you 'ad to go the other night.' Alex's voice is charged with the possibilities of what might 'ave 'appened if I 'adn't 'ad to go.

'Me too.' I am almost whispering. His voice in my ear does strange things to my stomach.

'Would you like to come to my place on Sunday? For breakfast? At about eleven o'clock?'

Breakfast at eleven … How very French. My mind flicks quickly through my activities for the weekend. I have a full day's work tomorrow. I should try to talk to Alex Two again and go and visit Professor Tanaka on Sunday. But we can do the afternoon visiting time … Or she can go by herself in the morning. Maybe the kiss moment needs more space. Maybe I need to work things out in my head first, before I try to work them out with her. 'Yes. That would be nice. Breakfast. At eleven.'

After our goodbyes, I flop back on the couch, my mind bubbling. I think I might have made a sexual assignation. Which is good: I need to start making progress on that front. Confusingly, Alex Two's kiss replays in my mind for a moment. I push the memory down. I can't think about that right now. Picking up my phone, I open Facebook and message Rosie – *Sunday is SA day.*

Her reply when it comes is not what I had hoped for.

The first time's kind of meh.

Chapter Twenty-three

Saturday passes in an auto-piloted blur. Sunday's breakfast looms on the horizon like a far-off shore where the inhabitants may or may not be friendly. The closer I get, the more foreboding it seems. Getting ready for breakfast with Alex takes most of Sunday morning. There is a lot to consider. I dig around in Mum's bathroom cabinet and discover a mud mask which promises to make my face clearer and brighter. I slap on the greyish goop before proceeding to my bedroom to decide what to wear. This requires great concentration. I am in the middle of considering my twentieth outfit when I notice a strange sensation – I can't move my face. I stop and try to raise my eyebrows, but it doesn't work. For a moment I think I have developed Moebius Syndrome, the one that freezes your face. This is going to ruin my date. Then I remember the mud mask and rush for the bathroom. My face emerges, pink, clean and – phew – mobile.

I experiment with make-up and scrutinise my underwear. None of it is suitable for viewing by a French Love God – I choose the least bad pair. I consider hair straightening again, but can't face the trauma. Instead I experiment with different hair arrangements.

From time to time I get a sick churning in my stomach. Will I make a fool of myself? Will it hurt? I wish Rosie was here to coach me.

I wish I'd teased out the implications of the word *meh* when I'd had the opportunity. It doesn't fill me with confidence. My nerves are jittering as I head for the door at ten-thirty. I am wearing my Number Five Amélie outfit – a little button-up white top with a lace collar teamed with a knee-length flowered skirt and black boots – and my hair is as untamed as usual. All the other arrangements made me look strange.

Don't expect too much and it will be fine, says Amélie as I head for the door. *Think of it like a trip to the dentist.*

'What?'

Oh yes. My first time was a nightmare.

Sex is one of life's great mysteries, says Billy. *And not to be treated lightly.*

'E was like a robot, says Amélie. *It wasn't until I met Dino I realised –*

'Enough.' I hold up my hand. 'Too much information.' I slam the door behind me.

While I wait for the train I text Alex Two. *Will visit PT in arvo session. Will you be there?* She doesn't reply. *Damn.* She's not talking to me.

I gnaw my lip and a strange restlessness fills my body. Like I need to run and run and run until it goes away. I've never been a runner so it's perplexing.

171

The city train comes and I get on. Alex One lives in an apartment in Spring Hill, close to the CBD. On the train, I inspect the baguette and Camembert cheese which I have brought as my contribution to the breakfast. I am unsure if the Camembert is appropriate for an eleven o'clock breakfast, but the baguette should be fine. And perhaps we will segue into lunch. *Segueing* is a very French thing to do. I try to imagine what this segue might involve ...

As I stride up the hill from Roma Street Station some odd symptoms make their presence felt. My mouth gets drier and drier. It's like there's a suction cleaner draining my saliva. At least I haven't got Fish Odour Syndrome. That must put quite a kibosh on romantic interludes.

I stop at Alex's door but I don't knock. Instead, I lean against the railing outside, trying to summon my courage. If only I'd brought a bottle of water. Or maybe a bottle of Scotch. My mouth is so dry I can't even talk. Being burnt at the stake now seems a sensible lifestyle choice. It would be so much easier to walk away and follow the Joan of Arc route.

.''Appy?'

Alex has opened his door. My mouth becomes even drier. I didn't think that was possible.

'What are you doing out 'ere?'

I lick my lips and cough. 'Enjoying ze view.' My Foreign Accent Syndrome is flaring up again. Clearly it's stress related.

Alex looks down his street at the dingy rows of flats and run-down houses. He looks back at me with a quizzical expression. 'Do you want to come in?'

I nod, although I'd rather lead my army into battle and get tried for witchcraft. Or run a marathon. Either would be fine, but I can't back out. As I walk up to the door, I try not to focus on how devastatingly French Alex is, but it is hard.

He is wearing a loose grey T-shirt and faded blue jeans. His feet are bare and his black hair is rumpled. He even has stubble on his jawline. He looks like one of those guys in that painting by Renoir, the ones lounging around near the Seine. He doesn't move aside as I reach the door, instead he puts his hands on my shoulders and kisses me on the lips.

I jump back with a squeak. I should have been expecting this, but I wasn't. I thought I'd get a chance to settle in, to acclimatise to his presence first. My heart palpitates like a salmon leaping upstream. 'I need a drink,' I squeal. 'Vater.' My foreign accent has switched to German.

Alex steps back. 'Do you want to come inside, or shall I bring it out to you 'ere?'

'No.' I step over the threshold. 'I'm in.'

Alex shuts the door behind me and walks away without a word.

Looking around, I find myself in a lounge room. Slumping onto the nearest couch, I take off my backpack and run my tongue around my lips. This is not going well. I need to pull myself together. Alex returns with a glass of water. I toss my hair back over my shoulder as I gulp it down. 'Sorry, it's hot out there. I needed that.' Thankfully, I am no longer speaking with either a French or German accent.

Alex looks relieved. He sits on the couch next to me and meets my eyes.

My face goes soft and I feel like I might slide off the couch and trickle away.

'Can we try again?' he asks.

I nod. If I'm going to sexually activate, I may as well get it over with.

He moves closer and puts his hand around the back of my neck. Leaning over, he kisses me. His lips are warm and I imagine myself as the woman in *The Kiss*, her lover holding her close on a busy street in Paris. But I hardly have time to form the image in my head, things are moving so quickly. His shirt comes off, exposing a tattoo of a wolf on his shoulder. My top comes off – the buttons flying apart under his fingers. He is half on top of me, undoing my bra, when I feel my baguette digging into my back.

The baguette reminds me we were supposed to have breakfast. Something snaps in my brain. This is all wrong. It isn't how I want it to be. Where is the seduction, the romance? He could have at least put some music on – it wouldn't have to be French, just something to show he's making an effort. Placing my hands on his shoulders, I push him. I must push harder than I mean to as he rolls right off the couch.

He lands on the floor with a thump. 'Ow. Merde. What the 'ell?'

I scramble for my shirt. 'You said breakfast. I'm hungry. I haven't eaten anything all day. I've been saving up.' I pull the baguette out from behind my back and brandish it at him. 'I brought a baguette.'

Alex sits up on the floor. 'What's got into you 'Appy? Why did you come 'ere if you didn't want to do this?'

'Not like this. Not so fast.' I button my shirt. 'We should have had breakfast first. Talked a bit. That would have been nice. It's not a race, is it?' Holding my baguette like a club, I stride towards the door as Alex gets to his feet. Hand on the doorknob, I turn to face him. 'I would have … I just wanted …' I blink fast. 'To take it slow.' I step out and shut the door behind me. My heart is thumping like I'm a marathon runner crossing the finish line.

Alex opens the door and calls something after me in French as I run down the street.

I don't bother trying to translate – whatever it was, I doubt it will make me feel any better.

I am hot and sweaty by the time I get back to Roma Street Station and my mind is on spin cycle. I glance at my phone. There are no messages, but I notice the time. My truncated breakfast date means I can make morning visiting hours at the hospital if I hurry, so instead of catching the train home I get on a bus to Wooloongabba.

I press my nose against the window as the bus starts off. I'm still rattled by my date with Alex One. Why did he have to be so pushy? It's like we were only there for one thing. Maybe I should have expected that, but I didn't. I thought … I don't know what I thought, but in retrospect the way I pushed him off the couch feels good. Maybe all those boys who were scared of me were justified. There are advantages to being strong.

Perhaps Alex Two will be at the hospital. The thought of seeing her is initially soothing, before I remember we are on strained terms as well. Sex sure messes things up. In the last twenty-four hours I have gone from having two Alexes in my life to maybe having none. I'm not sure if this is my fault. Perhaps I've been putting out confusing vibes. Given the level of confusion in my head, that would not be surprising.

Inside the hospital, I catch the lift to the third floor. I don't know what I'm going to say to Alex if she is there.

'Who are you visiting?' asks the nurse at the front desk.

'Professor Tanaka. Michiko.'

She blinks. 'I'm sorry but you can't see her right now.'

'Why not?'

'She's taken a bit of a turn for the worse.'

Chapter Twenty-four

I hold onto the reception desk, which feels like it is swaying. The lights are too bright, the clatter of trolleys and feet too loud. A nurse pushes a bed past me – I see a flash of red hair on the pillow and bile rises in my throat. 'Is she going to be okay?' I have to say this twice, as my voice doesn't work the first time.

'We don't know at this stage. Are you family?'

I shake my head. 'I thought she was getting better,' I stammer.

'Sometimes things change overnight. Are you all right? Do you need me to ring anyone?'

'No. No, thank you.' I turn and walk slowly back to the lifts. My mind is frozen. While I was fooling around with Alex One, Professor Tanaka was getting sicker. Pulling out my phone, I call Alex Two again. Her phone is turned off and I listen to her message. *Hey it's Alex, don't leave a message because I don't check them, send me a text.*

Alex, where are you? I text.

'Are you going up or down?' A nurse is standing next to me.

'Oh. Down.'

She presses the button for me.

I expect nurses are used to people who look like they've beamed in from another planet.

When I get home, Mum is ensconced in a novel – her usual Sunday pastime. She looks up and her gaze lingers. 'Are you okay, Happy?'

I shake my head.

She pats the couch beside her. 'What's up?'

Tears well up and roll down my face as I sit next to her. It is some time before I can explain. I tell her things have gone badly with Alex One – an edited version that makes him sound better than he was – and about Professor Tanaka's condition. 'I feel so … selfish. And stupid.'

'Oh, sweetie.' She puts her arms around me and rocks me. 'You weren't to know. Life is hard sometimes.'

I sniffle into her shoulder.

'I'm sure she'll be okay.'

'And my friend Alex Two isn't talking to me.'

'Why, darling? What happened?'

'I don't know.' I hardly know where to start. And it's not something I'm ready to talk to Mum about. Not yet. That's a different conversation.

But Mum looks into my eyes. 'This girl, Alex … Is she just a friend?'

'Yes.' My whole body turns hot. 'Why?'

'Just asking, sweetheart.' Mum runs her hand over my hair.

I go to my room and text Alex again, but there is still no reply. I think of messaging Rosie, but can't find the heart for it. As long as I don't push too hard, I can pretend we're still friends the way we used to be. That she's still there, waiting for my message.

Even Amélie and Billy don't have any words of comfort. Today they are just pictures on the wall. I flop on my bed and cry some more.

I pull myself together in time to do the evening shift at the cinema. As chance would have it we are showing *Summertime* or *La Belle Saison*. This is billed as a lesbian love story, set in the 1970s.

Kevin is in a bad mood. 'Can't wait until this bloody French Film Festival is over,' he moans as we shut the doors on the screening.

'Why?'

'Can't you smell it?'

'What?'

'The garlic. Bloody French film fans reek of the stuff.'

I shut my mouth tightly. Surely those snails aren't still working their way out of my system? I shake my head. 'Hadn't noticed,' I mutter through gritted teeth. When Kevin is occupied out the back, I buy myself some mints from the sweet bar.

I open the packet as I step inside the darkened cinema but one hour later when the lights come up they are still uneaten in my hand. Those two girls were mesmerising. Their tragic love story reminded me of *Brokeback Mountain*, which is about the saddest movie I have ever seen. Although it was nothing like it really.

I sigh deeply as I open the cinema doors. The movie has left me washed out, sad, confused and, yes, I admit, yearning. It has left me with a strong urge to talk to Alex Two.

On my way home I text her – *How are things?* But she doesn't reply. I ring the hospital and they tell me there has been no change.

On Monday I wake up feeling like I've run a marathon. When I drag myself upright my phone says it is eleven am. I look in the mirror and see a giant pimple erupting on my chin. I have cramps in my stomach and my eyes are red. My entire body is rebelling.

I try to ring Alex again, but she doesn't reply. I ring the hospital and they tell me Professor Tanaka is still not doing very well and I can't visit.

In desperation, I go to the Buc Buc Facebook page to see if Alex has written anything. The last entry is from two days ago. Posted next to a picture of Marie-Antoinette, the la fleche, it says: *Let them eat cake, I'm sticking with my French Elegance Chicken Feed (sponsored post).*

Sponsored post? Who on earth is sponsoring her posts? And then I remember that I am. I check her page and see she's got over two hundred likes. I renew the sponsorship for another week. She'll be happy about that when she notices. Her post has one comment again from that Sarita – *Really miss you, Alex, I hope you're going well xox.*

Who is this Sarita? I click on her profile and see a pretty brown-faced girl with long black hair. Her profile is private. An uncomfortable emotion fills me as I click her profile shut. I close my computer. I really need to talk to Alex.

Mum has left me a note on the fridge with twenty dollars pinned to it – *Thinking of you, buy yourself something nice xxx*. I stick the money in my bag and eat a quick brunch. Then I get dressed in my Number One Amélie outfit – the sleeveless red dress – pull on my tea cosy, walk to the ferry terminal and catch a ferry to West End.

It is so hot that even sitting out at the front of the ferry in the breeze doesn't help. Wearing the tea cosy doesn't help either, so I take it off and stick it in my bag. My phone tells me it's going to reach a top of thirty-six degrees. Storms are predicted later.

As I climb the hill to Alex's place, I wonder how things will be between us. Surely the awkwardness will have evaporated by now. I have no idea what I want to say, but my chest is filled with the need to see her.

The chickens are running loose around her yard and they rush towards me when I open the gate. I shut it quickly before any can escape. 'Hi, girls, where's the boss?'

The chickens stare at me blankly.

'Où est la patronne?' I try but, unsurprisingly, the chickens are circumspect. 'Hey, Marie-Antoinette, who's sponsoring your Facebook posts?'

She stalks away like a supermodel. Clearly she doesn't know I am bankrolling her ascent to internet stardom.

Climbing the steps to the front door, I knock but there is no answer. I hear a buc buc from below. The chickens have gathered at the foot of the stairs. They look up at me expectantly. 'You girls waiting to be fed?'

The chickens go buc buc and jostle each other in a hopeful way.

'Sorry, you're going to have to wait.'

I knock again and the door shifts a little. I push it open.

It is cooler inside. A cup and a bowl are draining on the sink. Everything looks tidy. 'Alex?' My voice comes out in a squeak. Should I go in? Maybe she's having a nap. I can't just leave. 'Alex?' I walk through the lounge room towards what I think is her bedroom. The door is ajar.

Alex's room is sparsely decorated with two posters. The Arc de Triomphe is Blu-Tacked to one wall and *Poultry of the World* decorates another. This poster looks vintage: the chickens are beautifully illustrated and the writing is in an old-fashioned font. I step closer and examine it. Down the bottom it says, *Portraits of all known valuable breeds of fowls.* I can see the appeal of chickens – they are rather attractive. Certainly, as an occupation, they beat reality TV.

Alex's bed is unmade and a pile of books rests on the table next to it. I scan their spines, noting titles by Freud, Sartre and Simone de Beauvoir. We haven't talked about these authors, only about Madeline. Has she been dumbing herself down for me?

A desk in the corner of the room is cluttered with papers and has a computer, which appears to be on standby.

I know I shouldn't, but I walk over and touch the mouse and the screen flickers to life. The French Tourism Board website fills the screen. I scan the page. *Office closed Mondays* it says at the top.

I tap my fingers on the desk and straighten up. I think I know where she is. I need to hurry. Sprinting down the stairs, I scatter the chickens, who cluck in an offended way. I click the gate shut behind me and run to the bus stop – it's quicker than the ferry – but a bus is pulling out. *Damn.* Now I've got fifteen minutes to wait. I pace in front of the shelter, checking my phone every few seconds, but there's no message from Alex. I try to ring her again, but her phone is still switched off. At last the bus comes and I am on my way to the city.

Jumping off the bus, I run towards the high-rise building that houses the French Tourism Board. It is seriously hot here in the CBD – a heat shimmer rises off the road. Stepping into the air-conditioning is bliss. I catch the lift to the basement. The Tourism Board's doors are closed. I press my nose to the glass, but can see no one inside. The next door along is an accounting firm and I stop at the reception desk there.

'Is there no one in today?' I point at the Tourism Board.

The woman shakes her head. 'Closed Mondays. That's what it says on the door.' She looks back to her keyboard.

'Has anyone been in at all?'

'Mm, maybe.' She keeps typing.

'Who? Did you see them?'

She doesn't look up from her keyboard. 'I can't keep an eye on everyone who goes past.' She types for a bit longer. When she looks up she seems surprised to see me still standing there. 'Might have been a pest inspection.' She clicks her mouse and paper churns from the printer.

'The pest inspector, was she young with black hair and a blue fringe?'

She looks up again. 'Might have been. I've got something I need to finish here, if you don't mind.'

'Okay. Thanks.' I go back to the Tourism Board and press my nose to the window again. Alex has been here, I know. I put my hand to the door handle and it turns. I glance over at the receptionist, but she has her back to me, pulling paper from the printer. Opening the door, I slip inside.

The lights are off, but a dim glow comes through a small window at street level. It takes a moment for my eyes to adjust. Posters are scattered across the floor, as if someone has pushed them off a desk: *French Food Festival, French Movie Festival, French Fashion Festival, French Literature Festival, French Wine Festival.* A vintage-style poster on the wall shows a painting of the Eiffel Tower with a young woman standing beneath it. *Find Yourself in Paris*, it says.

I stare at it. *Find Yourself in Paris* …? Is that the poster Professor Tanaka saw in the Tokyo subway? A sticky note is attached to the poster. I step closer and read it. *Vintage is in – new campaign idea?* Did they get that idea from Professor Tanaka?

Some cardboard boxes are stacked against the wall, their lids ripped open. I walk over and see mugs inside the first one. I pull one out. It has the same image on the side – *Find Yourself in Paris*. The second box has T-shirts in the same design and the third is full of *Find Yourself in Paris* caps.

I sink onto a chair, swivelling from side to side as I try to make sense of it. Alex has been here, I'm sure, but where is she now? I check my phone again but neither of my Alexes have been in touch. I don't suppose I'm ever going to hear from Alex One again anyway.

''Ello?'

I jump from my chair.

Alex One is standing in the doorway, backlit by the light in the corridor.

'What are you doing 'ere?' I ask.

He tilts his head to one side. 'I work 'ere. What are you doing 'ere?' He steps inside and closes the door behind him.

My pulse does a rapid pit-a-pat. I look around me at the mess on the floor. It looks like I've trashed his office in a fit of rage.

He leans against a desk and we eye each other silently.

'This isn't what it looks like,' I say.

'I'm sure there is a good explanation.'

I clear my throat. 'Yes.'

He waits.

'Oh, you want me to tell you? Um, in fact there is no explanation.'

He smiles. 'You are a funny girl, 'Appy. First you throw me off my couch, then you mess up my office. Why?'

I lift my shoulders and let them fall.

'It doesn't matter, I still like you.'

He still likes me? I stare at him, wondering why my insides aren't turning to creme caramel. I take in his dark brown eyes, his long legs in denim, his little goatee beard, his amazing French accent, but, right now … I don't care. I don't even care that he's seeing me with a giant pimple on my chin, I've got other things on my mind. 'Sorry about the mess. It was like this when I got here.'

'That's strange. It wasn't like this when I left.' His eyes meet mine. 'I'm sorry about yesterday. I misjudged things.'

'It's okay, but … I need to go.'

Alex looks bemused. 'Okay. Au revoir. Maybe I will call?'

I don't know what to say to that. I head for the door, but hesitate and turn back. 'Is Paris the most wonderful city in the world?'

Alex laughs. 'Paris is just a place, 'Appy. I like it because it's 'ome.'

'Yes, I thought that might be the case. Bye.'

Alex lifts his hand. He looks disappointed to see me go.

Out in the corridor I walk quietly to the lift and press the up button.

When I emerge onto the street, the shadows are lower. I walk to the river and flop onto the grass as the heat of the day dissipates. Dark clouds gather above the city, foreshadowing the predicted storm. I pull on my tea cosy again, not for warmth but for comfort. It reminds me of Alex. I am still sitting there at five o'clock when the workers stream out of their buildings and the shopfronts close.

Where is she? I think of her Facebook post again. Who is that Sarita girl? I wish I could talk to Rosie about all this. But maybe she wouldn't understand anyway. This is a strange thought, because I've always felt like Rosie understood everything about me. I'm not sure that she'd understand *this* though.

After a while the sky turns pink beneath the clouds and lights wink on. Across the river, the giant Ferris wheel lights up and starts to turn.

My phone rings and I snatch it up, but Dad's name is on the screen and I remember it's Monday. I let it go to message bank, as I'm not in the mood.

With my eyes half-closed, I imagine dusk on the Champs-Élysées or at the Eiffel Tower – that must look spectacular when the lights come on. *The Eiffel Tower* ... Could she be there? It's worth a shot. I jump to my feet and run for the nearest bus stop.

Chapter Twenty-five

It's a slow ride down Coronation Drive: the traffic is bumper to bumper. I get off opposite Park Road and cross the street. Car lights dazzle me as I walk up the street. The air is muggy and the dull rumble of thunder rises over the roar of cars. I pull off my tea cosy again to cool down.

Before too long I see the blue lights of the Eiffel Tower. Walking up to the base, I look around. Even though it's early for dinner, the Park Road restaurants are filling up and the footpath is bustling. There is no sign of Alex. Then my eyes are drawn to a small ladder running up the side of the tower. Lifting my gaze I see it meets a platform about halfway up.

I crane my neck to look up at the platform. 'Alex!' I yell. 'I know you're up there.' It's worth a shot. People turn to look at me on the street, but I don't care. 'Alex!' I yell into the bright lights of the tower, 'I need to talk to you.'

There is no response, I'm making a fool of myself. But as I squint into the blue lights, I think I see a shadow move. 'I saw you. I saw you, Alex,' I call. 'You may as well come out now.'

After a moment, a face emerges above the latticed fence that lines the platform. Alex looks down at me.

I wave at her and she raises one hand in reply.

'I went to your house,' I yell. By now I have a few onlookers. I have left my tea cosy near my feet and someone throws a coin into it. Perhaps they think it's street theatre – a reworking of *Romeo and Juliet*. 'I need to talk to you.'

'Why?' Alex yells back.

'The chickens are concerned about you.' I wish I could see her face but it's only a shadowy outline.

'The chickens worry too much,' she yells.

'I found out there was a pest inspection at the French Tourism Board.'

'It needed it,' Alex yells. 'It was infested with propaganda.'

A few more coins clink into my tea cosy. Some people are easily pleased. Maybe it's one of Kevin's Emperor's New Clothes situations where they don't understand what's going on, but they think they should.

'Alex. I went to the hospital,' I yell. 'I heard about Professor Tanaka.'

Alex looks over at me, her face outlined in the glow of blue light. She doesn't reply.

I look at the ladder. I'm not good with heights and I don't want to do this, but I'm going to have to. I run gracefully towards it, like it's part of the performance. I don't want anyone to stop me.

Putting my feet to the rails, I climb. When I reach the platform, I push at the trapdoor above me, but it is locked. The only way up is to climb around the outside of the fence. I have no idea how

Alex got up there; it looks pretty exposed. Then I remember she is a former circus performer. It probably wasn't too much of an issue for her.

'Alex?' I call. 'How do I get up there?'

I hear footsteps above me and a hand dangles over the edge. Letting go of the ladder, I grasp Alex's hand. Clambering around the barrier and onto the platform, I collapse to the floor, panting. My heart is thumping wildly. This Eiffel Tower might not be a patch on the real thing, but it's high enough for me.

When I focus, I see Alex sitting on the platform, resting her back against the railing, her feet stretching towards me. She is wearing a *Find Yourself in Paris* cap. Wisps of blue hair poke out around her face. It suits her.

She raises one eyebrow. 'Didn't expect to see you here, Happy.'

I stay lying down. It is too hard to move. 'Why didn't you answer your phone?'

'I didn't feel like talking.'

'I was worried about you.'

'Why? What did you think I'd do?'

'I don't know. I thought maybe … something stupid.'

She snorts.

'You could have texted me.'

'I didn't know you cared.'

'Well I do.'

We are silent for some time.

'Are you okay?' I ask.

She breathes deeply. 'Not really. Are you?'

'Not really.'

189

'Well.' Her tone is dry. 'Here we are then.'

Above us, the Savoir Faire sign winks on and off. For some reason this reminds me of the ginormous pimple on my chin. Hopefully Alex can't see it in this light. I reach out and touch her foot. She moves it away. I bite my lip. 'Do you come here often?' I ask.

She shakes her head. 'First time.'

'I'm surprised the police haven't come.'

'It was all pretty discreet until you got here.'

'I was gathering a following down there. They're waiting for the next act.'

'What happens in the next act?' Alex looks ethereal in the blue light, like a vampire lover. She is wearing shorts and a singlet and her arms and legs glow palely.

She is beautiful. I can't take my eyes off her. She looks different. Or maybe it is me who is different. 'I don't know. No one sent me the script. I'm making it up as I go along.'

Alex folds her feet and wraps her arms around her knees. 'There's something you haven't been telling me, Happy.' Her voice is strained.

'What?' My pulse thumps in my neck as if it knows something I don't.

Alex pushes her hair behind her ears. She meets my eyes.

My stomach prickles.

'Rosie?' she says.

Chapter Twenty-six

I curl my fingers around my thighs. 'Rosie?' I whisper her name. I want to cover my ears so I can't hear what Alex is going to say next. If I could talk I'd ask her to stop, not to say it. But there is no voice left in me.

She takes a deep breath. 'Happy, I looked at her Facebook page.' Her words hit me like a slap.

I turn away and press my forehead to my knees. A burning tide floods my chest. I lift my head again and stare at Alex. *Please stop*, I think, but she doesn't.

'Happy,' her voice is soft now. She stares into my eyes. 'Please tell me about Rosie.' Her eyes are luminous in the semi-darkness of the flashing sign.

Savoir Faire.

Alex puts her hand on my wrist and circles it with her fingers. There is no escaping her.

I take a deep breath. 'You want to hear about Rosie?' My voice is an angry croak.

Alex nods.

'Okay. I'll tell you then. About Rosie. Rosie has …' I pause. 'Rosie has crazy red curls and a Great Gatsby tattoo.' I stop and wipe my nose with the back of my hand. 'She has a weird sense of humour and … and she loves to dance.' I'm like a deep diver ascending. The only way out is up.

Alex doesn't say anything. She lets go of my wrist, fumbles in her pocket and passes me a tissue.

Rosie's story is a locked compartment I tiptoe around every day. Now Alex has opened it and there's no way I can shut it again.

'Her boyfriend, Rosie's boyfriend, he studies music at uni. We didn't see each other as much once she started going out with him. Things changed. Sometimes she didn't feel … so much like a friend anymore.' I wipe my cheeks. My tissue is a sodden mess. I ball it up and Alex hands me another one.

But strangely, my tears dry up now. I need to focus. To get through this. 'Then something … something terrible happened.' I pull my feet closer and hug my knees to my chest.

Alex searches my face.

I look away from her out at the lights. 'There was a car crash.' The lights blur. 'Four of them died – Rosie's boyfriend: Luke, and two other boys from uni, Joel and Xavier.' My shoulders shake. I hug my knees tighter. It's too much. I'm not going to make it out, there's no clear water above.

Alex touches my leg. 'You said four.'

I nod. 'Yes, four. Luke, Joel, Xavier …' My throat closes up again.

Alex is quiet beside me.

I don't want to tell her. 'Luke, Joel, Xavier.' I press my face into my knees. 'Luke, Joel, Xavier.' Tears roll down my cheeks and onto my legs.

'And Rosie,' I whisper. 'Rosie died too.'

I close my eyes and time passes. I am still breathing. Long, slow, deep breaths. I can feel Alex breathing beside me. I have made it to the surface. To the air.

Alex is quiet beside me.

I need to explain, but it hurts my head. 'I forget … I forget she's not around.' I don't look at Alex, because I'm scared of what I might see. If she thinks I'm crazy I'd rather not know. 'On Facebook, I can still see everything she's ever written.'

A waft of diesel fills the air as a truck goes past. I chance a quick glance at Alex. Her eyebrows are drawn together. She already thinks I'm crazy, so there's no point in stopping now.

'I send her messages, then I trawl through our old conversations and pick out replies. Ones that make me feel like she's still here.' I feel like I'm ripping a hole in a curtain – one that's been hiding my fantasy. My voice falters. I look out at the city so I can't see Alex's expression. The more I talk, the crazier I feel.

'Sometimes it doesn't work.' I cough but the tightness in my throat doesn't budge. 'Sometimes I go to places we didn't go together. Then she doesn't reply. And that's when I know she's stopped and I'm going on without her. Those times are … hard.'

I lift my head from my knees and look at Alex. It's hard to know what she's thinking. 'She was so … full of life. Someone like that doesn't vanish. Not all at once. They were just going down the road to get kebabs. *Bloody kebabs.* Rosie didn't even like kebabs. She was a vegetarian. That's ironic, isn't it?' I attempt a crooked smile.

But Alex doesn't smile back.

'I saw her in hospital afterwards. She looked flawless. As if she was asleep.' I wipe my nose with the back of my hand again. 'Maybe that's why I have trouble believing she's dead. The last time I saw her she looked so perfect. So alive. But she never woke up.'

Alex's hand is still on my leg. Her face is pale.

It's not fair of me to dump all this on her. She didn't sign up for it. 'I'm sorry. This is heavy, isn't it?'

'Yes.' Her mouth twitches. 'But I asked you to tell me.'

I meet her eyes, wiping the snot from my nose again. 'I'm a mess.'

She shrugs. 'Yes, you look like shit. Go on.'

'It took weeks for her to die. I was in and out of the hospital. In and out. When her parents told me she'd gone I felt – this is going to sound strange …' I wipe my eyes. 'I felt completely broken. But at the same time I felt like I'd been …' I swallow '… set free.'

'How?'

'The worst had happened now. I didn't need to worry anymore.' I touch my hand to Alex's and feel its warmth. She turns her hand palm upwards and I slide my fingers through hers. 'I felt like my life stopped and somehow started all over again in that moment.'

'How long ago was that?'

'Just over a year. I can't hold it in my head. I know she's gone but it keeps slipping out. I feel like she's still around. I can feel her presence. In Sydney, everyone knew … But in Brisbane, she was never here so it seemed like she could be alive again. I started to pretend. That's crazy, isn't it?'

'It's a little weird.'

I look at her. 'Only a little?'

'I'm trying to be tactful. It's weird but understandable. A year isn't long, Happy. Not long to get over something like that.'

'It seems long. It seems like forever.'

Above us the Savoir Faire sign winks on and off. Thunder rumbles again.

'Are you angry with me?' I ask.

'About Rosie?'

I nod.

'Not now … When I found out I felt, I don't know …'

'Like I'd been lying to you?'

'Yes.'

I don't want to ask her if she's angry with me about other things too. I don't have the strength right now. Later maybe. 'Can I put my head on your shoulder?'

Alex sighs. 'Sure. That would be okay.'

Chapter Twenty-seven

I am half-dozing on Alex's shoulder when my phone rings. It is Mum.

'Happy? Where are you? Are you coming home for dinner?'

'Um, I'm at the Eiffel Tower. In Milton.'

Alex looks at me.

'Mum,' I mouth.

'So when are you coming home?'

'When am I coming home?' I whisper to Alex.

She shrugs.

'Not yet. I'm ... with my friend Alex.'

'At the Eiffel Tower?'

'Yeah, we're here at the moment, but we may move on.'

'What about dinner?'

'We'll probably have dinner together.'

'Will you be home before midnight?'

'I should be. Don't wait up.'

'Okay, take care, love you.'

'Love you too.'

Alex glances sideways at me. 'So we're having dinner?'

I've been making assumptions. 'If you'd like to?' I can't let her go now. I feel tender, like I've been peeled out of my shell, and I need her to stay close.

'Yes, okay. Where?'

'I've got an idea. Follow me.' I stand and peer over the edge. 'How do we get off this thing?'

'I'll go first.' Alex climbs gracefully over the edge and onto the ladder. She holds out her hand.

I lean over and, taking her hand, clamber my way onto the ladder. It is scary and I'm glad of her grip. There is a smattering of applause from the café diners as we reach the bottom of the tower.

'Bravo,' calls one of the waiters.

'It was *Romeo and Juliet*, wasn't it?' says a woman with short dark hair. 'I've been taking bets.'

'Yes, that's right,' I say. 'It was a feminist retelling where Juliet rescues Romeo from the tower and neither of them dies.'

'I thought so.'

'Why can't you people leave Shakespeare alone?' says a middle-aged man at another table. 'What's next, *The Taming of the Shrew*, where the shrew's a man?'

'That's a great idea,' says the dark-haired woman. 'It's about time we had a good hard look at the misogyny in Shakespeare's plays.'

'It's people like you …' The two seem to be settling into an ideological argument.

'I'd take off quick if I were you,' says a suntanned man with white hair at the nearest table. 'The cops are on their way.'

'Thanks.' Alex jerks her head at me and we run down the street. A police car goes past and we duck into a shadowy shop entrance.

The headlights flash over us and disappear. 'I feel like a renegade,' I say.

The police car pulls over next to La Dolce Vita and two square-shouldered cops get out.

Alex and I walk quietly in the opposite direction until we are out of sight.

'Now, all we need for my dinner plan to work is something to drink,' I say. A little further down the street a corner shop is open. I pull Alex inside and buy two glass bottles of fizzy grape juice.

'Classy.' Alex gives me a small smile.

I smile back at her and my heart starts putting itself back together, piece by piece. 'You ain't seen nothin' yet, baby. Classy and me are like that.' I cross my fingers and hold them up.

'So where are we eating?' she asks as we walk towards the traffic lights.

'You'll see.' We cross over the road and I lead the way to the ferry terminal. A CityCat is coming and I walk down the gangplank, waving to Alex to follow.

Alex and I board the ferry and find a seat on the back deck, where it's not so windy. The boat chugs away from the jetty and a light breeze lifts our hair. The city is all sparkly and beautiful from the river. Lightning glows on the horizon. There is no one else around and it is surprisingly quiet out here.

'It's nice out here on the water,' says Alex. 'Do you think Paris is better than this?'

'Mm, imagine Notre Dame and the Arc de Triomphe lit up at night. All those cathedrals and fancy shops.'

'True. That'd be awesome to see.'

I open my backpack and pull out the day-old baguette and Camembert that have been there since my failed breakfast date. They are only slightly squashed and Camembert improves with age anyway. 'Ta da.'

'Why are you carrying around a baguette and some Camembert?'

'Just a safety precaution. In case I should be called upon to host an impromptu meal.'

'Well, we're in luck, because …' Alex reaches into her bag and pulls out a jar of honey and some walnuts.

'Can I ask why you are carrying around a jar of honey and some walnuts?'

'There was a market in the park down the street this morning. You realise what we have here, don't you?'

I survey our ingredients. 'No.'

Alex pulls a tiny penknife from her wallet.

'Did you used to be a girl guide?'

'I wanted to be, but my father had an ongoing feud with the pack leader, so, no.' Alex slices a piece of baguette, spreads honey on it, puts a slice of cheese on top and sits a couple of walnuts on top of that. 'Traditional French recipe as served at Le Petit Escargot.'

'Really?' I take the bread.

'It should be goat's cheese, but it doesn't matter.'

I take out the sparkling grape juice and hand one to Alex.

She chinks her bottle to mine. 'Here's to …' She looks at me questioningly.

To Paris, to Rosie, to love? 'To Professor Tanaka,' I say.

'Yes, to Professor Tanaka.' Alex gives me a lop-sided smile. 'May she get back to Paris one day.'

We are quiet for some time, sipping on our drinks. 'Have you ever seen *Midnight in Paris*?' I ask eventually.

Alex shakes her head.

'In *Midnight in Paris*, Owen Wilson finds this portal where he can slip into Paris in the 1920s. He meets Ernest Hemingway and F Scott Fitzgerald, the author of *The Great Gatsby*.'

'I know who F Scott Fitzgerald is.'

'Right. Well, wouldn't it be great if Professor Tanaka could slip through a portal back into Paris in the 1960s and this time, whatever it was that went wrong, would go right for her?'

'Nice idea, Happy.' Alex smiles. She holds her bottle up and chinks mine again. 'Here's to Professor Tanaka finding a portal to Paris in the 1960s.'

We both take a sip of our drinks.

The ferry stops at Toowong and a few people get on and off. 'It makes you think.' Alex stares out at the river.

'What?'

'About life. And how you can spend so much time wanting something else.'

'Instead of appreciating what you have?'

'Yeah.'

200

'I know. I do wonder if, when I eventually get to Paris, it will be as amazing as I expect.'

Alex takes a gulp of her drink. 'So, how do you feel about that?'

Another ferry goes past in the opposite direction and we sway up and down in its wake. The motion is comforting.

'I feel …' I take a sip of my drink. 'I don't know. It's hard to put a finger on.'

'Aha. Let me try out some of my psychological training on you.' Alex pulls a notebook and pen from her bag.

'Do you have any psychological training?'

'No. But I will have soon, so that counts, doesn't it?'

'No, but I expect that's as good as it's going to get for me right now, so carry on.'

Alex gives me a mock salute, opens her notebook to a clean page, frowns and writes for a couple of minutes. 'Okay. I'm going to read you out the list of basic emotions and I want you to score each one out of ten to describe how you feel about going to Paris. Got it?'

I cough. 'Got it.'

Alex reads from her notebook. 'Fear.'

'Seven. No, seven and a half.'

'Whole numbers only.'

'Okay, eight.'

Alex nods and makes a note. 'Anger.'

'Um, four?' I feel as if we're playing Grandma's Footsteps and any moment Alex is going to catch me out. I don't know why I feel this way.

'Interesting. Joy.'

'That's a tough one. Six?'

Alex scribbles again. 'Disgust.'

'... Three.' I sound doubtful, even to myself.

Alex raises her eyebrows. 'Trust.'

I frown.

'Go with your gut instinct.'

'Two.'

'Anticipation.'

'Eight.' I speak quickly. I just want to get this over with.

Alex looks at her notebook. 'Last one. Sadness.'

I must have known it was coming. Heartache hits again like a tidal wave. 'Ten.' My voice is a whisper. I chew my lip to stop the tears.

'Ten?' Alex meets my eyes. Her voice is soft. She shuts her notebook and puts it back in her bag. She gazes out at the river for a moment then turns back to me. 'Why so sad about going to Paris, Happy?'

The ache in my chest is expanding to fill my body. 'Because ...' I swallow hard.

Alex looks at me steadily.

'Because Rosie won't be there and the plan always was that we would go together.'

Alex nods and looks into my eyes. 'I don't know what to say.'

'It's okay. You don't have to say anything. Just being here is fine. It's more than fine. I haven't talked about her before. Not like this. I guess I felt like if I never admitted she was dead, maybe she wasn't. Maybe she was in Sydney, hanging out with Luke and too busy to talk to me. And in November, when it was time to go to Paris, there she'd be, ready and waiting and we'd be off, off and away.'

Alex smiles at me. 'She was lucky to have you as a friend, Happy.'

'No, I was the lucky one. If you knew her you'd know. She was effervescent. When Rosie walked in the room, the party began.' I smile back weakly. 'Life's so strange sometimes, huh?'

'Sure is.' Alex squeezes my hand.

The boat bumps and shudders as it pulls in at a wharf. We are still alone here on the back deck.

'We always said to each other – it was a joke really – if one of us died the other had to scatter her ashes in Paris.'

'But you didn't?'

I shake my head. 'I couldn't. I mean I told her parents, but they had enough to deal with. I let it go. I felt like I'd failed her though.'

'You didn't fail her. You were her friend.'

Lightning flickers on the skyline. The air smells moist, like wet dust.

'I'm not ready to lose anyone else from my life.'

Alex pushes her fringe out of her eyes with her free hand. 'Professor Tanaka will be okay. She's way tougher than she looks.'

'I hope so.' I keep hold of Alex's hand. 'So, all of that, the Rosie thing, I think that's partly why Mum moved us to Brisbane. She thought a change of scene would do me good. It was good for her too though, to get away from Dad, and she loves her new job.'

'Has it done you good?'

'Didn't seem like it at first. I hated the place.' I meet her gaze and give a small smile. I am exhausted, like I could sleep for a million years, but underneath that is a calmness I haven't had for a long time. 'I don't know. Maybe. It kind of feels like it now.'

Alex and I sit in silence for some time, holding hands, watching the river go by. I am all talked out. Seems like she is too.

The ferry reaches the end of the river and all the passengers except us get off. No one else gets on.

'This is the end of the line, guys,' says the ferry operator, a suntanned blonde woman.

'We're sightseeing,' says Alex.

Her eyes flicker over the remains of our dinner and she taps a sign next to her. *No eating on board*, it says. 'Be discreet, ay?'

'Thanks.' I smile at her and she smiles back.

We all look skywards as a loud clap of thunder is rapidly followed by a jagged flash of lightning. A fat raindrop plops onto my head.

'I'd be getting home if I were you.' She pulls up the ramp and the ferry backs out into the river.

Alex and I lean back, watching the shore. The banks are dark here and mangrove-lined. We could be on a boat in the Congo, or South America. I almost expect a hippo to rise out of the water. The thunder and lightning flashes add to the exotic mood.

'I've never had a ferry to myself before,' I say.

'We're like millionaires on our private yacht.'

'Only this is better.'

'How's that?'

'It's unexpected. It wouldn't be the same if you owned the boat.'

'So true,' says Alex. 'It makes you wonder why you bother organising anything at all when the random stuff is much more fun.'

'Though you can't drift along waiting for things to happen. You need to get yourself into the right position for the fun stuff to come about.'

'True. Maybe it's fifty per cent planning, fifty per cent chance.'

'I'd say sixty per cent planning, forty per cent chance.'

'Ah, you're a goal-setter, Happy.'

'I am.'

'The gods of random chance are watching over us tonight though.' Alex pauses. 'So you tracked me down to the French Tourism Board, huh?'

I look at her. It seems like that happened in another lifetime now. 'It wasn't that hard. How did you get in there, anyway?'

'Remember the escargot incident?'

'How could I forget?'

'I'm not a bad pickpocket. Learnt it in clown school.'

'You stole Alex's keys? Did you drop those escargots on him on purpose?'

'Maybe.'

'I think you did. So what did you find out in there?'

'Nothing much.'

I stare at her. 'There was no grand conspiracy?'

She shakes her head.

'Just a whole lot of marketing merchandise?'

She nods. 'How did you know?'

'You left the door open. I went in.'

'Did you see that poster? The one Professor Tanaka talked about?'

'Find Yourself in Paris? Yes.'

She pulls a square of paper out of her pocket and unfolds it to show me the Eiffel Tower picture. 'Look. I took a copy. To remind me. Hey, they might be sponsoring my Buc Buc Facebook page.'

'The French Tourism Board?'

Alex gives a half-smile. 'I sent them an email asking if they'd like to support the promotion of French chickens.'

'That's pretty random.'

'I never heard anything back, but all of a sudden my posts are sponsored.'

I decide not to fill her in. 'Sleeping with the enemy, huh?'

She gives me a long look. 'I'm not the one who's doing that.'

My face flushes. 'Neither am I.'

'Oh yeah?' Alex's eyes linger on me, then she shrugs. 'I don't know if I even care about Paris Syndrome anymore. Now Professor Tanaka's so sick, it all seems …'

'Pointless?'

She nods.

My stop comes, but I don't want to leave. I stand and baguette crumbs fall to the deck.

'I'll walk you home,' says Alex.

'Cool.' I put out my hand and pull her up.

It's late now and the streets are quiet except for the rumble of thunder. The storm is moving away again. Only the odd drop of rain splatters the footpath, raising the scent of wet dust.

When we reach my apartment I can see the light on inside. Mum's waiting up for me. 'See you tomorrow?' I say.

'Sure.'

I watch her go and when she reaches the streetlight on the corner she turns around. I can't see her face but I think she is smiling. She bends over and throws herself into a handstand, holds it for a few moments then backflips to standing.

'A circus trick,' she yells, 'for special occasions.'

I clap as loudly as I can.

Lightning flashes behind her as she waves. I wave back and I watch until she is out of sight.

Chapter Twenty-eight

Tuesday is the last day of the French Film Festival, which is strange. I hardly feel like the same girl who walked into the cinema with her resume two weeks ago.

I pass a streetlight on my way to work, which, obscurely, reminds me of Alex's handstand last night. A warm glow fills my stomach but underneath is a twinge of anxiety. Will things be strange and awkward between us now? Does she think I'm a nutcase? I wouldn't blame her.

This morning I looked through Rosie's Facebook posts and sent her a message as I always do. *Missing you, Happy xxx*. It was different this time though. I didn't search her feed for a reply.

Today we are screening *Jean de Florette*, a wistful story set in the south of France. As I stand in the dark watching it, the sun-dappled green fields and lichen-covered rock walls transport me into a trance of longing. *One day.*

Kevin pumps his hand in the air as we shut up after the screening. 'Made it through the French Film Festival. Yahoo,

Hollywood blockbusters here we come. Suppose you're cut up about that.' He pulls an electronic cigarette out of his pocket and sucks on it. The tip glows futuristically blue, like a robot cigarette.

'Yes, I am a bit sad, and I think you are too, secretly. Go on, confess, you've developed a new love of French cinema, haven't you?'

'Uh-uh, no way. If I never see another bloody baguette or a flipping scooter riding past the Eiffel Tower, that will be fine with me. Bring on the shoot-'em-ups.'

'Oh, come on, you must have had a favourite?'

He shakes his head and exhales a faint cloud of vapour.

'One you disliked less than the rest?'

Kevin frowns. 'What was that one about the balloon? That wasn't too bad.'

'*The Red Balloon*?'

'Yeah, that's the one.'

'What did you like about it?'

'It only went for half an hour. That was bearable.' Kevin ponders. 'Women like this French stuff though, right?' He gestures towards the *Amélie* poster on the wall.

'Yeah, they do.'

'They think it's romantic.'

I nod. I have no idea where he's going with this. 'Why? Have you got a woman you want to impress?'

Kevin's ears turn red. 'Say I did. French stuff would be the go, huh?'

I smile at him sideways as I wipe the counter. 'Yep. The more French stuff the better, I reckon.'

Kevin nods thoughtfully. 'I've paid two weeks' wages into your account.'

'Oh, thanks.'

'No worries. You've done all right. I was worried at first. The French speaking and all that, but you're one of the better assistants I've had here.'

Coming from Kevin, this is a ringing endorsement.

'Only a week until the Boxing Day new releases. Goes crazy then so it's good you're trained up.'

When I step out onto the street after my shift, Alex is perched on a bench outside. Alex Two, that is, not Alex One. A flutter in my chest tells me this is the Alex I want to see.

She is wearing faded jeans and a black singlet and looks like an extremely hot rock star. 'Hey.' She flicks her blue hair out of her eyes.

'Hey.' I am preposterously pleased to see her. I examine her face. She doesn't appear to think I'm a nutcase.

'Good news. Professor Tanaka is getting better. They say we'll be able to visit tomorrow.'

A breeze blows up the street, lifting my hair in a fuzzy cloud. I smile broadly. 'That's fantastic.'

'What are you doing now?' Alex gets to her feet.

'Nothing much.'

'Want to go to the Gallery of Modern Art and see the new French modern exhibition?'

'Awesome. You have such good suggestions.'

'I do my best.'

We walk towards the train station. I examine her out of the

corner of my eye. She has slid on a pair of John Lennon–style sunglasses. Her hands are in her jeans pockets and she walks with easy grace. I feel acutely conscious of the space between us.

'France invented modern art, you know,' Alex says.

'I didn't know that.'

'Oh yes. Why do you think Picasso and Chagall painted in France? They weren't French.'

'Since when were you such an art expert?'

'Since I read the exhibition website this morning.'

'I'm impressed.'

She gives me a crooked smile. 'Excellent. I aim to impress.'

We sit next to each other on the train, but there seems to be a lot of distance between us on the seat. I remember the books on her bedside table. 'I saw those books in your bedroom. When I went around to find you.'

'You went in my bedroom?' Alex frowns.

'Sorry. I was worried about you. I didn't touch anything.'

'It's okay.' She shrugs. 'I have no secrets.'

'Have you read Jean-Paul Sartre and Simone de Beauvoir?'

Alex looks at me over the top of her glasses. 'No, I just keep them there to impress anyone who might wander into my bedroom.' She pauses. 'Yes, I've read them. Why?'

'There's more to you than just chickens, isn't there?'

Alex smiles. 'Yes, Happy, chickens are just the most obvious facet of my incredibly well-rounded personality.'

I feel the need to broach the topic of last night's confessions. 'So, I'm sorry about last night,' I say. 'I kind of downloaded on you. It was pretty intense.'

211

'Don't be silly – I'm the one who started it. I wanted to know what was going on with you.' She touches my arm and meets my eyes. 'I'm happy you felt you could talk to me.'

'Thanks. Just thought I should, you know, mention it.' I exhale like a surfacing whale.

Alex smiles.

'You don't think I'm crazy-mad?'

'Madness is a continuum, right? Crazy-mad?' She ponders, 'No. I'd say we might both be somewhere on the spectrum though.'

We smile at each other and my stomach skips. How have I not noticed before that her lips are so pink?

We get off at South Bank and walk up to the art gallery. *French Modern*, says the banner at the entrance.

A vibrant display of artwork extends before us as we go through the glass doors into the gallery. I stop to read the sign at the exhibition entrance. *Twentieth Century French art developed out of the impressionism of the Nineteenth Century …*

Alex and I wander on. The first canvas we come to is an enormous hodgepodge of blue paint. Alex reads the sign. 'Anthropometrie de l'Epoque Bleue. *This painting was made by covering naked women in blue paint then getting them to roll around on a canvas in front of an orchestra and a formally dressed audience.*' She looks at me and laughs. 'I'd like to have seen that.'

I blush hotly. I don't know why.

My blush is infectious and Alex blushes too.

We stand there staring at each other's red faces.

'What's going on here, Happy?' Alex asks at last.

I know she isn't talking about the painting. I bite my lip. She's so beautiful and I like her so much, but only last week I thought I was in love with Alex One, and now … I'm confused. 'It's hard to put into words.'

She sighs. 'How are you feeling?'

'I'm not sure.'

She reaches into her bag and pulls out her notebook. 'Should I do the emotion thing?'

'No, no, wait, I can do it. Happy – nine out of ten, nervous – seven out of ten, confused – seven out of ten,' I pause and look into her eyes, 'and tentative – eight out of ten. How's that?'

Alex gives me a long look then shrugs. 'I guess we work with what we've got.'

Her voice is neutral, but her shoulders look stiff and I feel like I've said the wrong thing.

We walk past a wall painted in red stripes and a wildly indecipherable painting in shades of grey, towards some works that look more recognisably like art as I know it.

'Professor Tanaka would have liked this,' says Alex.

I hold up my hand to stop her. 'Look.' I point at the painting on the opposite wall. 'Is that …?'

Alex comes to a startled standstill. 'It looks like it.'

We walk closer. Yes, it is definitely the painting that was used in the *Find Yourself in Paris* poster but this one, which must be the original, has no text. The painting is much larger than the poster and I notice something new as I look at the young woman in front of the Eiffel Tower. 'She's Asian.'

'I noticed that.'

'Does she remind you of anyone?'

Alex meets my eyes. 'Yes, she does.'

The woman's smile is radiant as she looks towards the artist.

'She looks like she's in love,' I say.

Alex reads the sign. '*Jacques Brasseur, 1967 oil painting titled* Michiko. *The identity of the model is not known.*'

'Michiko,' I say.

'Yes.'

'Is it her?'

'Maybe,' says Alex.

'It's got to be her. Don't you think?'

Alex stares at the painting. 'That's pretty amazing.'

'And kind of confusing.'

Alex nods. 'Considering she told us she saw the poster in Tokyo.'

'And she never told us she was in it.' I gaze at the painting of Michiko smiling with joy, and for some reason tears spring to my eyes.

Alex glances at me. 'It makes you think, doesn't it?'

I nod. 'One moment you're like this,' I gesture at the painting, 'and the next–'

'She'll be okay.' Alex's cool fingers touch my arm.

Back at home that night Alex calls me when I'm reading in bed. 'Hey you,' she says.

Her voice ignites a range of symptoms. *Rapid pulse. Weak legs. Stupid smile.* Clearly, I have a big, fat crush and I just need to admit it. 'Hey.'

'Still nervous?' she asks.

I hesitate and my stomach flutters. 'Six out of ten.'

'I suppose that's progress. It's Professor Tanaka's birthday tomorrow, according to Facebook.'

'I can't believe you two are Facebook friends. How old will she be?'

'Seventy-five.'

'That's a big one.'

'We should get her a cake.'

I catch sight of my *Amélie* poster and she gives me her usual mischievous smile. My chest fizzes and at once I know what we need to do. 'We can do better than that, can't we?'

Alex is as excited as I am about my suggestion. 'Okay, let's get organised.'

We work out a plan of attack. 'Alex,' I say, when we finish our planning, 'let's not talk to Professor Tanaka about the painting yet. There must be a reason why she hasn't told us that she's on the poster. I don't want to upset her. Not while she's sick.'

'And we don't really know if it's her.'

I agree, although I am already sure it is.

'Bye then. Sleep well.'

'Bye. See you tomorrow.' As I hang up, I yawn. I'm tired, but I can't sleep. There's so much to do. I check the tattoo fund in my bank account. This project is going to almost clear it out but I still have my cinema earnings.

As I commence preparations, my mind churns.

'Is what I think is happening with Alex really happening?' I ask Amélie and Billy.

Why don't you kiss 'er and see what 'appens? says Amélie.

'But what if it doesn't work out? Would we still be friends?'

It's tricky, says Billy.

Why don't you set a treasure 'unt and leave clues around town? Amélie suggests.

I love Amélie's suggestions but they can be difficult to implement. Thinking about Alex makes me reassess lots of things. The guy with the sea slug tongue, all those guys who couldn't beat me in arm wrestles … Even the way I felt about Alex One. Was it just his Frenchness that attracted me? Or was it him? I don't know.

I also think back on other things – my obsession with Amélie for instance and that art teacher, Miss Simpson, I was fixated on in Year Eight. More than anything though, I think about Rosie.

It's so hard to know what to do.

On Wednesday I get up early, which is tough because I went to bed late. I slide my hand over to the bedside table and check my phone. I have a text from Alex. *Operation Joyeux Anniversaire commences 10.00.*

'You're up early.' Mum is dressed in her Zumba gear – stretchy pants and a singlet – and looks very fit. She leans over and ruffles my hair as I spoon out my muesli. 'Are you working today?'

I nod. Explaining to Mum what is on my schedule for today would take more energy than I currently have and I'm not sure Mum, being a health professional, would approve of our plan. Alex and I have divided the tasks. She, due to her connection with Le Petit Escargot, is on food duty. I am tasked to ambience. This is a broad area with no clear boundaries.

'What do you think of when I say ambience?' I put my bowl in the sink.

Mum tilts her head to one side and sips her coffee. 'Mood, I guess.'

'Hmm, so how do you create it?'

Mum smiles. 'Are you developing an interest in interior decorating, Happy?'

'Maybe.'

'Well, you create ambience with lighting, music, smells, decoration ... That kind of thing.' She gestures at our utilitarian kitchen. 'As you can see, it's not my forte.' Mum glances at her watch. 'Gosh, look at the time. I'd better skedaddle.' She pauses on her way out the door and turns back. 'You're not throwing a party, are you, Happy?'

I shake my head.

'You can if you want, I'd like some warning, that's all.'

'Who would I invite to a party?'

Mum bites her lip and blinks several times. She rushes back and plants a kiss on my forehead. 'Have a wonderful day, darling.' And with a patter of gym shoes she is gone.

Ambience. Dad told me once that George Bush said the French have no word for entrepreneur. I'm sure he would have said the same about ambience if he'd thought of it.

You 'aven't seen ambience until you 'ave seen Paris, says Amélie as I'm ferreting about in my drawer for a clean T-shirt.

Nobody does ambience like the French, Billy agrees.

They are in agreement. This is a first. 'Well, that's setting the bar high. I'd better get cracking.' I give myself a quick once over

217

before I rush out. Jaunty red neckerchief. Blue T-shirt. White shorts. *Ambience level at three out of ten and rising.*

Three hours later I am riding up the lift in the hospital, a large backpack on my back. If anyone asks me what I am up to, I will say I am delivering laundry, or maybe cleaning products. But no one cares, which is lucky.

I hover in the corridor, waiting until the nurses' station out the front is unoccupied. I don't know what the rules are around surprise birthday parties, but I suspect they are frowned upon. At last the nurse walks away down the ward and I stride confidently past her desk to room 303. I pause at the door and peek in through the glass window. Professor Tanaka looks pale and still. She must be sleeping. It is ten am – visiting hours. I push open the door. Where's Alex?

By ten-thirty I have set up my sound system, draped red, white and blue streamers around the room, placed blue cellophane over the bedside lamp and turned it on, and have some rose-scented oil warming on Mum's aromatherapy heater. I hope Alex turns up soon. I don't want to face the wrath of Nurse Debbie on my own.

I have been quiet in my preparations and Professor Tanaka hasn't stirred at all.

At last the door creaks and Alex backs in, carrying a large tray. Her face is flushed and her hair messed; she looks kind of frazzled. She looks around her and smiles. 'Wow, Happy,' she whispers, 'this is great what you've done here. Sorry I'm late, the croissants weren't ready.' On her tray she has an assortment of goodies – deliciously aromatic croissants, jam, butter, delicate petits fours, a rich-looking chocolate gâteau and – by way of contrast – a plate of pungent garlicky snails. 'I know you don't like snails, but ...'

'I know, they're traditional. And actually I might be developing a taste for them. Hey, you're wearing the French colours. Is that deliberate?'

Alex is dressed in red jeans and a white T-shirt. Her blue hair completes the tricolour. She smiles. 'Totally intentional.'

My eyes are drawn to the way her jeans hug her thighs.

She catches me looking. 'I know, they're too tight, but they're all I could find in red.'

'No, you look great.'

Her cheeks are already pink but they become a little pinker. She places the tray gently on Professor Tanaka's bed as it is too big for the bedside table. 'No sign of the dragon?' she whispers.

'Not yet.' I shake my head.

She looks at Professor Tanaka. 'Has she been asleep the whole time?'

I nod. 'Maybe they gave her something.'

Alex and I look at each other for a moment. 'Well, let's get this party started,' she says.

I touch my phone and 'All the Girls and Boys' warbles from the little speakers I've set up on the bedside table. It took me until one o'clock this morning to put together a compilation of suitable French music. The tune warms the sterile atmosphere of the hospital room. Put together with the lighting, the streamers and the scent of rose, it makes it ... not exactly homey, but a lot less scary. All we need is for Professor Tanaka to join the party. I look at her again, but nothing has changed. She is still quiet and pale. I have a twinge of doubt about whether this party is a good idea.

Alex and I sit on the bed next to the tray of food. There is plenty of room as Professor Tanaka is so tiny.

Alex's leg brushes against mine, but she shifts away.

I would like to sit closer to her, but I need to get my head sorted and an occupied hospital bed is not the place. I survey the gâteau, the croissants, the petits fours, the snails. 'How are we going to get through all this?'

'Little by little. The cake comes last.'

'I suppose we may as well start.' I pick up a tiny petit four and place it whole in my mouth. 'Mm, del–'

'What on earth are you two doing?'

Alex and I jump like frightened rabbits.

Nurse Debbie shoulders her way into the room. She puts her hands on her hips and her eyes roam around, taking in the streamers, the lighting, the music and coming to rest on the food. Her nose crinkles. 'Are those snails?'

I chew rapidly and dust at the scattered petit four crumbs on my lap. In the cold light of Nurse Debbie's gaze, the surprise party now definitely seems like not such a good idea. Amélie has led me astray.

'It's Professor Tanaka's birthday,' says Alex.

'Well, I'm sorry, but she's not in a fit state to enjoy it. I need you to pack all this up straight away. It's against regulations.' Her eyes rest on the snails. 'And unhygienic.'

I don't know what makes me turn – maybe a small noise, an intake of breath, but when I look at Professor Tanaka, her eyes are open. 'Look.' I nudge Alex.

220

She turns too. 'Happy Birthday, Professor Tanaka.'

'Happy Birthday,' I repeat.

Professor Tanaka blinks.

The door creaks at that moment and an accordion pushes its way through the entrance, followed by Tony the accordion player, resplendent in a red waistcoat with upswept black hair. 'Ees this the right party?' He squeezes his accordion and a lively note hangs suspended in the air.

Chapter Twenty-nine

Nurse Debbie folds her arms and glares at Tony.

I look at Professor Tanaka and she smiles and gives a small nod.

'Yes, this is the right party.' I wave my hand at Tony. 'Please begin.'

Tony squeezes the accordion and the first notes of 'Non, Je Ne Regrette Rien' fill the air. The red, blue and white streamers sway in the draft from the open door and things are a little festive at last.

Another nurse pokes her head in the door. 'All right in here?'

'Call the duty doctor.' Nurse Debbie moves over to the bed. 'Do you want these people here, Michiko?'

Professor Tanaka's dark brown eyes survey me and Alex. She smiles again. 'Yes.' Her voice comes out in a whisper. She turns her head to the accordion player. 'I don't think we've met before?'

'Bonjour. Je suis Tony.' He bows and continues playing.

'Help me sit up, please,' says Professor Tanaka.

Nurse Debbie adjusts the bed and plumps the pillows, pulling Professor Tanaka into a sitting position. She takes her pulse. 'Do you know what day it is?'

'It's my birthday.' Professor Tanaka looks at the tray on her bed. 'I always have snails on my birthday.'

'I'm going to talk to the doctor.' Nurse Debbie pauses at the door. 'You have half an hour, no more. Don't overdo the snails.'

'How are you feeling, Professor Tanaka?' asks Alex once Debbie is gone.

'I feel fine.' Her voice is faint. 'Thank you for coming to celebrate my birthday. Such a wonderful surprise.'

'Would you like a snail?' asks Alex.

Professor Tanaka has a bit of trouble with the fork, so Alex helps her, holding the snail to her lips.

'Mm, delicious,' she murmurs.

I take a snail too, pop it in my mouth and chew. 'I'm definitely getting a taste for these.'

Professor Tanaka looks around the room. 'What a lovely job you have done with the decorations. It's like I am in Paris. And the music ...' she sways her head, '... wonderful.'

'It's so good to see you looking better,' says Alex.

'It was just a silly turn.' Professor Tanaka smiles and her eyes crinkle. 'I am so much better now. I hope you weren't worried about me.'

'We were a bit,' I say.

Professor Tanaka laughs mischievously. 'I'm still around for a little while yet. And you two – what have you been up to the last few days?'

Alex and I exchange a glance. If you take out my fiasco with Alex One, the uncertain status of my relationship with Alex Two, the raid on the French Tourism Board and the poster at the art gallery, there is not all that much left to tell. Surely something we've done is suitable for bedside chit-chat?

'We've been riding on the ferries,' says Alex. 'It's beautiful at night.'

Professor Tanaka smiles. 'There is nothing like riding a ferry on the Seine at night.'

We nibble on the petits fours for a few minutes. 'I feel like I am at the Cafe de Flore,' says Professor Tanaka. 'They have the most delicious petits fours there.'

Tony switches to the theme music from *Amélie*. As one, our heads and feet move in time with the music.

'Ah, Amélie,' says Professor Tanaka. 'You can't listen to that tune without being happy.'

'We'd better cut the cake,' says Alex. 'Before they kick us out.' She pulls two candles – a seven and a five – out of her pockets and presses them into the icing. Pulling some matches out of her other pocket, she lights them.

Alex and I are singing 'Happy Birthday' to an accordion accompaniment when a doctor in a white coat comes in through the open door. He waits for us to finish.

Professor Tanaka leans over and blows out the two candles.

Alex hands her a knife. 'Now you have to cut the cake and make a wish.'

Professor Tanaka pushes the knife through the cake and closes her eyes briefly. When she opens them, she smiles. 'I have wished.'

'Better leave Michiko to rest,' the doctor says.

Tony the accordion player plays a few more notes, bows, waves and departs.

Professor Tanaka lifts her hand to wave. 'He was charming.'

Alex cuts a slice of cake and places it on a paper plate next to her bed. 'I'll come and see you tomorrow,' she says.

'Me too,' I add.

Professor Tanaka smiles. 'Thank you for such a lovely birthday. It was the most memorable I have had for many years.'

Nurse Debbie comes into the room and clears her throat in a meaningful way.

'Let me take your blood pressure.' The doctor takes Professor Tanaka's arm.

Nurse Debbie points at the door and gestures for us to depart.

I lean forward and give Professor Tanaka a kiss on the cheek. She is frail to the touch and smells papery, like dry leaves.

Alex gives her a kiss too. They smile at each other for some time. 'I'll take the rest of the food and leave it at the nurses' station, so that should make us popular,' she says.

Nurse Debbie shoos us out.

'We'll see you soon,' says Alex.

Alex and I put down our leftover food at the nurses' station. We are about to leave when Nurse Debbie comes out of Professor Tanaka's room. She smiles wearily when she sees us. 'Well, that was the first surprise party I've ever had in hospital, but it did brighten her up.'

'She's looking much better, isn't she?' says Alex.

Debbie nods in a guarded way.

'She'll be all right, won't she?' I ask.

'Look, I shouldn't say this, because you're not family, but there doesn't seem to be anyone else ...'

'What?' I ask.

'She's a trooper. She should be all right for a while, but it could happen again. Then again, it might not ...' She looks at the plate of petits fours and the gâteau. 'I've never been to Paris. Kind of like to now. I shouldn't, but ...'

'Je ne regrette rien,' says Alex.

Debbie reaches out, takes a petit four and pops it in her mouth. 'Mm, delicious.' A smile transforms her face. 'You're right. Je ne regrette rien.'

Alex and I say goodbye and make our way out of the hospital. We sit next to each other on the bus on the way home, our shoulders brushing, and though neither of us says anything I know we are both thinking about what Nurse Debbie said. *It could happen again.*

Being on the bus from the hospital reminds me of the last time, when Alex kissed me. She catches my eye. Is she remembering it too? If she kissed me now, I'd kiss her right back. But she doesn't. Maybe she's decided she doesn't like me in that way anymore. Perhaps she's waiting for me to kiss her instead.

'What's up?' she asks.

'Nothing, why?'

'You were frowning.'

'No I wasn't.'

She lifts her shoulders. 'Whatever.'

We finish the bus ride in a slightly disgruntled silence. I wish I knew what I should do.

I have an afternoon shift at the cinema. We are showing the latest Hollywood shoot-'em-up. I thought Kevin would be thrilled to have seen the last of France, but strangely, an attack of nostalgia has struck him down.

'You like that movie, *Amélie*, don't you?' He glances at the poster.

'Like it? I love it. It is the best movie ever made. When I watch *Amélie* I feel like everything is right with the world.'

Kevin pulls a pack of mints out of his top pocket, takes one and offers me the packet.

I take one too.

Kevin sucks on his mint. 'Hypothetically, if I was trying to impress a woman – the kind of woman who likes *Amélie* – what would I do? Let's say I wanted to give her a present. A Christmas present.'

'Tell me more about this hypothetical woman. What sort of woman is she?'

A far-off look comes over Kevin. 'A sophisticated woman. A woman who knows her mind and isn't afraid to speak up. An independent, intelligent and beautiful woman.'

'Wow. She sounds amazing.'

Kevin nods. 'She is amazing.'

'Well, for a woman like that, you're going to have to pull out all the stops. First, to get her warmed up and create the impression you are a sensitive New Age guy, you can give her a DVD of *Amélie*.'

Kevin's brow puckers. 'I resent your implication that I am not a sensitive New Age guy.'

'Sorry. No offence intended. I see now you are.'

Pacified, Kevin nods. 'Go on.'

'If the DVD goes well, I'd follow it up with a traditional present, some French perfume, or maybe a scarf.'

Kevin looks at me intently. 'Then what?'

'You want to give her more presents?'

He nods. 'No expense spared.'

'Okay, to show her what a sophisticated and worldly kind of guy you are, I'd give her a food hamper.'

'Wait.' Kevin holds up his hand. He rushes over to the counter and finds a pen and some paper. 'Okay. *Amélie* DVD, perfume, scarf.' He scribbles. 'So, what's in the food basket?'

'A baguette and some honey, goat's cheese and walnuts.'

Kevin frowns. 'What's she going to do with that?'

'Test it out. It's delicious.'

'Doesn't sound too good. I've never had goat's cheese before.'

'I hear it's what all the sensitive New Age guys are eating.'

Kevin snorts. 'If I have to. Ta for that.' He rips the page out of his notebook and places it in his pocket.

'Good luck.'

He smiles and smooths his hair over the bald patch. 'She'll be putty in my hands.'

Ew. Maybe I shouldn't have helped Kevin with his plans, but it's too late.

When I step out of the cinema, a familiar but unexpected shape is leaning on the streetlight outside.

''Ello.' It is Alex One. He is wearing a black T-shirt and loose jeans and when he smiles his teeth flash white against his olive skin. A *Find Yourself in Paris* cap is perched on the back of his head.

Although he is as cute as ever, no bizarre bodily symptoms manifest themselves. 'What are you doing here?' I ask.

'I came to see you, what else?'

'Oh, right.' It is flattering of course. He is still very good-looking – and French – even if I no longer turn to jelly in his presence. I hadn't thought we were on visiting terms, though.

'I 'ave brought something for you.' He pulls a pen out of his pocket. 'They 'ave just come in. I thought you might like one. They are very good pens. It is a Christmas present.'

This is rather surprising. I take the pen and inspect it. It has a picture of the Eiffel Tower on one side with *Happy Christmas* superimposed over it and *Find Yourself in Paris* written on the other. It looks like the kind of pen you might pay a lot of money for. 'Thank you,' I say.

'We got them made, just for friends of the Tourism Board.' Alex sticks his hands in his pockets. 'I miss you, 'Appy. Can we get together some time?'

He misses me? I fiddle with the pen. It was nice of him to come all the way over here to give it to me. 'Um, yeah, sure.' It's hardly a definite commitment.

He smiles. 'Okay. I will call. Goodbye.' He raises his hand and walks away.

I watch his long legs stride away from me and I feel … nothing much at all, which is in itself a strange feeling. I slide the pen into my pocket – it is, as he said, a very good pen.

229

Chapter Thirty

Back home, I lie on my bed thinking about Alex and the way she smiles – that mixture of shyness and confidence. Of how funny she is – her snorty laugh, her fondness for chickens. My mind plays with the memory of her long legs in the red jeans and the way her blue fringe flops over her eyes. I imagine kissing her and a hot tide sweeps across my body.

It's confusing.

How can it be that one minute I am swooning for Alex One, and now ... It's pretty strange. All I know is that I like her. And totally In That Way. I need to do something about it.

My mind turns to Professor Tanaka. She looked so radiant in the painting in front of the Eiffel Tower. She couldn't have had Paris Syndrome then. So what happened? Did the city turn against her?

I look up at my *Amélie* poster. 'If Professor Tanaka was your friend, what would you do, Amélie?'

Find a way to set things right.

'But how?'

Disguise yourself as a Frenchman and write a secret message …

Talk to the artist who painted the picture, says Billy. *He knew her in Paris before things went wrong.*

'That is an excellent idea, Billy.' Sitting up, I pull my laptop off the bedside table and Google his name – Jacques Brasseur. He has a website and is still living in Paris. After some thought, I compose a careful email and send it.

Is that it? asks Billy. *You're just sending an email?*

'What else am I supposed to do?'

What about finding a cure for Paris Syndrome?

'It's not that easy.'

If it was easy, everyone would be doing it. Doesn't mean it can't be done.

Billy is right: I need to try. 'I'll give it a go.'

Amélie nods approvingly. *Everyone needs a little help sometimes. You need to be creative.*

Billy sniffs. *God helps those who help themselves, girlie.*

After work on Thursday I head over to Alex's house. I have a plan I need to discuss with her. She isn't expecting me, but when she opens the door her blue eyes crinkle up in a smile. Her hair is plastered back from her face like she's just got out of the shower.

I smile back at her, almost forgetting why I'm here.

'Come in. Cup of tea?'

'Love one.'

'Professor Tanaka's back home now,' she says. 'Looks like our birthday party did the trick.'

'That's awesome. Have you seen her?'

She shakes her head. 'I told her I'd come around this afternoon.'

Alex yawns loudly as she busies herself with the kettle and the teapot.

'Tired?' I say.

She nods. 'Went out dancing last night with a few friends.'

Dancing? Since when does she go out dancing? Irrationally, I feel slighted. Why wasn't I invited?

'I'd have asked you,' Alex says, as if she's read my mind, 'but, you know, clubs. You need to be over eighteen.'

'Do you have lots of friends in Brisbane?'

Alex shrugs. 'I've been here a year. I've met people.'

'Do you miss your old friends in Toowoomba?'

Alex takes a while to answer. She bangs some cups on the bench then turns around with a small smile. 'Yes, but life moves on. I don't think ... I don't think those friends were people I could go on with.'

Again, I want to probe the mystery of her move to Brisbane, but her stiff shoulders warn me off. Outside, the chickens cluck contentedly. 'So, do I get to hear the chickens play the xylophone now?'

She shakes her head. 'We're still in rehearsals. They've mastered "Three Blind Mice", but we're working on a few jazz numbers.'

'Can't wait.' I watch her long arms as she pours water in the teapot.

'It's going to be pretty special.' Alex turns with the teapot. 'What?'

I blink.

'You look like the cat that got the cream.'

'Do I?' I fiddle with the edge of the tablecloth, embarrassed. 'It's nice here. With you and the chickens.'

Her mouth pulls up on one side. She looks amused. 'Thank you. It's nice here with you too.'

My chest tightens. I don't know how to move this along. I wish Alex would kiss me again and take things out of my hands.

Alex puts the teapot on the table and touches my shoulder. 'I know this is a new thing for you, Happy. I'm not going to drive it. You need to work it out for yourself.'

She's read my mind again. I hesitate. 'Everything's a new thing for me.'

'Oh.' She draws out the word. 'Really?' Her hand is still warm on my shoulder.

I sit as still as possible, hoping she'll leave it there.

Alex takes her hand off my shoulder. 'You know what, Happy? My theory is that if you meet the right person it doesn't matter what gender they are.' She walks back over to the kitchen bench and picks up a plate. As she comes back to the table she gives me a half-smile. 'Works for me.'

I reach for my cup of tea and look up to meet her eyes. Something flips in my stomach. 'Maybe that works for me too.'

Alex bites her lip as she sits opposite me. 'Well, good. Because the chickens have got attached to you and I wouldn't want to disappoint them. They might stop playing the xylophone.'

'I had no idea they felt that way.'

'Well, they do. It's obvious. Listen to them.' She gestures towards the clucking chickens outside. 'That's their happy cluck they only make when you're here.'

I smile. 'I'm deeply touched.'

Alex places a bowl of whipped cream on the table and a jar of jam, then pulls a tea towel off the plate to reveal scones. 'Ta da. I've been baking.'

'Far out.' I take a scone, add the jam and cream, and bite into it. 'Mm. You are incredibly multi-talented. Chicken trainer, gardener, waitress, psychologist, dancer, gymnast and scone-maker. You should be on a reality TV show.'

'*My Chicken Rules*?'

My scone catches in my throat as I laugh. I take a sip of tea to wash it down. 'I've been thinking about Professor Tanaka.'

Alex nods. 'Me too. And?'

'We have to get her back to Paris.'

'How'd you figure that out?' Alex bites into a scone. She ends up with a blob of cream on the end of her nose, which looks very cute.

'This Jacques guy, the painter, was obviously her lover – you saw the way she looked in the painting. She couldn't have been happier. But for some reason she got Paris Syndrome. Why? You've got cream on the end of your nose, by the way.'

Alex wipes her nose and shrugs. 'Who knows?'

'But she adores Paris and it's just wrong if she never goes there again. She might have died this week … We need to get her back there.'

'We can't force her.'

'If we found a cure for Paris Syndrome, she'd go.'

Alex looks sceptical. 'That's a big if, Happy.'

I wave my scone around. 'Come on. We've done all the research. You've got the data there in your bedroom, right? We're two smart girls: we can figure it out.'

'If it was that easy someone would have done it.'

'Phoo.'

'Phoo?'

'Yes, phoo. People are discovering new things all the time. Maybe no one's tried. Not in the way we have. We're probably the world's leading experts in Paris Syndrome. You want to be a psychologist, here's your opportunity.' I place my teacup on the table with a bang. 'Let's psychologise.'

'I suppose we can give it a go.'

'Think positive, Alex. We're going to do it.'

'Yeah, we're going to do it.' Alex punches the air with her fist, but she sounds unconvinced.

I decide to ignore her ironic attitude. 'That's the Joan of Arc spirit. We're not going to rest until we find a cure for Paris Syndrome.' I jump to my feet.

Alex stands, pushing her chair back. 'Or until we get burnt at the stake. Whichever comes first.'

Chapter Thirty-one

Alex and I sit at her desk with the piles of questionnaires in front of us in a stack.

'What now?' she asks.

'I'm just the motivator. You're the psychologist.'

Alex frowns. She pulls out a sticky note, writes *Exhibit A – interviews* on it and sticks it to the front.

'Good. I like your sticky-note technique. Clever. What else can we stick notes on?' I see the poster of Professor Tanaka in front of the Eiffel Tower on the edge of the desk. I write on another sticky note *Exhibit B – victim* and stick it to the roll of paper. 'Now what?'

Alex opens a drawer and pulls out a small stack of paper. A photo flutters out and falls to the ground. I bend and pick it up. It is a photo-booth shot of the girl who posted on Alex's Buc Buc Facebook page, Sarita. She is wearing a trilby hat and has an easy smile that shows off her white teeth.

'Who's that?' I ask.

Alex takes the picture from me and tosses it back in the drawer. 'An Indian exchange student who lived here for a bit.'

'Where is she now?'

'She went back to India.' Alex leafs through the papers, her voice casual.

I lean over her shoulder. The page in her hand looks vaguely familiar. 'Hey, how come you've got a copy of my essay?' I snatch at it, but Alex pulls it away.

'I helped Professor Tanaka judge the essay competition. These are all the entries.'

'And you chose mine?'

Alex smiles. 'It wasn't hard. It was a standout. The decision was unanimous.' She writes on another sticky note – *Exhibit C – high risk of Paris Syndrome* and sticks it to the front.

I roll my eyes. 'Okay, now what?'

'We're making good progress, aren't we?'

'Excellent progress. We're smokin',' I say.

We gaze intently at our three piles.

'I'm unsure how to progress this.' Alex taps her fingers on the desk.

'It's like that emotions test you gave me. We need to find out what it is about Paris that stirs people. Why don't we look for key descriptive words that reoccur?'

'Good plan.'

'Okay, I'll look, you type. Ready?'

I flick through the surveys and call out words that seem important. '*Thrilling, joyful, exciting, stirring, fabulous, awesome, wonderful, desire, longing, absorbing, adorable, bohemian,*

237

sophisticated, beautiful, cultured, tasteful, elegant, delicious, pleasurable, fashionable, delightful, surprising, stimulating, bold, eclectic, creative ...' I go on for some time. 'Got all that?'

Alex stares at the list of words on her screen. 'It's like a thesaurus of positive words, isn't it? People think about Paris and they go gaga.'

I tilt my head to one side and study the screen. 'It's kind of the opposite of having a phobia, isn't it? What do you call the opposite of a phobia?'

'An obsession?'

'How do psychologists treat phobias?'

'They try to break the link between the object of the phobia – say spiders – and the fear response.'

'So we need to break the link between Paris and the excitement response. Too much positivity builds false expectations.'

Alex nods. 'True.'

We study the screen for a while.

'I've got it.' I almost jump from my seat.

Alex covers her ears. 'Ow, Happy, no need to yell. You've got what? A cure?'

'Not exactly a cure. Prevention is better than cure, right?'

'So?'

I lean back in my chair and put my hands behind my head. 'This is going to sound a bit obvious, but I think the key to avoiding Paris Syndrome is to ensure that your expectations about Paris are really low.'

'Easier said than done.'

'Wait.' I hold up one finger. 'Every time a positive image of Paris comes into your head you need to be able to question it and replace it with a negative one.'

'Right.' Alex sits up straighter and her eyes sparkle. 'Aversion therapy.'

'Isn't that where you give people electric shocks every time they think of something? I'm not sure if Professor Tanaka would go for that.'

Alex shakes her head. 'It used to be like that, but these days it's more about mental conditioning. They've found imagining something negative works better than real threats like shock treatment.'

'Interesting.' I look at the words on the screen. 'So every time you think *exciting*, you need to replace it with *boring*. Or if you think *elegant*, replace it with *ugly*.'

'Yes. It's about re-training your mind so your expectations are at rock-bottom and when you get to Paris, it can only be better than you expect.'

'And voilà. No Paris Syndrome.'

Alex smiles and twirls her chair back and forth. 'It's counter-brainwashing. I bet this is the sort of thing cult busters do all the time.'

'Exactly. That's what we are – Paris Syndrome cult busters. We need to stage an intervention. What do you think? Can we train Professor Tanaka so she's safe to go to Paris?'

'It's worth a shot.'

'Okay. So what we need is a structured program of aversion therapy to break down years and years of brainwashing, right? It's not going to be easy.'

'But we're the team to do it, Happy.' Alex puts up her hand and I high-five her.

Alex and I labour away together for a couple of hours. We sort through the movie theatre surveys and the Le Petit Escargot interviews. We carefully read through all the essays, highlighting appropriate sections. This gives us around two hundred obsessive statements about Paris, which Alex types into the computer.

'Wow.' Alex scrolls down her list. 'The rot goes deep.'

'Okay, now to fight back.' I read out the first statement, which happens to be from my essay. *When I live in Paris, accordion players will pop out from quaint little wooden-shuttered shops to serenade me as I pass.* I imagine the accordion player, the wooden shutters, the cobbled streets. *Oh, to be in Paris.*

'Happy.'

'What?' I jump.

'You're supposed to be critiquing that statement, not succumbing.'

'Oh, right.' I mentally slap myself around the face.

'Okay. I want you to imagine the quaint little shop with wooden shutters, but, instead of an accordion player, what is going to pop out?'

'A pickpocket?'

Alex nods. 'Maybe.'

'An evangelising Christian with pamphlets? Someone who wants to show you thousands of holiday photos on their iPhone? Someone who wants to sell you a cheap and nasty Eiffel Tower keyring?'

'Now we're getting there.' Alex makes a note on the screen.

We move through our list. *You may as well not be eating if you're not eating French food*, becomes *The French mainly eat intestines, gizzards and garden pests.*

It is hard work and eventually we stop for a break. Alex prints out what we have done and, while she makes cheese on toast for afternoon tea, I read through it, making a few notes for improvement.

Alex puts a plate down next to me. 'Nice pen.' Her voice is dry.

I am holding my *Happy Christmas – Find Yourself in Paris* pen. My cheeks burn. 'Oh, yes.' Although I have nothing to hide, I feel like I do. And then I remember that I agreed to see Alex One again. I do, in fact, have something to hide.

She sits next to me. 'I didn't see those pens when I raided the Tourism Board office.'

'Didn't you?' I don't want to explain how I came by the pen. It will sound peculiar – like something is happening which isn't. It almost certainly isn't. Instead, I take a large bite of the toast. 'This is great.'

Alex puts on a French accent. 'It ees special Kraft cheese from a little-known village called Brisbane.'

'Do they milk the cows themselves?'

'Naturellement.'

The awkward moment seems to have passed. I stash the pen away in my backpack at the first opportunity.

After our break, it takes a couple more hours but in the end we have two hundred flashcards, all of them headed with the title *Paris Syndrome Busters*. I feel mentally exhausted and, I never thought I'd say this, completely sick of the very idea of Paris.

'It's working,' says Alex. 'When I think of Paris now, I feel a sense of deep ennui. In fact, it almost makes me want to vomit.'

'Me too.' I ponder. 'You know, even the thought of going to Amélie's café in Montmartre doesn't excite me. It makes me feel tired and cross.'

'I picture myself standing on top of Notre Dame and I yawn. Why would you bother?'

'If you offered me a baguette, I'd hit you over the head with it.'

'We must be finished,' says Alex.

I look at our pile of cards. It's quite an achievement. 'Do you think Louis Pasteur felt like this when he discovered pasteurisation?'

'Absolutely. It's a great moment in science.' Alex tucks her fringe behind her ear and her blue eyes sparkle. 'We have discovered the Happy and Alex Paris Syndrome Inoculation Technique.'

'HAPSIT.'

'It's got an acronym, even. Do you think there'll be a Nobel Prize in this for us?'

'Definitely,' I say.

We meet each other's eyes, and smile. And in the glory of the moment it seems quite natural to lean over and touch my lips to hers.

It is electrifying. My pulse pounds in my neck and her breath is warm on my cheek. My whole body glows with longing. I should have done this ages ago.

But Alex pulls her head back and stares at me. Her face is serious.

'What?' I swallow, yearning to close the gap between us.

She runs her hands through her hair. 'I ... I don't think you're ready for this, Happy.'

Chapter Thirty-two

My brain feels numb as I stare at Alex. I can't believe it. I've finally plucked up the courage to kiss her, and now ... she's not into it. My cheeks burn. 'Do I smell of garlic?'

She shakes her head and swivels to and fro on her chair. 'Don't be silly. I'm just ... worried.'

'About what?'

She frowns. 'It's complicated.' She glances at her watch and jumps to her feet. 'Can we leave it for now? Professor Tanaka should be home. Let's go do it.'

I don't get up from the desk.

Alex gives me a lopsided smile and holds out her hand.

I take it and she pulls me up.

She places her hands on my shoulders and looks into my eyes. 'I like you Happy. I really like you, but ... Let's not rush things. Okay?'

I take a deep breath, forcing myself not to kiss her again, then nod. 'Okay.'

Alex and I make small talk as we catch the ferry to St Lucia and walk to Professor Tanaka's door. The air between us feels magnetic and full of tension. Acting normal is a huge effort and I'm not totally successful.

At the front door, Alex turns to me and smiles. 'Don't look like that, Happy.' She touches my cheek.

My stomach does flip-flops. 'But, I don't understand. Why?'

She draws breath, but then the door opens.

'Ah, I thought I heard you here.' Professor Tanaka beams out from the doorway. 'Come in, come in. How lovely to see you.' She looks a little tired, but her step is lively as she leads us down the corridor to the lounge room. The smell of coffee wafts towards us. Coffee smells so much better than it tastes.

Professor Tanaka sinks into her armchair with a sigh of satisfaction. 'I'm so happy to be home.' She waves her hand at the table. 'Please, help yourself.' Although it is now five o'clock, as always, she has croissants laid out for us.

Usually when I eat croissants I imagine I am in Paris, but now, as I bite into one, the thought of Paris fills me with torpor. It is a strange sensation. Our Paris Syndrome–busting method is powerful – I have immunised myself in the process of developing it. I shoot a look at Alex. 'I bet the croissants in Paris aren't as good as these.'

Alex sips her coffee. 'I reckon the coffee wouldn't be as good, either.'

Even in our awkward state we are working well as a team.

Professor Tanaka frowns as she turns her gaze from me to Alex. 'Oh no, girls, the coffee and croissants in Paris are much,

much better. These,' she flaps her hand disdainfully towards the plate, 'are the merest imitation of croissants et café au lait in Paris.' A faraway look comes over her. 'Ah, I have such fond memories of sipping coffee in the Cafe de Flore.'

'Professor Tanaka,' I ask, 'would you go back to Paris if you were sure you weren't going to get Paris Syndrome again?'

'Of course,' Professor Tanaka waves her croissant emphatically. 'I can imagine nothing more wonderful. Paris is so sublime, so exciting. There is no other place with such elegance and sophistication.'

Alex and I exchange a glance and I'm sure she is thinking what I am – *sublime, exciting, elegance and sophistication* ... Professor Tanaka will be a tough nut to crack.

'Well ...' I pause and glance at Alex.

Alex picks up two teaspoons and gives a little drum roll on the table.

Professor Tanaka looks at her quizzically.

I jump in. 'Alex and I have developed a cure for Paris Syndrome.' I smile broadly.

I am expecting Professor Tanaka to be excited, but her face is neutral as she puts down her croissant.

'Ta-da,' I add.

Professor Tanaka lifts her eyebrows again.

Alex smiles. 'It's true. We have.'

Professor Tanaka frowns. 'I'm sorry, girls, but I find that hard to believe. The best psychologists in the world ...'

'But we have. We've been working on it for ages. At least half the day,' I say.

Alex nods. 'It's developmental, but it's effective. We've tried it on ourselves. Happy and I are already immune to Paris Syndrome, aren't we?'

I lean forward. 'If you dropped me in Paris right now, no matter what happened, I'd be completely indestructible. When I bite into a croissant,' I take a bite to demonstrate and speak with my mouth full, 'it's just a croissant, not a symbol of Paris.'

Professor Tanaka still looks dubious but she gives a small smile. 'Well, tell me about it.'

I explain our Paris Syndrome–busting technique. 'We've all been fed so many romanticised images of Paris our whole lives that it's positively imprinted in our brains. The only way to counteract that is to train ourselves to think of Paris in entirely negative terms. It's like learning a new language. Look.' I pull out the cards. 'We've developed flashcards.' I hold up a picture of a quaint Parisian café with a red awning and elegant people sipping coffee out the front under red umbrellas. 'What words come to mind when you look at this picture?'

Professor Tanaka tilts her head to one side. 'Ah, such a charming café. What joy to sit there watching people go by, listening to the melodious sound of French being spoken, and–'

I hold up my hand and turn over the flashcard. *This café has dirty toilets, weak coffee and rude service*, it reads.

Professor Tanaka frowns.

'Read it out,' I say.

'*This café has dirty toilets, weak coffee and rude service,*' Professor Tanaka reads, but she doesn't sound like she means it.

I turn the card over so she can see the café again.

She smiles again. 'Those beautiful awnings … Why don't we have those on cafés here?'

'Professor Tanaka.' Alex speaks sternly. 'You're not trying.'

I turn the card over and tap my fingers on the words.

'*This café has dirty toilets, weak coffee and rude service,*' Professor Tanaka intones again.

'Again,' says Alex. 'This time with feeling.'

'*This café has dirty toilets, weak coffee and rude service,*' Professor Tanaka says with a little more emphasis.

'Say it like you hate it,' I say. 'This is the worst café you have ever encountered. This café has ruined your life.'

Professor Tanaka's face screws up in an expression of disgust. '*This café has dirty toilets, weak coffee and rude service,*' she spits out.

'Good.' I smile. 'You're getting it.'

Her face clears. 'I see how this works. *This café has dirty toilets, weak coffee and rude service,*' she reads yet again in a loud voice and laughs. 'This is fun.'

'Okay, time to move on.' I hold up another flashcard. It shows a boat going down the Seine past Notre Dame Cathedral.

'Ah, the Seine, Notre Dame,' Professor Tanaka enthuses. 'Look at it. Such superb architecture, those soaring turrets, the incredible fierceness of the gargoyles–'

I hold up my hand and turn over the card.

'*The tour boat is crowded, it is raining, there are pickpockets and an unfriendly ticket seller,*' Professor Tanaka reads. Her smile broadens. She repeats it again and again, until I am there with her on the tour boat from hell. I can practically feel the rain trickling down my back and a pickpocket's hand in my coat pocket. Professor Tanaka shudders in an exaggerated way. 'What a horrible, horrible boat tour. I don't know what I ever saw in it.' She puts down her coffee cup and looks from one of us to the other. 'Did you think of this yourselves? The two of you?'

Alex and I nod.

'It is brilliant. Brilliant. Give me more.'

Alex and I go through the flashcards. We have Paris laneways lined with dog shit, expensive dress shops that make you queue for an hour to get inside, Monet's *Water Lilies* that you can hardly see for the crowds in front of them, restaurants serving overpriced and dried-out fish and chips ... It takes over an hour to go through them all but Professor Tanaka never wavers. 'Another one,' she says every time she has summoned the right amount of disdain for the feeble offerings of Paris. At last we come to the end of our stack.

'That's it.' Alex leans back in her seat.

We are silent for some time. I feel like we've been through something together – something almost mystical. We have unwrapped Paris and given it a shake out, and things will never be the same.

'How do you feel?' I ask eventually.

Professor Tanaka shakes her head in a bemused way. 'Different. Drained, a little sad maybe, but also fresh, as if I've been spring-cleaned. Paris seems so much less like a paradise. It is almost like ...'

'Just another place?' suggests Alex.

Professor Tanaka sighs. 'It's strange. For so long it has been so much more than that – a fantasy of perfection.'

'So the method works?' I ask.

Professor Tanaka pauses, gazing around her room at the Parisian photos on the wall. 'I think if I kept doing this training, perhaps it might be safe for me to travel to Paris.'

'Really?' says Alex.

'Yes, I do.' Professor Tanaka sounds bemused.

Alex and I smile at each other and I forget for a moment that we are on difficult terms.

'So, are you going to book a trip?' I ask. 'We'll keep training you. As much as you need. Until you feel safe.'

Professor Tanaka nods slowly. 'Maybe I will.' She smiles. 'I can't believe it. Can I really go to Paris again?'

'Absolutely,' says Alex. 'When will you go?'

'As soon as possible. It has been way too long.' Professor Tanaka gets to her feet with an alacrity I have never seen in her before. 'I'm going to look at flights right now.' She claps her hands. 'I must go right away. Paris is so wond—' She stops herself. 'Paris is an ugly city with little to recommend it.' She smiles. 'But I would like to go there anyway.'

And even though I have spent most of the afternoon coming up with examples of the numerous ways in which Paris can disappoint, I can't resist the squeal of excitement that bursts from my lips. 'Paris! I'm so excited for you. J'aime Paris so much.'

Professor Tanaka and Alex frown at me.

I put my hand over my mouth. 'Oops. Sorry.'

'We'll have none of that sort of talk from now on, Veronica,' says Professor Tanaka sternly.

●

'I don't know what came over me.' I bite my lip. 'Ho hum. I suppose it might be bearable.' But inside, I am hooting and yelling. Professor Tanaka is going to Paris!

Alex and I walk back to the ferry together in silence. Now we are alone I am again conscious of the pull between us. It seems completely irresistible. But maybe it's just me? I start and stop several sentences in my head, but none of them seem right.

'How about that, hey?' Alex says after we sit on a bench at the wharf to wait. 'We found a cure for Paris Syndrome.' She glances at me. 'It seems like it might really work.'

'We're pretty awesome.' I shuffle my feet. There is another long silence. I should be jubilant at our success, but instead I feel tense. All I want is to touch her again. I inspect my fingernails and cough. 'What did you mean before when you said it's complicated?' I can't look at her without wanting to kiss her, so I stare out at the river.

Alex taps her feet on the ground. 'Lots of things ... That girl whose photo you saw. Sarita. Stuff happened between us. I'm not totally over it.'

'Oh.' I sit on my hands and swallow hard. 'Is she your girlfriend?'

'No.' Alex touches my arm.

I turn to her.

'It's finished. But ...' she sighs. 'I'm a little gun-shy. I just don't feel sure ... It's not just that, there're other things too.'

'What do you mean?' A hard ball fixes itself inside my chest.

'You've never had a relationship with a girl before, have you?'

'No, but–'

'You're experimenting.'

'I'm not experimenting. Why would you say that? I don't understand. Why did you kiss me if you're still in love with Sarita? You started it, not me.'

'I know I did.' Alex pulls her hands through her hair and fixes her blue eyes on mine. 'It was an impulse. You're beautiful, Happy. I really like you. But I've ... reassessed things, that's all. I don't want to lose you as a friend, Happy.' Her voice is soft.

I turn away from her eyes. I don't know what to say. *Friends.* I don't even know if I want that, but I make myself reply. It seems the polite thing to do. 'I don't want to lose you either.'

'Cool.' She smiles in a relaxed way, as if it's all sorted out.

I'm relieved when her stop comes and she gets off the ferry.

She waves as the ferry chugs off and I raise my hand in response.

Back home, I flop onto my bed. My mind is spinning. All I can think of is Alex's lips and the crazy, overwhelming sensation that filled me when I kissed her. The kiss replays in my mind over and over. *It's complicated.* It's a wonder people get together at all when it's so difficult.

Amélie and Billy look down at me with concerned faces. *What's wrong?* asks Billy.

'I'm in love with a girl.'

Well, hallelujah, says Billy.

I shake my head. 'She just wants to be friends. Or maybe not. At any rate, it's complicated.'

Ouch, says Billy.

Amélie sighs. *If only two people could want the same thing at the same time.*

I am almost asleep when I remember what Alex said – *you're beautiful, Happy*. With everything else happening, the words had slipped by me. I touch my lips, thinking of hers and stretch out in my bed. *You're beautiful.* It's something to hold onto.

Chapter Thirty-three

The days leading up to Christmas are rather bizarre.

On Friday morning Mum comes inside holding a basket. 'Is this for you?'

I walk over and have a look. Inside is a DVD copy of *Amélie*, resting on a bed of red, white and blue tissue. I know immediately who it is from. Beside it is a note. *To the beautiful madam in number 91.*

I look at the note. 'Nuh-uh. I'd be mademoiselle, wouldn't I?'

Mum eyes the basket with suspicion. 'If this is something you're cooking up, Happy, it's not going to work.'

'I'm as surprised as you are.' This isn't totally true. I'm not surprised to discover the object of Kevin's affections is Mum. I'm not too sure how I feel about it though.

At the cinema that morning, the *Amélie* DVD hovers between Kevin and me like a ghost in the room. We go about our usual ticket-selling and door-closing routine. Who will be the first to acknowledge its presence?

Kevin whistles while we clean up.

I'm not sure if this is an expression of a good mood or an attempt to fill the awkward silence. I suspect the latter.

Eventually his whistling peters out. 'How's your mum going?' He empties out the popcorn maker.

I stop what I'm doing and stare at him. 'Pretty good. Seems like she's got a secret admirer.'

'Oh yeah?' He avoids my eyes and his face reddens. 'What does she think about that?'

I put my hands on my hips. My first instinct is to quash this unsuitable romance in the bud, but Amélie's poster looks at me with a twinkle in her eye and I have a rethink. Who am I to stand in the way of Kevin's crush? It's not like it's going anywhere – he's hardly Mum's type. I can let nature take its course. 'I think she likes it. He seems to have good taste in movies.'

Kevin meets my eyes and turns a deeper shade of red but makes no admissions.

That evening, Mum and I watch *Amélie* together. I already have it downloaded on my laptop of course, but the arrival of the DVD is an occasion. It is as delightful as always. The streets of Montmartre glow on the screen with the romance of Paris and with Amélie's elfin charm. Despite my Paris Syndrome–busting efforts I am again as infatuated with the city as ever. Clearly a one-off inoculation isn't enough and constant vigilance is needed to maintain the cure.

At the end of the movie, Mum sighs. 'There's just something about Paris, isn't there?'

'You're not the first to think so.'

'I know.' Mum picks up the DVD and inspects it. 'Do you know who's behind this, Happy?'

I shake my head. 'Could be anyone. I'm sure there are plenty of men out there who'd be interested in you.'

'Hardly.' Mum's cheeks have a bloom of pink as she puts the DVD away.

It's nice to see her like that; she could do with some amusement in her life. *Kevin and Mum*. I suppose stranger things have happened.

'What about you, Happy? How are things going with Alex?'

I stare at her. How does she know about Alex and me? But she means Alex One of course. Alex Two is a whole different conversation – one I'm not ready to have. 'Oh, um, it didn't work out. He was a bit of a dick.'

Mum strokes my arm. 'Plenty of boys in the sea, Happy.' She hesitates, giving me a quick glance. 'And girls.'

I meet her eyes. I can't believe she said that. 'Am I putting out gay vibes?'

She smiles. 'I'm your mother, Happy. I'm not stupid.'

Wow, that came out of the blue. Has everyone except me known all along? She seems to be waiting for me to say something, but I'm not sure how to start or what to say. It's weird talking about this kind of stuff with your mother anyway.

After a few moments Mum stands and stretches. 'It's probably a statement of the obvious, but I want you to know that you being gay or bi or anything else is … you know … the same as being straight. As far as I'm concerned. Okay? When you're ready to talk, I'm ready to listen.'

I give her a lopsided smile. 'Thanks, Mum. When I've got anything to report you'll be the first to know.'

Mum gives me a big hug and heads for bed.

I lean my head back on the couch and all I can think about is Alex. *It's complicated. You're beautiful.*

The next day a silk Dior scarf and a bottle of Chanel perfume appear on our doorstep in the morning. Again, these are addressed to the beautiful madam in number 91.

'Goodness.' Mum gazes at her presents. 'I wonder who it is. They seem quite sophisticated. And generous.'

'I don't know about that. They may be following advice. On the internet or something.' I pick up the scarf and inspect it. 'It might be a cheap knock-off from Thailand.'

Mum looks at me sharply. 'You do know something about this, don't you, Happy?'

I shake my head vigorously. 'Someone has obviously been admiring you from afar. I'm not surprised at all.'

Mum grimaces, but she looks secretly pleased. She hums as she gets ready for work.

Kevin looks up expectantly as I come into the cinema, but he doesn't say anything.

I tease him for a while, getting the popcorn maker started and setting out the flyers for the upcoming movie.

Out of the corner of my eye I can see him polishing the handles of the doors in an agitated way. Kevin never polishes the door handles – that is my job.

I decide to put him out of his misery. 'Mum liked your present.'

Kevin blushes violently, his hand drops to his side and he turns to face me. 'How did you know it was me?'

'Kevin, I'm the one who advised you on what to give her, remember?'

'Yeah, but, your mum, she must have lots of admirers ... A woman like her.'

I decide not to tell Kevin he is currently the only contender for her affections. Instead, I roll my eyes. 'I'm not stupid.'

'You don't mind?'

To be honest, Kevin's pursuit of Mum makes me feel a bit weird. I am tempted to tell him so, but I think of Mum's face when she opened the present. 'It's none of my business.'

'Do you think I've got a chance?'

How can I answer this tactfully? I mentally compare Kevin with Dad. Dad is a handsome, dynamic human rights lawyer who is also, as it turns out, a complete arse, while Kevin ... I study him as I formulate my response. Kevin is looking different. He is still wearing his Hawaiian shirt, but his hair is no longer combed over his bald spot. 'You've had a haircut.'

Kevin runs his hand over his buzz-cut hair. 'What do you think?'

I put up my thumb. 'Major improvement.' I smile. It's strange but I have become fond of Kevin – maybe Mum could do worse. To give him credit, he's trying hard. 'Keep it up. I'd say you're in with a chance.'

Kevin smiles broadly. 'I've never felt like this about a woman before. Your mother, she's so–'

I hold up my hand. 'I'm not going to stand in your way, but I don't need to know the details. She's my mum, all right?'

'Got it.' Kevin walks away with a bounce in his step.

The third day, Christmas Eve, brings exactly what I expected – a basket containing a baguette, walnuts, honey and goat's cheese. This time the note says, *Happy Christmas. From a secret admirer.*

'Who can it be?' says Mum. 'Maybe it's one of the doctors I met at the in-service training last week.'

I survey the basket's contents. 'They seem to like France. They can't be all bad.' Even though she and Kevin are incompatible, I'm happy to see Mum looking so chuffed. I remind myself how hard the months after Dad left were for her. Every morning she'd come into the kitchen with puffy, bloodshot eyes. She thinks I didn't notice, but I did. That's it. I've decided. If Kevin can make her happy, I wish her all the luck in the world.

Christmas Day is a quiet one. Mum is on call, so she can't go too crazy. This also means that we are stuck in Brisbane. Dad asked me to go down to Sydney for a few days, but I didn't want to leave Mum here by herself. Besides, there is Alex to think of. It has taken exceptional willpower not to contact her since her *just friends* announcement, but I don't want to stray too far from Brisbane.

Although it is just Mum and me, a large pile of gifts has gathered under the tree. From Mum, I have a new pair of green ballet slippers, a polka-dotted sun and rain umbrella, a vintage-style swimsuit and a brooch which is a large, green fake flower. I try them all on. 'These are perfect, Mum. I love them.' I give her a big hug.

She beams at me. 'I thought they were your style.'

From Dad, I have a music voucher, a clothes voucher and a book voucher, all safe bets. Very practical. I suspect Hannah played a part in this.

I have spent the last of my tattoo money and some of my wages buying presents. For Mum, I bought a bonsai banksia in an earthenware pot.

She squeals when she sees it. 'That is exquisite. I never knew you could make a bonsai banksia.'

'It's kind of bizarre, isn't it? Like a miniature kangaroo.'

Mum laughs. 'I love it.'

Last year, Dad cooked a turkey, but Mum and I decided that a seafood salad is more appropriate to a Brisbane summer.

It is, but to be honest I miss having Christmas with all the trimmings.

When Dad rings, I thank him for his presents.

'Are you doing okay, Happy?' he asks.

'I'm doing fine, Dad.' This is not true. I am missing Alex so much it's like I've had an amputation. But tomorrow Professor Tanaka flies out to Paris and I will see her then. Even if we're *just friends*, I can't stop the hum of anticipation this gives me.

That night, I lie in bed thinking about Professor Tanaka getting ready for Paris. She must be so excited. The thought of Paris inevitably leads back to Rosie. Even though I've stopped messaging her, she is always on my mind. I take her copy of *The Great Gatsby* out of my bookcase and flick through it before I go to bed.

When her parents asked me if there was anything I wanted to keep, I thought of the book straight away. It reminds me of how much Rosie loved the twenties and how, like Daisy, she lit up every room she walked into. When I look at the book, I can almost hear her laugh and see her catlike dancer's walk. Rosie was so graceful.

As I put *The Great Gatsby* back in the bookshelf, it occurs to me that Rosie was like Daisy in other ways too. She could be careless with the people who loved her.

Chapter Thirty-four

The next day Alex, Professor Tanaka and I meet up at Toowong Station to catch the train to Brisbane airport.

Alex smiles when she sees me, her eyes crinkling up and my heart leaps like a crazy grasshopper before I tamp down my excitement. It is good to see her, but also painful. We all wish each other Happy Christmas and exchange notes on what we got up to yesterday. Professor Tanaka went out to lunch with her best friend Professor Wilkins, who had just returned from New Zealand. Alex had a picnic at South Bank with some friends. My stomach clenches at this news. Why wasn't I asked? I assumed she'd have gone home – Toowoomba's not that far – but this doesn't seem the right time to ask her why she stayed in Brisbane.

Professor Tanaka is in high spirits. She is pulling an enormous suitcase and dressed in a chic white pantsuit – not the best colour for travelling but I'm sure she'll pull it off.

'I can't believe it,' I say once we're settled in our seats. 'You bought a ticket and – just like that – you're jetting off to Paris.'

Professor Tanaka's eyes crinkle up. 'I'm not blasting off to Mars.'

'You may as well be,' I say. She has nine hours' flying time to Kuala Lumpur and from there it is thirteen hours to Paris. To a girl who has gone no further than New Zealand, this seems like an incredible journey.

Professor Tanaka has been diligent with her pre-trip Paris Syndrome inoculation program. She tells me Alex has been drilling her every time she comes over to do the gardening.

'I am not excited at all,' she says, but she has a sparkle in her eyes.

At the airport she surveys the departures board with the resigned air of someone travelling overseas for a business meeting. 'Such a long journey. I must buy myself a magazine.'

Alex and I sit on the plastic chairs while Professor Tanaka heads for the newsagency. It must be a special occasion because she's gelled back her fringe and is wearing jeans instead of shorts, with a red racer-back singlet which shows off her shoulders. She looks amazing. I, myself, have chosen my Number Three Amélie outfit, the green polka-dot dress and boots, in honour of Paris. I have also added, in honour of seeing Alex, the green fake-flower brooch that Mum gave me for Christmas.

'So, has the Paris Syndrome inoculation thing been working for you?' I ask. 'Are you still jaded by the thought of Paris?'

'Not exactly.' Alex shakes her head. 'I imagine that Professor Tanaka is going to be followed around by handsome accordion players from the moment she gets off the plane. How about you? Have you brought your expectations into line?'

'Mm-hm, my expectations are pretty realistic. I mean, obviously the light in Paris will have a rosy, soft-focus glow, like someone's smeared Vaseline over a lens. And all the women will look like Julie Delpy and all the girls like Madeline. That's not delusional, is it?'

'Oh no, that's quite realistic.' Alex waves her hand dismissively.

I laugh. 'We have no problems at all with our expectations.' Our banter is easy and the knot in my stomach recedes. We see Professor Tanaka approaching. 'Enough of that.' I put a finger to my lips.

Alex gives me a cheeky wink and my stomach flips. *Damn.* I don't want to be just friends.

'Paris will be exceedingly dull and I wish you didn't have to go,' I say to Professor Tanaka.

'Likewise,' says Alex.

Professor Tanaka sighs. 'It will be dreary, but what can I do?'

They are calling her flight. We all stand.

'You be careful over there, Professor Tanaka. Paris is a big city. There are pickpockets, and … don't talk to strangers,' I say.

'You forget I grew up in Tokyo. Paris is small in comparison.' She pauses. 'Though perhaps not as safe.'

'I have a favour to ask.' I pull a book from my shoulder bag and hold it out to her. It is Rosie's copy of *The Great Gatsby*.

Professor Tanaka's eyes widen. '*The Great Gatsby*. I haven't read that for such a long time.'

'It belonged to a friend of mine who would have liked to go to Paris. I was wondering … can you leave it in Paris? Maybe in Amélie's café? She would have liked that.'

Professor Tanaka meets my eyes. 'Of course, Veronica.' She takes the book from me and inserts it in her handbag without looking at it again.

In the front of Rosie's book I have written: *This book belonged to Rosie who adored Paris and would have loved to travel. Take it with you on your journey or pass it on. I want this book to see the world.* I have included my email address so people can update me on the book's travels if they choose. At some stage, maybe, it might wend its way back to me.

Alex and I stand there waving as Professor Tanaka queues to go through the scanner. The line is long, so this gets a little strange. She turns around every now and then and waves at us and we wave back frantically. It is a relief when she gets through the scanner, gives one last wave and heads for the departure gate.

'It's like watching your only child head off on a backpacking tour of Europe,' says Alex.

'We've taught her everything we know. It's time she learnt to be independent.'

'Yes, we've given her the best start we can.' Alex turns to me. 'This calls for a cup of coffee.'

'I'll have tea.'

Alex gives me a quizzical look. 'You're never going to make a good Parisian if you don't drink coffee.'

I shrug. 'I'll be a non-conformist tea-drinking Parisian.'

We head for a café. Outside the windows planes are lined up on the runway, each one singing of far-off lands. It still seems a little like magic to me, how you can just hop on and end up in another world. Alex and I order at the counter, sit at an empty table and look out at the planes.

'I brought you something.' Alex reaches into her shoulder bag and pulls out a brown paper bag. 'Happy Christmas.'

I open it and find a red and green tea cosy. 'It matches my dress.' I smile and pull it on my head. 'Thank you, I love it.'

'It's a good look,' Alex says.

'As it happens, I have something for you.' I rifle around in my shoulder bag. I wasn't sure if we were on present-giving terms, but as Alex has jumped the gun, it's lucky I came prepared. I hand her a small package, wrapped in the Santa Claus paper that is de rigueur around my place.

Alex rips the paper off to reveal three little ceramic chickens. She smiles broadly. 'You know me too well.'

I touch the tea cosy on my head. 'From your mother?'

Alex nods. 'Is that strange? Re-presenting is a thing, isn't it?'

'Yeah, re-presenting is hip, or if it wasn't before it is now.' I decide the time has come to broach the topic of her family. 'How come you didn't go home to Toowoomba for Christmas?'

Alex's shoulders tense and I think she's going to fob me off again, but then she sighs. 'Neither of my parents has spoken to me for almost a year.'

I stare at her. How can a parent not speak to you for a year? 'Why not?'

The waiter puts down our drinks. Alex waits until he leaves.

'I told them I was gay.'

'What?' I put my teacup down with a bang. 'No way. That's crazy.'

She gives an ironic smile. 'Hadn't you noticed?'

'Yes, what?'

'I'm teasing. They're heavy-duty Christians. I used to be too, until I discovered there wasn't any place there for weird people like me.' Alex picks up her coffee and takes a sip. She looks like she's having trouble swallowing.

I want to touch her, but I'm not sure if I'm allowed. 'When was that?'

'When I was fourteen, I was right into it all before that – Sunday School, Youth Group … But then the priest gave a sermon about the evils of homosexuality and I realised he was talking about me.' Her mouth twists. 'I didn't come out to my parents until last year though. They acted like I was doing it to spite them. They wanted me to go and talk to the priest.' She gives a sardonic smile.

'Wow. I'm sorry. I didn't know people still thought that way.'

Alex gives me a funny look. 'Guess we've been mixing in different circles. I suppose I've got used to it. More or less.'

A number of things fall into place. 'You said you had a falling out with your school.'

Alex nods. 'Christian school. My parents delivered me up to the priest and he told me I needed to have conversion therapy to cure my affliction. I walked out and never went back.'

'That must have been tough.'

'Yeah.'

'I can't imagine … being kicked out of home.'

'It was about as awful as you'd expect. So I moved to Brisbane to finish school.' She smiles. 'New start.'

'And your friends in Toowoomba?'

'They were mainly church friends.' She taps her fingers on the table. 'But, oh well, I've made new friends.'

'And the tea cosies …'

'I know, right? The tea cosies keep coming. Bizarre, huh?'

I feel like she's skating over the surface and I want to know more, but she finishes her coffee and looks out at the planes. 'One day.' She lifts her hand and makes a noise like a plane taking off.

My smile feels crooked. 'Rosie used to do that, whenever we talked about Paris.'

Alex fixes her eyes on me. 'How did it begin, the Paris thing? I mean, was it Rosie, or you?'

'It started with *Madeline*, we were both crazy about it as kids, and it grew from there. You couldn't say it was Rosie who drove it, or me. We were both mad about Paris.'

'A folie à deux.'

'Pardon?'

'It's where a syndrome or psychosis transmits itself from one person to another. I'm surprised you don't know that – you being so into syndromes.'

'Well, I'm surprised too: it's a dreadful omission on my part. Folie à deux, so it's a French thing, huh? That's appropriate. I never thought it was a folly though. It was a shared passion. It was only after Rosie died that it became more like an obsession than a passion. I felt like I had to hold onto the dream. Does that sound strange?'

Alex shakes her head. 'Not at all.'

I nibble on the little biscuit that came with my tea, but I have to force it down. 'You know how I told you four of them died in that crash?'

'Yes.' Alex holds my gaze.

'There was a place in the car for me too.'

'But you didn't take it?'

I shake my head.

'What happened?'

'We had an English test the next day. I was studying. Rosie rang at about eleven o'clock and told me they were going out for kebabs and they'd pick me up. I could tell she'd been drinking. I didn't want to go. She got angry with me, so I told her I'd go, to keep the peace. I hated fighting with Rosie.'

'What stopped you?'

'This is going to sound peculiar, but we've got this photo at home of my great-great-grandmother. Here, I've got it on my phone.' I pull out my phone and show Alex the picture of Billy and her six sisters.

'Wow, she looks awesome.'

'I know, you can tell, she's such a powerhouse. Anyway, I sort of feel like she's my guardian angel. Like we're connected. Because she's got hair like mine, and because she went to Paris when she was seventeen.

'That night, their car was outside and I was about to head out the door when I saw her photo. I felt like I heard her voice in my head.'

'What did she say?'

'*Don't let anyone else tell you what's right for you, Happy.* And I went outside and told Rosie I wasn't going. It was hard. She was … forceful sometimes.'

You're such a bore, Happy.

'That was the last time I ever spoke to her.'

We are silent for some time.

'I'm so glad you said no.'

'Afterwards I felt guilty. Like I'd betrayed her. Like it would have gone differently if I'd been there.'

'But it wouldn't, would it?'

'No. I know that now. It taught me something.'

'What's that?'

'It's like Billy said. You have to listen to yourself, not to anyone else.'

Alex sips her coffee and looks at me. Her eyes are as blue as the sky outside. 'You haven't let go of her, have you?'

I shake my head. 'The funeral was ... It felt all wrong. I don't remember much of it, to be honest.' I take a deep breath. 'Just all these kids crying. All these kids who didn't even know her.'

'I don't think we do grieving very well,' says Alex. 'There's got to be a better way – a pagan ceremony or something.'

'I guess so. It's hard to know what would have helped though.'

Alex toys with her cup. 'Were you in love with Rosie?' Her voice is low.

My breath catches. The question is completely unexpected, but also makes complete sense. My mind goes blank. 'I don't know.'

Alex's mouth twitches. 'Really?'

'I didn't ...' I didn't feel the way I feel about you, I want to say, but the words won't come out. 'I don't know,' I repeat.

Alex looks at me for a long time, then there is a roar outside and we look up. 'There she goes,' she says.

The plane lifts into the air and now Professor Tanaka is cocooned in a metal canister rocketing towards Paris.

'Jealous?' asks Alex.

After a moment I shake my head. 'It's strange, but no. Paris will be there for me when I'm ready. I hope Professor Tanaka's going to be okay.'

'She'll be fine.' But Alex sounds as uncertain as I am. She reaches over and touches my hand.

At that moment my phone goes ting, announcing the arrival of a text. I glance at it quickly; it is from the other Alex. I turn off the phone without reading it, but Alex removes her hand and sits up straighter. Did she see his name on the screen?

'Let's go, ay?' she says.

We catch the train back towards the city. Alex's stop is before mine. She needs to change lines.

Alex stands as the train slows. 'I might not be able to see you for a while. I've got some other stuff on,' she murmurs. She doesn't meet my eyes.

My stomach contracts. I think of her other friends, of her life I know nothing about. I felt like she was letting me in for a moment there, but now the doors have closed again.

The train comes to a standstill and the doors swish open. Alex gives me a wave, leaps onto the platform and is gone.

I press my face to the window, looking at the place where she vanished, willing her to reappear, but she doesn't. I wipe away a solitary tear as the train pulls out, my mind numb. What just happened? What did I do wrong? Should I have got out and chased her?

I am almost in Toowong when I remember to look at my phone.

Would you like to meet up some time soon? says the text from Alex One.

I don't reply.

Chapter Thirty-five

On Wednesday morning I lie in bed and pull my phone towards me. Alex One's text is still there, but there is no word from Alex Two. *Would you like to meet up some time?* Dropping the phone, I stare up at the ceiling. *Do I want to meet up?* I fiddle with my hair while I imagine how this *meet up* might go ...

I go around to Alex One's flat for 'breakfast' again. I am wearing my Number One Amélie dress as it is, I suppose, a special occasion. I am not as nervous as I was last time and I haven't brought any food. I'm not expecting to eat.

But he doesn't rush me; in fact he is kind of sweet. He kisses me at the door and offers me a cup of coffee. 'I 'ave some croissants too.'

I'm not in the mood to linger though. 'Where's your bedroom?' I ask.

He gives me a funny look, like he's not sure what's going on, but he leads me to his room.

There is a double bed next to the window and maybe a print of Uluru on the wall. I assume he rents his flat fully furnished. The room is very neat. Or is it? Would he tidy up for me? Maybe not. *The room is very messy and I sit on the bed, taking my boots off, then unbuttoning my dress.*

Alex still has a funny look on his face as he watches me, but he pulls off his T-shirt and unbuttons the top of his jeans.

I hang my dress over a chair then lie on the bed in my underwear. For the purposes of this fantasy, it matches and is rather becoming.

Alex is down to his boxers. His clothes are in a pile on the floor. He lies on the bed facing me, his head propped on his elbow.

We haven't touched since the kiss at the door.

'You 'ave done this before, 'aven't you, 'Appy?'

I force a laugh. 'What do you think?'

This takes care of any last-minute scruples.

When he is on top of me, or maybe underneath me, *I will look at the wolf tattoo on his shoulder and it will remind me of the first time I met him in the tattoo shop and how crazy I was about him then ...*

My fantasy vanishes with a puff of smoke. It's like Professor Tanaka says: it's strange how we can desire something so much, which will only disappoint when it is acquired. I pick up my phone again and reply to Alex One's text. 'No thank you.' I pause before sending. It seems a little unkind. After all, I did like him once. 'It's not you, it's me,' I add then send it off on its way.

So, there we go. I could have had a French lover, but it wouldn't have transformed me. Afterwards, I would have been exactly the same person, with the possible exception of a little minor chafing.

*

I do an afternoon shift at the cinema. We are in the post-Christmas blockbuster phase now and the cinema is packed with families and gangs of teenagers. I miss the French Film Festival crowd.

In the evening I lie on my bed in a disoriented but curiously emotionless state. I look at my pictures on the wall. 'Well, my love life is stagnating,' I say to Amélie and Billy.

Oh, says Amélie, *you just 'aven't met the right man yet. It wasn't until I met Dino that I knew what love was about.*

'Maybe,' I say. But if I substitute Alex Two for Alex One in my fantasy, it has a completely different outcome – one that makes my whole body tremble. I stretch my arms out over my head and point my toes and for some reason I laugh.

'But Amélie, I am totally crazy about a girl,' I say out loud.

Chapter Thirty-six

On Thursday, when I get home from work, Mum is stirring a pot on top of the stove. About once a month she gets an urge to go beyond the usual recipes and impersonate a domestic goddess. I suspect she, like me, may be affected by moon cycles.

'Smells good.'

'Pumpkin soup.' Mum frowns at the pot. 'It's not supposed to be so lumpy.'

I peer over her shoulder. It looks like something that might emerge from the top of a volcano – steaming liquid interspersed with boulder-like chunks. 'I'm sure it'll taste good,' I say.

We are finishing dinner, which is actually not too bad, when my phone announces the arrival of an email. I reach for it, but Mum grabs my hand.

'No phones at the table.'

'What if it's Professor Tanaka?' I've had no word since she left and I'm getting worried.

Mum lifts her hand. 'Okay, go on, have a look.'

I scan my phone quickly. 'It's from her.'

'Do you want to read it out?'

'Okay.' I read.

Dear Alex and Veronica,

It was early morning when my plane arrived in Paris. I had slept only a little and felt dazed and rumpled, but as I looked out the window the city appeared below me in the dawn light and my tiredness fell away.

Such was my excitement I had to pull out a flashcard — Paris is the most overrated city in the world *— and this settled me down at once. It is a good system you have developed.*

I am writing to you from the Café de Flore, which as you know was Jean-Paul Sartre's favourite café in Paris. Soon I will have a meeting with some of my colleagues at the Sorbonne.

Paris is in the grip of winter and there are not many tourists around but I am enjoying the cold weather.

I have had some trials and tribulations already so it is lucky I was prepared for the worst. Yesterday I was a little slow getting out of an automated toilet and it commenced its cleaning cycle. Water sprayed from the walls and it was terrifying. By the time I got out the door I was waterlogged and had to go back to my hotel to change. I did feel a fool.

A few hours later when I visited the winter markets on the Champs-Élysées, a canvas flap on one of the stalls came loose and tipped a bucket-load of icy rain water down my neck. I had to go back to the hotel and change again.

Despite these setbacks, it has been glorious [though of course entirely overrated]. I have gazed at the paintings in the Louvre. I have walked

along the Seine and browsed in the Shakespeare and Company bookshop. I
have bought cheese at the cheese market and flowers at the flower market.
As yet, however, I have not climbed the Eiffel Tower. Neither have I
been to Montmartre. I have been saving this treat up. One night before I
return home, I will have dinner at Amélie's café, Les Deux Moulins.

The Café de Flore is busy inside, so I am drinking my hot chocolate
outside next to a heater. The hot chocolate is expensive, eight Euros, but
it comes in a little jug and tastes like rich melted chocolate so it is worth
it. It is cold, but I can watch the Parisiennes go by with their little dogs,
looking chic in their winter coats, hats and scarves. That goes for the
people as well as the dogs.

Yesterday I went to the Ritz Hotel, where I heard an interesting
story about Hemingway. He was the first person to have a drink at the
hotel after Paris was liberated from the Germans in 1944. It had been
the German Army Headquarters in Paris — Hemingway came into
the city with the American troops with the sole aim of liberating his
favourite drinking location.

I have attached a photograph of Hemingway that was on the wall at
the Ritz.

Thank you both for making this journey possible. I have not even a
touch of Paris Syndrome!

Love,

Michiko Tanaka

I click on the photo of Hemingway. He is sitting at a table with a
few friends. They all look dashing in their American army uniforms.
At the table behind him is a curly-haired woman of around fifty in
what might be a French army uniform. The photo is taken side-on

and you can't see her whole face. She is leaning into the shoulder of another woman in the same uniform. 'Billy,' I practically yell. I thrust my phone at Mum. 'Look. It's Billy.'

She stares at the photo. 'Where?'

'There at the table behind Hemingway, with the curly hair. Next to that other woman.'

Mum touches the screen and enlarges the photo for a better look. 'Mm, could be …'

'It's her, isn't it? Look I've got her old photo here too.' I flick through my photos to the one of Billy in the white bow.

Mum glances at the photo then flicks back to the one with Hemingway. 'It looks like her, it's hard to be sure though.'

'It's Billy, I'm sure of it. I can't believe she was there with Hemingway in 1944. I wonder what became of her after that. Did she never get in touch with her family?'

Mum shakes her head. 'You know the story. I don't think they were in contact. She was the black sheep of the family.'

'Maybe she fell in love with a soldier, got married and changed her name.'

'Maybe. I guess we'll never know.'

Mum hands me my phone back and I stare at the photo. Billy, if it really is her, looks like she has fulfilled the promise of her feisty teens. She has a small liqueur glass in front of her and a broad smile on her face. She is having a blast. I notice the easy way she leans against the woman next to her. They are obviously good friends, or maybe more than that …

Mum leans over my shoulder and looks at Billy. 'There was a bit of a story behind her going to Paris, years earlier, just after

278

World War I in fact. She left her daughter, my grandmother, behind as a baby. My nana was brought up by the other six sisters.'

'Why haven't you told me that before?'

'I don't know, really. I wasn't deliberately hiding it from you, but … no one ever talked about it in my family. I only found out after my grandmother died – there were some papers. It was shameful. Things were different then, you know. She was unmarried.'

'And she was shuttled off to Paris to get her out of the way?'

'Maybe. She was a dancer. Dancers were needed in Paris in the twenties.'

I look at the Hemingway picture again on my phone. Billy – I am almost sure it is her – looks like she is dying to leap out and take on the world. I speak before I have time to censor myself. 'Do you think that woman is her lover?'

Mum looks startled, but takes the phone from me and looks at the photo again. 'Mm, I can see why you would think that. Maybe.' She gives me a tender smile. 'Do you and Billy have that in common too?'

I blush. 'It seems so.'

Mum puts her arms around me. She buries her face in my hair. 'Want to tell me about it?'

All my pent-up emotions press at my chest like they need to get out. And it seems like I'm ready to talk. So I tell her about Alex and how I feel about her, about how confusing it's all been. About how she kissed me first, but I didn't know what to do. About how I kissed her back, but then things went a little strange.

'You sound like you really like this girl.'

I nod. 'Her parents kicked her out of home.'

Mum's face tenses. 'For being gay?'

I nod again. 'She had to do the last year of school by herself in Brisbane.'

Tears come to her eyes. 'Oh, Happy. That girl has had a lot to deal with. You need to be sensitive to that.'

I toy with a broken edge on one of my fingernails. 'I don't know what to do.'

'Does she know how you feel about her?'

'I don't know. I think so …'

'Maybe you need to tell her.'

Just then I hear the plaintively familiar notes of an accordion outside our apartment. It is the theme song from *Amélie*. Mum and I run to the window. Tony the accordion player is standing under a streetlight. He nods at us, without pausing his playing.

Another figure emerges from behind the giant fig. He is wearing a Hawaiian shirt and holding a piece of cardboard. As he reaches the glow of the streetlight he holds up his sign – *Rhonda, will you have dinner with me?*

Chapter Thirty-seven

On Friday morning I wake to find a new email in my inbox. It is from Jacques Brasseur, the painter I contacted over a week ago. I had given up on hearing from him.

> *Dear Happy,*
>
> *I am sorry for my slow response, but I have been in confusion since I received your email. You have awoken many memories. The woman in my painting Michiko is Michiko Tanaka, and she was twenty-five in 1967 as you said, so I think she is the same person. Michiko and I were close once but that was a long time ago. Sadly, we are no longer in contact.*
>
> *Regards,*
>
> *Jacques Brasseur*

I read over the email again. *Michiko and I were close once*. I remember her radiant face in the painting, like she was looking at someone she loved. But everything went wrong. I read the last line again: *Sadly, we are no longer in contact*. He obviously has fond memories of her, and now she is right down the street … *What would Amélie do?*

I tap my fingers on the keyboard. I know Alex said she had stuff on, but this is an emergency. Professor Tanaka is only in Paris for another week. I forward the email to Alex and write at the bottom, *Can we talk?*

I check my emails every few minutes and after an hour at last she replies. *Okay, come on over* ☺

The smiley face is encouraging and within the hour I am in Alex's kitchen again. She is wearing cut-off denim shorts and a loose, white singlet. She looks sure in her body as she moves around the kitchen, finding plates and cups.

My heart is thumping so loudly I'm surprised she can't hear it. I can't take my eyes off her. 'It's good to see you again,' I say.

She turns from the kitchen bench and gives me a small smile. 'It's good to see you too.'

I get down to business with difficulty. 'So, that email from Jacques Brasseur. We need to talk to him.'

Alex raises her eyebrows. 'We do?'

'Of course we do. She's in Paris; he's in Paris. Paris is the City of Love …'

Alex gives me a stern look.

'Sorry. I mean Paris is the most overrated city in the world.'

'That's better. Okay, so we need to talk. What are we going to say to him?' Alex beckons me towards her room.

We sit in front of her computer and compose a careful email back to Jacques, asking if we can set up a time to Skype each other. *It's urgent,* I add and press send.

'Let's see where he lives,' says Alex. She Googles his street address, which is on his website as he has a gallery there. Jacques lives in Montmartre, like Amélie. Google Street View shows us a five-storey apartment building, rising off a narrow cobblestone street.

I sigh as I look at it. 'It looks like Amélie's apartment.' I snatch the mouse from Alex and move down the street. 'Look,' I squeal.

Alex puts her hands over her ears. 'Ow, that hurt.'

'It's Amélie's greengrocer, just down the road.' I zoom in on the shop. It looks exactly like it does in the movie, with fruit and vegetables arrayed enticingly under a green awning.

Alex takes the mouse back. 'Let's find her café.' The computer screen zooms down narrow cobblestone laneways and steep steps, past an apartment block with plants on each balcony and there it is – Les Deux Moulins.

I can hardly breathe for excitement. Alex and I smile at each other. 'I can't believe he lives right near Amélie's café. This is fate,' I say.

Alex nods. 'You're right. Amélie is going to bring them both together.'

Now we've dispatched our business, I suppose it's time for me to leave. I get up from her desk, searching for a way to prolong our conversation. 'It's my birthday in a week, fifth of January.'

'Is that right?' Alex smiles at me. 'Eighteen?'

'Yep.'

She leans back in her chair. 'Well. Coming of age. What are you going to do?'

I sling my bag over my shoulder. 'I don't know.'

'Maybe the chickens and I can organise a surprise party for you.'

'I'd like that.' It will be another excuse to see her anyway.

'They can invite all their friends from Buc Buc.'

'I'm still waiting to hear them play the xylophone too.'

'Okay, it's a date. We'd better get practising. I think we'll skip "Chopsticks" and go straight to "Happy Birthday".'

'Can they really play the xylophone, or are you bullshitting me?'

'They can play. It's hit and miss though. They get performance anxiety.'

I stand there in awkward silence while Alex shuts down the computer.

'So, I guess we'll talk again when we hear back from Jacques?' I say.

'Sure.' She stands and walks me to the door.

I hesitate at the top of the steps, wanting to say something more, but not knowing what. I start going down.

'Have you been well, Happy?' she asks when I'm halfway down.

I turn back to look at her. 'No, not really.'

We hold each other's gaze and she doesn't smile.

'I've missed you.' I find myself blinking back tears.

'Are you still seeing that French guy?' she asks.

'No.' My mouth drops open. 'Of course not. Nothing happened between us.'

She is still standing at the top of the steps watching me. I can't read the expression on her face, but her lips part. 'Would you like to go swimming at South Bank tonight?'

The unexpected joy of this makes me laugh.

'What?' Alex smiles.

'I would *love* to go swimming at South Bank tonight.'

That evening I sit out the front on the ferry to South Bank, the warm wind blowing my hair into a fuzzy tornado. I think about Alex's face as she stood on the steps, the way she smiled. A nervous patter fills my stomach. Is this a date? I wonder what form it will take ...

Alex and I stroll hand in hand along the river. The multi-coloured lights of the Ferris wheel slide across her face and the breeze lifts her hair. She buys a single rose from a stall and hands it to me with a kiss. Everyone we pass smiles warmly at the young lovers ...

My fantasy goes pop right there as the ferry judders against the wharf. That part is definitely not going to happen. Not in Brisbane anyway and probably not anywhere else either. Though I have heard that Berlin is very cool that way.

I can't see Alex when I get to South Bank pool at bang-on eight pm. The lights are on, sparkling over the water's turquoise shadows. A couple of older women are breast-stroking calmly across the middle, but other than that, it is empty.

I pull off my dress and perch on the edge of the pool with my back to the river. I am wearing the swimsuit Mum gave me for Christmas. It is red with white polka dots and has a halter-neck top and a little frill around the bottom. I feel very classy in it, very Parisian. Or maybe, now that I think about it, very Berlin. The night is so warm and a palm tree rustles next to me in the gentle breeze. I feel like I am somewhere exotic – a Pacific Island hideaway.

Suddenly a splash right in front of me showers me with spray. I squeal as Alex's head emerges from the water, her hair seal-sleek, droplets running down her face. She squirts a spray of water out of her mouth towards me.

I laugh and slide into the pool. It is body temperature, the water surrounding me like a soft blanket. Alex ducks underwater again. I sink under too, opening my eyes and see her, pale in a black bikini, stippled in moving light and shadow.

She waves at me.

I wave back – we are two astronauts meeting in space. She opens her mouth and bubbles rise, gleaming, to the surface. Then she turns and swims away, still underwater. Her kicking legs are white, fluid, graceful against the blue. The pool scene from *Three Colours: Blue* comes into my head. As it turns out, it isn't only the French who can swim mysteriously. Alex is otherworldly, wraith-like. I am enchanted.

I follow her receding form, stretching my arms through the water, enjoying the weightlessness, the warmth, the sense of being out of place and time. She glides into a little pool off the main one – an empty shadowy place – and stops. Again, she turns to me and waves underwater before breaking the surface. My head bursts out of the water next to hers and her arms go around me. My body presses against hers, our legs tangle, our lips meet and her tongue touches mine. I've imagined this so often, but the reality is so much more. I never knew it could be like this. I dissolve.

Alex and I kiss for a long time in the shadows, our bodies entwined, half-floating, like tangled-up jellyfish. Eventually we drift away from each other slightly, still holding hands.

Alex smiles at me, her face half-lit. 'Maybe we should take things a bit slower, Happy?'

'No, I don't think we should.' I pull myself closer, my legs touching hers, my heart still pounding.

She strokes my face. 'You're something else.'

I am? I close my eyes to her touch.

'I don't want ...' Her voice is soft.

My eyes flash open. 'What?'

She swings her legs through the water, creating a gentle current which rocks me. 'I don't want to compete with Rosie.'

I open my mouth to protest, but she puts up her hand.

'I'm not good with rejection. I've had too much of that in my life. I like you. I like you a lot, but ... I don't want to jump in too fast. Baby steps, okay?'

I think of what Mum said, *that girl has had a lot to deal with*, and I squeeze her hand. 'Okay.'

Chapter Thirty-eight

A couple of days pass and we don't hear from Jacques. I think about Alex constantly, but she doesn't get in touch. About fifty times a day I fight off the urge to message her. *Baby steps*. Images of our legs intertwined in the pool float through my mind like drifting sea creatures.

Professor Tanaka emails again to say what a great time she is having. It is only five days now until she comes home.

On New Year's Eve, Mum and I catch the ferry into South Bank for the evening fireworks over the river. They are spectacular, blazing up across the city skyline. There are so many people and I keep thinking I see Alex. Every girl with short, dark hair makes my pulse race, but none of them are her. None of them are anywhere near as beautiful as her. We don't hang around until midnight, Mum has work in the morning.

'Are you making any New Year's resolutions, Happy?' Mum asks on the way back on the ferry.

I ponder this. 'Just the usual – try to remember what year it is, get my head around my sexuality, cut back on the Milo.' I pause. 'Forget the last one, that's not going to happen. How about you?'

Mum laughs and squeezes my hand. 'Remain open to new adventures.'

'Yeah, that too.' I pause. 'So are you going to go out with Kevin?'

Mum gives me a Mona Lisa smile. 'I think I might.'

Dad rings on Monday. 'Happy New Year. What's new, Happy?'

'I'm totally in love with a girl,' I say before I can have second thoughts. 'Her name's Alex.'

There is silence on the end of the phone for a few moments. 'Wow, that's a surprise. I don't mean in a bad way, I just mean it's a surprise.'

'I don't seem that way to you?'

Again, there is silence. 'Maybe, now I look back on things … Have you told Rhonda?'

'Yes, of course.'

'I'm proud of you, Happy.'

'For falling in love with a girl?'

'Not just that, but yes, for knowing your mind and not being afraid to tell me. For being yourself.'

'Thanks, Dad.'

'I'm sorry I can't be there with you. You know I love you, don't you?'

'I guess I do, yeah. I love you too, Dad.' After a bit more chit-chat, we hang up.

'I'm glad you guys are getting along better.' Mum has come into the room during the end of our conversation. She smiles at me.

'He's still an arse, but, you know, he's my dad.'

She shrugs. 'You've only got one of him, love.'

I send Jacques another reminder email on Tuesday and, at last, on Wednesday he replies. *I can see I will get no peace until I talk to you.* He suggests a time for a call. Hooray! I forward the email to Alex and we make a time to meet up.

On Thursday evening, the day before my birthday, I go over to Alex's house. My heart is dancing a jitterbug, my mouth is dry and my hands are sweaty as I knock on her door. I am almost scared to see her again. Is this thing between us as amazing to her as it is to me?

She opens the door looking exotic and mysterious in a shin-length turquoise kimono covered in pink butterflies.

'You look like a secret agent after-hours,' I say.

She twirls. 'I got it at the West End market. Isn't it cool?'

We stand there, staring at each other. I want to kiss her, but her bright body language, the way she holds herself, makes me uncertain.

Alex makes the first move, giving me a quick hug and a kiss on the cheek. 'Come in, come in.'

I flush. Her manner is so far from the way it was at the pool I almost feel like I've been slapped.

'We don't want to be late.' She points at the clock. It is almost seven.

We have arranged to Skype at eleven am Paris time – seven pm our time.

The man who appears on the screen is undoubtedly old, his hair is grey and thinning, but he exudes vigour. He smiles tentatively when I click the link so he can see us too. 'Bonjour.'

Behind his head, I can see his apartment is lined with paintings and full of weathered but comfortable furniture.

I touch Alex's arm as Jacques gets settled and mute the speaker. 'Do you hear what he's playing?'

Alex smiles. '"All the Girls and Boys".' We exchange a look. I unmute the speaker.

'This song,' Alex gestures towards the screen, 'Professor Tanaka plays it a lot.'

Jacques smiles and rubs his chest. 'Does she?' He is silent for some time.

'That painting you did of her in front of the Eiffel Tower,' I begin, 'I'm confused. She told us she saw it on the Tokyo underground and it made her want to go to Paris. But yet she is already in Paris in the painting ...'

'Is that what she said?' Jacques sighs. 'It is all so long ago. The mind plays tricks as you get older. Fifty years ago feels like yesterday, but yesterday is 'ard to remember.' He taps his fingers on the table.

'Maybe we misunderstood her,' says Alex. 'She said the poster made her long for Paris but I don't know if she ever said it was the reason she went to Paris.'

Now Alex says that, I realise it is true.

'Can you tell us about how you came to do the painting?' asks Alex.

Jacques leans his elbows on the table in front of him. 'I met Michiko in Cafe de Flore in 1967. She was reading *The Great Gatsby*. She looked so cute, I asked if I might share 'er table even though there were other tables spare.' He pauses to sip his coffee. 'Well, you can guess … We fell in love. I painted 'er in front of the tower. She was in love with Paris, in love with me. And I was in love with 'er. I showed 'er all the secret parts of the city tourists don't see. We 'ad so much fun. I've never 'ad so much fun again. But she 'ad to go back to Japan to finish 'er research. It was a year before she could come back. I should 'ave gone to Tokyo, but I 'ad an exhibition 'ere to plan for. It seemed important at the time.'

He pauses and I notice something I hadn't seen before. Behind Jacques's back is the poster, *Find Yourself in Paris*. He has put it in an old art deco frame that suits its vintage style. I nudge Alex and she nudges me back.

'We wrote to each other,' Jacques says, 'and agreed she would come back to me at the end of the year. We planned to live together in Paris. But a year is a long time when you're young. I was too young and stupid to realise Michiko and I had something that only comes along once in a lifetime.

'She came back a year later and it was good again between us, as it was the first time. But she found out I 'ad been with another girl. There was a scene. She took it 'ard. Very 'ard. Before I could make amends she was gone. She left me a note – *You can't repeat the past*. It was a quote from *The Great Gatsby*. She used to love that book.'

I remember Professor Tanaka refusing to talk about her copy, and her startled reaction when I handed her Rosie's book at the airport.

'I kept writing to 'er but she never replied. I even flew to Tokyo. I met her brother, but 'e would not tell me where she was. I was devastated.'

'What about the poster?' I ask. 'When was that produced?'

'The next year, the Paris Tourism Commission saw my painting and decided to use it to 'ead their tourism campaign. I 'ad no idea Michiko would see it ... I suppose that was stupid of me too. It must 'ave been painful for 'er.' He spreads his hands. 'It was so long ago, but I've never forgotten 'er.'

'She told us she had to go home because she had Paris Syndrome,' I say.

'Paris Syndrome? Oh yes.' He smiles in a lopsided way. 'That's where you are so disappointed in the city you 'ave a breakdown.' He shakes his head. 'I don't know. Maybe she did 'ave a breakdown.' He pauses. 'That would explain why 'er brother wouldn't let me see 'er. But Paris Syndrome? I don't know. She loved Paris fine when we were in love. Take it from an old guy, being in love in Paris is a very fine thing.'

'She was hospitalised,' I say.

Jacques's mouth twitches. 'Michiko was sensitive. Some mistakes you never get to repair.'

My eyes wander to the poster on the wall behind him.

He turns and follows my gaze. 'Michiko was pretty, wasn't she?'

'She still is,' I say. 'She is also smart and funny and kind.'

Jacques runs his hands through his hair. 'Yes, I remember 'er well.'

Alex and I meet each other's eyes. She gives a slight nod.

'She's having dinner at Les Deux Moulins down the road tomorrow night,' I say.

'Michiko? She's in Paris?'

'Yes.'

'Would she want to see me?' He touches his face. 'I am not the man she knew before.'

'I think she'd like to see you,' I say.

Jacques puts his hands behind his neck and looks at the ceiling, then smiles and shakes his head. 'Thank you. Thank you for tracking me down.'

'You're welcome.' We wave at each other and disconnect.

'That is exactly what Amélie would have done, isn't it?' Alex smiles at me. 'Well done, Happy.'

I look into her blue eyes and my body sways towards her, but she jumps to her feet.

'I've forgotten to feed the chickens,' she cries and strides from the room, her kimono flying behind her.

It must be time to go home.

She waves at me from the garden shed when I come down the steps and it's hard to see her face in the shadows.

'See you tomorrow?' I call.

She turns to lock the chickens away then walks over to me and takes my hand. 'I've been thinking, Happy ...'

Her voice is strained. *She's going to break it off.*

But Alex continues, '... about what you said about Rosie's funeral. About how it was all wrong. I was thinking maybe you need to have a farewell ceremony. For you and Rosie. One that means something to you.' She pauses. 'What do you think?'

This is so far from what I thought was coming, I feel a little blind-sided. 'Like a pagan thing, you mean?'

'Something like that. I just thought ... I thought it might help.'

'It might help me, you mean?'

She nods and squeezes my hand. 'I think it might help me too.'

I don't speak for a while. 'That sounds ...' I hold her hand to my cheek and clear my throat. 'That sounds like it could be good.'

Alex lets out her breath. 'I didn't know if I should say that to you.'

'No, it's okay. You're going to make a good psychologist one day, Alex.'

She smiles. 'I'm sorry I'm so weird, Happy. Intimacy does strange things to my head. I'm working on it. I'm trying to be brave.'

'No, I understand, I think I do anyway. I'm weird too.'

'Well, clearly.' She puts her arms around me and we stand there for a long time, listening to the chickens make their night-time clucks.

Chapter Thirty-nine

La Dolce Vita, ten-thirty pm, Friday

I mistime the ferries and am half an hour early for my catch-up with Alex. The air smells moist, like rain is on the way. Luckily I have brought my Christmas umbrella. La Dolce Vita is just closing, but as I approach I see one table is still occupied. I can't believe it: it is Kevin and Mum. I freeze, then creep closer, ducking behind one of the marble pillars to watch them.

Kevin smooths back his hair as he always does when he is nervous, but his hand encounters only bristles – he has forgotten it's been shorn.

Mum looks beautiful. Her spiky red hair shines in the glow of the Eiffel Tower.

Kevin clears his throat. 'Thank you for coming.'

Mum smiles. 'Least I could do. Thank you for all the presents.'

The restaurant is so quiet I can hear every word.

Mum glances up at the Eiffel Tower. 'I haven't been here before. It's romantic, isn't it?'

'It reminds me of a scene in a fantastic French movie I watched the other day,' says Kevin. 'Have you seen *The Red Balloon*?'

Mum smiles. 'No, I haven't seen that one.'

'It's about this young boy ...' Kevin is in his stride.

Mum toys with her almost empty wine glass as he talks, but her head is cocked to one side and her eyes crinkle up in the way they do when she is having fun.

Kevin waves his hand towards the sky. '... and the balloons fly over the Eiffel Tower.'

Mum's gaze follows his hand. 'That sounds like a wonderful movie. Do you watch a lot of French movies?'

The first few drops of rain wet the pavement, but Kevin and Mum are sheltered beneath their umbrella.

Kevin nods. 'Have you seen *Cafe de Flore*?'

Mum shakes her head. 'What's that one about?'

He looks into her eyes as he talks. He gives the impression that he enjoyed all those French movies very much.

Eventually they notice they are the only customers here. 'I suppose we should go,' says Mum.

Kevin jumps up and jogs around the table to pull her chair out.

Mum usually pulls out her own chairs, but she doesn't say anything. I think she must ... like him.

Kevin holds an umbrella over her head and her laugh carries back to me as they walk down the street.

Well, who would have thought? I pull out my phone to check my messages and there is an email from Jacques. My eyes flick to the subject line.

Les Deux Moulins seven pm, Friday.

The days are short in Paris at this time of year so it was dark by the time I reached Les Deux Moulins. A warm glow lit the window and as I approached I could see Michiko sitting by herself. Her hair was still black and it fell softly around her face as it used to all those years ago. She hadn't changed one bit.

I came to a halt. I was nervous. Would she want to see me? Why would she? It had been so long. I almost turned to go, but then I noticed she was holding a copy of The Great Gatsby, *just as she had been in the Cafe de Flore all those years ago. I couldn't walk away now.*

I approached her table. 'Bonsoir, Michiko,' I said.

She looked up and her face was transformed by surprise. I leant over and kissed her on both cheeks. As I sat I saw a picture of Amélie smiling at us from the wall.

Michiko stared at me. 'How did you know I was here?'

'Your young friends, Happy and Alex, told me.'

'Ah, those two,' she said, 'I should have known.'

'You are still reading The Great Gatsby.*'*

She looked at the book as if she had forgotten it was in her hands. 'No, I haven't read The Great Gatsby *since I was last in Paris. I am fulfilling a request from Happy that I bring it here.'*

'You ran away so quickly. I never got to say I'm sorry, Michiko.'

Michiko smiled. 'It's so long ago, Jacques.'

'Do you forgive me?'

'Yes, of course. I was stupid to run away.'

I glanced at the picture of Amélie. There was a strange vibration in the air: it made me say words I hadn't planned. 'What do you say, Michiko, do you want to try again?' I reached over the table and took her hand. It was as small and smooth as it used to be.

Michiko smiled and glanced at her book. 'Can you repeat the past, Jacques?'

Snow fell outside as we held hands across the table. It landed on the awnings and settled on the cobbles in the street.

'Repeat the past? Why, of course you can, Michiko,' I said.

She placed the book on the table when we left. 'The waitress looks like a traveller,' she said.

I imagine you know what that meant.

Your grateful friend,

Jacques

'Hi, Happy.'

I look up from my phone. Alex is here. It is raining steadily now and the restaurant is completely quiet. Drops of rain catch in the light as we climb the tower. They look like snow. I am not as scared this time and follow Alex over the railing without much trouble. When we reach the platform, the street is laid out before us, its lights twinkling.

'Have you got them?' asks Alex.

I reach into my backpack and pull out a folded sheaf of computer printouts. I read a line from *The Great Gatsby*. *'There are all kinds of love in this world, but never the same love twice.'*

'Nice.'

My eyes scan the pages of Rosie's Facebook posts. Her voice sparkles in my ears as I read her words.

Gatsby was a dreamer. He held onto his bright star.

Welcome to insanity.

You and me and gay Paree.

Scatter my ashes in Paris.

Funny, sad, witty, mundane, they all remind me of a moment with Rosie. I can't scatter Rosie's ashes in Paris, so this is the best I can do. Crouching, I pull some matches out of my bag, place the pages on the edge of the platform and hold a flame to them. They flare and burn so rapidly that soon only a tiny pile of ash is left. Leaning over, I blow and the ashes fall and float among the raindrops. It is hard to tell one from the other. Tears slide down my cheeks as I stand.

'You know, Happy, Gatsby was misguided but he was admirable. He had a loyal heart.' Alex puts her hand over mine and squeezes it.

I look at her. 'Are you saying I'm Gatsby?'

'We're all Gatsby sometimes.'

I turn my hand and squeeze hers as I watch the rain fall in the street. We stand there for some time. The feeling of her hand in mine makes my heart race and my body warm. I don't move. I don't want to break the spell.

'Are you still crazy about Paris?' asks Alex.

I ponder the question. 'Not in the way I was. I mean, I'm glad to know it's there and I hope to get there one day, but … I can wait. Paris was about Rosie. Without her, it's not the same. How about you?'

Alex flashes me a quick, considering glance. 'Maybe Paris is my Gatsby moment.'

'A misplaced dream?'

'Mm, I still think Paris rocks, but really it was ... just a way of getting to know you.' She stares out at the streetlights. 'True confessions.'

A glow lights my stomach. 'Can I put my head on your shoulder?'

'Sure.' I rest my head on her shoulder and she touches my hair.

'So fluffy. They could make jumpers out of this.'

'Now I feel like a sheep.'

'You are nothing like a sheep.' After a few moments she lets go of my hand.

I let out my breath.

'Hey, I almost forgot, I've got something for you.' She pulls her phone out of her pocket and taps it. 'I made a video. Look.' She holds it out.

Four of her chickens are standing in front of a xylophone. They peck at it in a random way, producing a plunking sound. Alex's hand comes into vision and she gives them some pellets.

'Cool, huh?' she says. 'Do you recognise the song?'

'Play it again.'

She replays the video. It sounds like nothing I have ever heard before, but I make a wild guess. 'Happy Birthday?'

She smiles. 'I'd get them to do it for you live, but sometimes they get distracted, so I thought I should record it while they were on fire.'

'Awesome. I had no idea they were so talented.'

We climb back down from the tower. At La Dolce Vita we pause at an empty table with two chairs companionably drawn together. One of the wine glasses on the table has a lipstick stain in Mum's shade of red. For a moment I think I can hear her laugh.

Alex reaches out and takes my hand again.

I squeeze her warm fingers and look into her eyes. I suppose she's about to say goodbye and tell me we need to keep taking baby steps.

She clears her throat. 'Want to come back to my place?' She meets my gaze.

The way she looks at me makes my face burn. 'Yes. I'd like that.'

'I don't mean to play Monopoly.'

I smile. 'I don't want to play Monopoly.'

'Are you sure?'

'Absolutely, I'd thrash you and make you feel bad.' I laugh at the look on her face. 'I'm teasing. I know what you mean. And yes, I'm sure.'

'I'm scared about this. About us.'

I stare at her. 'You're scared? What of?'

'I'm scared I'm falling hard for you. I'm scared that you might be just playing.'

'I'm not playing. What makes you think I'm playing?'

'Some girls like to notch up the experience. It's fashionable. Katy Perry and all that. That's what happened with me and Sarita. I thought it was serious, then she went and got married to this guy her parents lined up for her.'

'Well, you're safe with me on that count. I've never, ever done anything fashionable in my entire life.'

She smiles. 'Might be time, right?'

I lean over and touch my lips to hers and it is like the pool kiss all over again. I am conscious of nothing except the way she feels, the thumping of my heart against her chest, our legs pressing together. The kiss goes on and on until a passing car beeps at us.

I breathe deeply as we step apart. 'When I kiss you, I feel like I'm underwater.'

'Me too.' Alex gives a slow smile. 'We need to get home. I've made you a birthday cake. The chickens contributed too, of course.'

We run down the street to the ferry, sheltering under my polka-dot umbrella, our shoulders brushing together. The street looks magical as the lights catch the falling rain.

Over in West End, the restaurants are shut, but people are still milling around. I pause as a sandwich board outside a little shop catches my eye – *tattooing*. I glance at my watch. 'I've been eighteen for over twenty-four hours.'

'So …?' Alex looks at me inquiringly.

I gesture at the sandwich board.

'Oh, right. You're legal.' She shrugs lightly. 'Go for it if you want.'

Alex and I look in the window. Inside it is clean and minimalist white – a far cry from the gothic splendour of Trev's Tatts. If Rosie were here she'd pull me inside to get inked at once.

The door to the shop opens and a pale man with long hair so blond it's almost white emerges. He is wearing a white nightie and wraps a silk scarf a little tighter around his neck as he picks up his sandwich board. 'Do you want a tattoo? I'm about to shut otherwise.'

I visualise the tattoo on my foot. *Je suis une Parisienne.* I'm not sure if that's true anymore. I may at some stage be a Parisienne, but what if I change my mind? What if I decide to live in Tokyo? Or Rome? Or Berlin? Will I wish I'd had *Ich bin ein Berliner* tattooed on my foot instead? I hesitate, then shake my head. 'No. I thought maybe I did, but I've changed my mind.'

He nods. 'Good idea. It's easier to change your mind before rather than after.'

This seems profound. We say goodbye and Alex and I walk on down the street. A sudden gust of wind blows my umbrella inside out. I try to fix it, both Alex and I getting soaked in the process, but all the spokes are warped now and it won't go back.

'Doesn't matter.' Alex holds out her arms to catch the raindrops. 'It's a warm night.'

'You're right.' I tuck the bedraggled umbrella under my arm.

We climb the hill through the rain towards Alex's house. My mind turns to Michiko, heartbroken in Paris, Billy, who disappeared there, and Rosie, who would have danced for joy had she ever made it to the City of Light. It's a night for beginnings, but also a night for endings. I turn my face to the sky and let the rain wash over it.

At the top of the hill is an old wooden gazebo and we run inside to get out of the rain. We can see all of Brisbane spread out beneath us and right now I wouldn't be anywhere else.

'It's hard to know what to make of it all, isn't it?' I lean on the railing, looking out at the lights. 'The way we're here and suddenly we're not.'

'This transient life?' Alex's arm is warm beside mine.

'Yeah.'

'We'll always be here in this moment, Happy. Even when we're not.'

I turn and stare at her. Her face is green in the glow of the streetlights and her hair is plastered to her head. She is without a doubt the most beautiful person I've ever seen. 'That is the most ridiculous thing I've ever heard, Alex.'

She gives me a quizzical look.

'But I'm a ridiculous person, so it makes sense to me.' I smile.

So we hold hands and run out of the gazebo and up the street as the rain soaks through our clothes. And Alex is right, because whatever comes next, I know this is a moment that will stay with me forever.

Glossary

absolument	absolutely
Arc de Triomphe	iconic arch monument in Paris
bonjour	good morning
bonsoir	good evening
Café des 2 Moulins	Two Windmills Café
Champs-Élysées	world-famous avenue, lined with luxury shops
chez moi	my home
Crèvecoeur	one of the oldest French breeds of chicken
cuckoo Marans	breed of chicken from the French town of Marans
de jour	of the day
de rigueur	fashionable
déjeuner au bord du fleuve	lunch by the river
eh bien	well

faux pas	misstep
folie à deux	delusion shared by two people
Gallic	French
Gauloise	strong French cigarette
hauteur	haughtiness
Je suis amoureuse	I am in love
Je suis une Parisienne	I am a Parisian
J'aime Paris	I love Paris
La Flèche	rare French breed of chicken
La Vie en rose	song, 'Life in happy hues', sung by Edith Piaf
Le Petit Escargot	The Little Snail
Louvre	world's largest art museum
mademoiselle	miss
mais oui	but yes
mais oui, un petit peu	but yes, a little bit
ménage à trois	three people romantically involved together
merci beaucoup	thank you very much
merde	damn it
monsieur	mister
Montmartre	artistic and character-filled part of Paris
Non, je ne regrette rien	song, 'No, I regret nothing', sung by Edith Piaf
Notre Dame	most famous gothic cathedral of the Middle Ages
Où est la patronne?	Where is the boss?

pâtisserie	pastry shop
poulets	chickens
pour moi	for me
rue	street
sacrebleu	goodness
salut	bye (and hello)
savoir-faire	sophistication
s'il vous plait	please
très	very
très bon, merci	very good, thank you
voilà	that's it

Famous French people

Jean-Paul Sartre	philosopher, political activist, novelist
Audrey Tautou	actress, famous for the movie *Amélie*
Marion Cotillard	actress, starred in the movie *Midnight in Paris*
Juliette Binoche	actress, starred in the movie *Three Colours: Blue*
Yves Saint Laurent	fashion designer
Simone de Beauvoir	writer, philosopher, feminist, political activist
Edith Piaf	cabaret singer, songwriter, actress

French food and drink

andouillette	pork sausage made with intestines
baguette	bread stick
boeuf bourguignon	traditional French beef stew

café au lait	coffee with milk
camembert	creamy cow's milk cheese from Normandy
cassoulet	slow-cooked casserole
cervelle	animal brains
Chablis	white wine from the Chablis region of France
crème caramel	custard dessert with layer of soft caramel on top
croissant	crescent-shaped buttery, flaky pastry
escargot	cooked land snail
gâteau	rich cake, usually containing layers of cream or fruit
haute cuisine	elaborate cuisine, served in gourmet restaurants
manouls	guts and stomachs of sheep
petits fours	bite-sized sweet or savoury appetizers

Acknowledgments

Thank you to everyone who has helped me on this journey – it's quite a roll-call.

The HarperCollins Children's Books team have been a joy to work with. Thank you to my publisher, Lisa Berryman, and editor, Eve Tonelli, for their passion and dedication in bringing *Paris Syndrome* to publication.

Paris Syndrome was supported by a Litlink Residency from the Varuna Writers Centre, which included invaluable advice from Jody Lee. Thank you to my fellow residents at Varuna for their encouragement: Joanne Riccioni, Fiona Britton, Donna Cameron and Diana Sweeney, who so kindly read an early draft.

The Byron Writers Festival staff past and present have been a source of support over many years.

Kathryn Heyman and Alexandra Nahlous provided insightful feedback, as did Kate O'Donnell who whipped my errant timeline into shape.

My writing group: Helen Burns, Jane Camens, Jessie Cole, Siboney Duff, Michelle Taylor and Jane Meredith, provided good cheer and wise advice.

Thank you to my agent, Jane Novak, for hugging her iPad after reading the manuscript.

Steph Spartels designed the gorgeous cover – I smile every time I look at it.

My family: John, Simon, Tim, Sue and all my extended family too. Thank you for your love and support – it takes a village to write a book.

And finally, thank you to my readers. Writing is one of my chief joys and I wouldn't be able to do it without you.

Lisa Walker lives on the far north coast of NSW where she is completing a PhD in creative writing.

Lisa has had a radio play produced for ABC RN and was the winner of the Byron Writers Festival short story award. She was a finalist in the ABC Short Story Award and won second place in the Henry Savery and Port Stephens Literature Awards.

Lisa is the author of *Liar Bird* (2012) and *Sex, Lies and Bonsai* (2013) and her debut YA novel is called *Paris Syndrome* (2018).